ALREADY TAKEN

Already Taken

This novel is a work of fiction. Any references to real people, events, establishments, or locales are intended only to give the fiction a sense of reality and authenticity. Other names, characters, and incidents occurring in the work are either the product of the author's imagination or are used fictitiously, as those fictionalized events and incidents that involve real persons. Any character that happens to share the name of a person who is an acquaintance of the author, past or present, is purely coincidental and is in no way intended to be an actual account involving that person.

ISBN- 13: 978-0-9895370-0-1

ISBN- 10: 0-98953-700-5

First Printing June 2013

Printed in the United States of America

Editors: Jamie Pender, Nichelle Johnson, and Lateria Wilcoxson
Typesetting: Jamie Pender

Cover Design by Brittani Williams
www.tspubcreative.com

Already TAKEN

Love N. Lee

Chapter 1

"Bitch, I told you to quit tryna be cute with them damn heels on," Shantreis joked playfully, eying her friend's five-inch Prada heels. "Save that shit for the club."

"Forget you, ho." Fallon stuck her middle finger up at her friend teasingly before she took a seat. She rubbed her sore heels as she looked around the crowded food court at Crabtree Valley Mall in Raleigh. She and her friend, Shantreis, had been shopping for hours and it was evident from all the bags they carried.

"I'll go get our food," Shantreis offered with a laugh.

Fallon nodded as she reached into her purse for her iPhone. She always felt awkward sitting alone and needed to occupy herself even if for only a few minutes.

"You might as well gon' head and save my number in ya phone while you got it out."

Fallon frowned as she looked up with agitation at the young man attempting to holla at her. His expression was cocky, as if he knew that she wouldn't turn him down. He was cute, brown-skinned with shoulder-length dreads, reminding her of Lil' Wayne from his 'Hustler Muzik' days. His looks weren't the issue, but his approach was. It indicated to Fallon that he was *way* too young and immature to try and spit game at her.

The dude hadn't missed the annoyance on her face and quickly scowled in response, "You frownin' at a nigga and shit and ain't even heard what the fuck I got to say. I should a' known you would be one of them stuck up females."

Fallon sighed, hoping to diffuse the hostile situation that she could sense coming on, "Look, I'm not trying to seem rude. I'm just tired."

"Don't take that shit out on me, shawty. I'm not the one! For real!" he yelled belligerently, drawing a few stares from other patrons in the mall.

What the hell? Fallon thought, looking around for Shantreis to help her out. Shantreis was a hood chick in every sense in the word, and would have no problem cussing him out. Fallon, on the other hand, preferred to avoid the drama. She didn't want to cause a scene and the murderous glare in the young man's eyes made her uneasy. It seemed like anything would set him off.

Just as she opened her mouth, another dude walked up. "Chill, Ghost. All that shit is uncalled for."

"Fuck that shit, Strap. Bitch tryna play me. She ain't all that no fuckin' way."

Strap turned to Fallon, embarrassed by his companion's juvenile behavior, "My fault, shawty. He—"

Fallon looked at him thoughtfully and squinted her eyes as if trying to see him better, "Oh my God… Damien?"

Strap blinked, surprised to hear his government name. It was one that he never used anymore and in turn, one that rarely anyone knew—unless they went back the way they did. "Aw shit, Fallon…" he muttered, realizing who she was. He didn't know how he hadn't recognized her immediately.

She hugged him enthusiastically and Strap savored the feel of her in his arms. "I missed you!" Fallon exclaimed. "Look at you! My lil' brother's all grown up."

Strap grinned, but hated the fact that she still looked at him as a younger sibling. She was only two years older than him but they'd met back when he was fifteen, so that had a lot to do with it. When she used to work at Foot Action, he used to come in and flirt with her. She found it flattering, but he was too young for her so she handled him like a lil' nigga. Strap had hated that, but he had been determined to make her his woman.

Fallon was a different breed of female. She wasn't a hood bitch by any means. She'd grown up in the suburbs, completely naïve to the harsh realities of the street life. The world she lived in was completely different from the one that Strap was just barely surviving in. Their worlds were on two different sides of the spectrum. She was pure, untainted by the cruel world and she was on her grown woman shit. It was what had drawn him to her, and coincidentally also drew his older brother, Cash.

"How have you been?"

"Shit. I'm straight…" Strap brushed a hand over his waves modestly. Slyly, he looked her over, admiring how much more beautiful she had become.

Fallon's eyes were still as green as a Granny Smith Apple and her dark brown hair stopped past her shoulder blades. He didn't know if it was a weave or not, but it looked damn good. Her heels accentuated her shapely legs and made her ass sit at attention. The form-fitting blazer and skinny jeans she wore gave her a sexy, innocent look. No doubt about it, Fallon was bad.

"You're all grown up," she commented. "And I see you cut your dreads…" She nodded her head in approval. "Now you look even more like Souljah Boy." Fallon laughed playfully. He had always hated to be told that but it was true.

"Whatever, man," he smiled slightly, loving the way her laughter seemed almost melodic. "Where you been at though? I ain't seen you in forever."

"I was in school so I'd been real preoccupied with that…" Her eyes were downcast and the mood of the conversation changed. Suddenly she asked, "How's uh… Damontrez?"

Strap was hoping that she wouldn't ask but he knew better than that. After Damontrez—or 'Cash' as he was known in the streets—met Fallon, any thoughts that Strap had of being with her completely vanished. She fell for his brother *hard,* and so did Cash. Fallon had that effect on niggas. Sometimes Strap wondered if he had never been shot and left for dead that night, if that would have stopped the two from meeting.

Strap was leaving the mall late that night, solo dolo. Normally he moved with at least two other niggas, but he had just wanted to stop by and see Fallon alone. He was almost to his car when three boys ran up on him in an attempt to rob him. His older brother's words echoed in his head, telling him to always fight for his. Foolishly he refused to empty his pockets, instead attempting to take them all on. Strap was winning despite the unfair odds but after one of the boys pulled out a gun, he lost. They left Strap in a pool of his own blood and took all of his shit.

"Oh my God!" Fallon had cried out when she noticed him struggling to breathe. He'd been shot in his side and the blood that was leaking out of him looked gruesome. "Hold on, Damien. I'm gonna get you some help!" She was hysterical but somehow her hands were steady enough to dial 911 and give the paramedics their location. Strap felt her tears on his face and tried to wipe them away before he passed out.

Everything that happened after that was still fuzzy to

him. He remembered Fallon being by his side in the ambulance as well as sitting in the room with him. Her presence comforted him and it felt good to know that somebody gave a fuck about him. Strap knew his mother was probably somewhere in someone's trap house shooting up dope and it infuriated him. He wanted to call out to Fallon to thank her, but he was so heavily sedated that he could barely keep his eyes open.

He slipped out of consciousness constantly but he didn't miss Cash and Fallon talking and laughing in the room as they awaited his recovery. Cash was thankful that she'd saved his little brother's life and offered to take her out to dinner after the ordeal was over. She accepted the invitation and the rest was history. Just like that, Cash had swooped in and taken Fallon's heart and Strap's hopes with him.

"You know how my brother is. Still doing his thing out here … Caught up with his business," Strap said shaking his head in mock shame. "That's how it goes when you're the boss."

"I guess I'm not surprised…" Fallon said with a sigh.

"Yeah," Strap nodded as he hiked his cargo shorts back up his waist, "But listen, I'm a' hafta holla at you, alright?"

"You be good, okay, Damien?" She gave him one last hug and he nodded his head, although he knew that he wouldn't be able to honor that request.

Strap wished that he could stay a little longer but he had business to handle. Their trip to the mall had not been to shop like it had been for the girls. No. He had way more important things to attend to than that.

"How the fuck you know that bitch?" Ghost asked as soon as they were out of earshot.

Ignoring his question, Strap stopped in his tracks and spun on him angrily, "Nigga, you was drawing a lot of unnecessary attention earlier! Suppose that nigga woulda saw us and left?!"

Ghost sucked his teeth, hating to be chastised. "That wouldn't happen. He don't know we was sent here to get his ass!"

Strap looked back in the direction of the man they had been watching for the past forty minutes. "Shit, you don't know! You better focus on what the fuck we here for."

"Yeah, yeah…" Ghost waved him off. "You was the one playing catch up wit' ole girl for five minutes and shit."

Strap was quiet, trying to take his own advice and stay focused. He quickly glanced back over at Fallon and shook his head. She was a distraction in the worst way. He hadn't seen her in a year—ever since she and Cash called it quits. Strap didn't think it was possible for him to still have feelings for her after that long, but he did and he just couldn't shake it.

"That nigga leaving!" Ghost whispered loudly, snapping Strap out of his thoughts.

"Aiight. Let's go."

"What happened?" Shantreis asked with a frown as she sat down with their food. "Was that Ghost and Strap you was talking to?"

"Yeah," Fallon answered softly, watching the men retreat out the door. "Why you say it like that?"

"Them lil' niggas stay in some fuckin' trouble. Strap ain't the same innocent teenager you knew from back in the day. He—"

"Well, I remember he had started selling a little weed here and there."

"Bitch please, he past that. Him and Ghost body niggas now. They got one hell of a reputation..." Shantreis shook her head. "Why the hell you think they call him Strap?"

"What?" Fallon asked in shock, not believing her ears. Even looking at Strap now, she still thought of the teenager that once had a crush on her. But it was obvious that he was a grown ass man now, carrying himself older than his twenty years. "And who is Ghost exactly?"

"They lil' brother… Well, him and Strap is twins." Noticing the way Fallon raised an eyebrow at their differences in appearance; Shantreis quickly spoke up, "Fraternal twins. Ghost been in juvie since he was like twelve or some shit. That lil' nigga is Looney Tunes, for real. Strap and Cash act they got some sense but not Ghost…" She shook her head again.

"Wow…"

"Yup." Shantreis smacked her lips as she picked at her Stromboli. "So that's what Cash got them doing—"

"How's Cash been?" Fallon asked, cutting her off and asking a little more eagerly than she'd intended. She knew that Shantreis' boyfriend, Outlaw, was his main general so she was sure that she knew something.

"Just wondering," she added quickly after noticing the surprised look on Shantreis' face.

Shantreis rolled her eyes at the way her friend tried to play it off. "The same," she answered in a matter-of-fact tone. "Y'all need to quit playin' and get back together. I don't even know why y'all broke up!"

Fallon sighed. She wished that it was that simple. She and Cash had been together for nearly three years but he couldn't leave the block alone. He was a dope boy and his work always came first. Cash really tried to make time for her, but he couldn't give her all the attention she deserved or needed. She had finally given him an ultimatum: her or the drug game. It was a decision he couldn't make, so she made it for him. Fallon was tired of being the mistress, his main bitch being the streets. When school returned for the semester, she said 'Goodbye' to Cash for good.

Ever the hopeless romantic, Fallon thought—no, she *wanted* for him to run after her… To assure her that she was more important than his work, but he never did. He let her walk right out of his life.

"You know you still love that nigga and he crazy about you too!" Shantreis took a sip of her drink as she paused, knowing that Fallon was anticipating what she was about to say next, "He be askin' bout you sometimes too."

"What? How you know? And why didn't you tell me?!" Fallon practically yelled at her.

Shantreis shrugged. "I thought you was over him. You never mention him or anything. So whenever he asks, I just tell him you good."

"You should've told me."

"Well, I'm tellin' you now, bitch," she stated in her usual manner.

'Bitch' and 'ho' were terms of endearment when Shantreis used it. It used to bother Fallon back in high school but she had come to accept her figures of speech. Shantreis had transferred to Garner High after moving from Virginia after her parents' divorce.

"We can set some shit up." Shantreis smiled as she pulled out her phone and started singing off-key, "*Reunited and it feels so goooooooddd.*"

"I'm supposed to be seeing Kevin, remember?" Fallon reminded her, knowing that he was just her excuse.

"Whatever, bitch. Whenever I try to push you on Kevin, you always say that the shit ain't that serious. Now that I'm tryna push you back on Cash, you sayin' some other shit!" Her voice trailed off as her phone went off. "Hold up, girl, it's Outlaw."

Fallon was quiet as she listened to her friend chatter away on the phone. She wondered if Cash was really missing her like she claimed or if Shantreis was just putting too much into it. She was known to over dramatize situations so it was a possibility that Cash had only been asking as some sort of courtesy.

Get over it, Fallon, she thought, *He obviously has or he would've tried to get up with you. It's almost been a year. The shit just isn't meant to be.*

"Whatever, Outlaw. You just come and go whenever the fuck you want, so I can too," Shantreis yelled into the receiver. "Bye, nigga! I said, bye!" She rolled her eyes as she looked back at her phone and noticed that Outlaw had hung up in her face first. "Girl, let me gon' on home. Outlaw trippin'."

Fallon had to laugh. She and Outlaw were a trip. They argued like a married couple and would break up to make up almost every other day. It was usually due to the fact that Shantreis was always accusing him of cheating. Fallon didn't know if he was or not, but hearing the two of them fight was hilarious at times. "All right then. I guess I'll go too. I'm so ready to relax anyway."

"Don't forget I wanna go out Saturday! Bodi, Flashbacks," she rattled off the names of a few clubs, "I don't give a fuck where. I'm just ready to shake my ass on somebody's dance floor! The baddest bitches in the 919 will be in *somebody's* muthafuckin' building!"

"That's if Outlaw lets you go," Fallon added with a giggle.

"Chile, boo!" She waved her off. "Outlaw don't run shit! At least not Shantreis Demetria Teasley."

"Whatever." Fallon laughed at her, but agreed. It had

been a long time since they had gone out so Saturday night was sure to be memorable.

"Okay. I'll call you later." Shantreis picked up her bags and turned back to Fallon, "And don't forget what I said. I can hook you up, girl!"

Chapter 2

"Greg, let me holla at'cha, nigga!" Ghost yelled as they followed behind a man in the parking deck.

Strap cut his eyes at his brother, but Ghost either didn't notice or didn't care. He was deviating from the script and Strap was pissed off, to say the least. He hated how reckless Ghost could be at times. He didn't have any concern for the fact that they were at a shopping mall full of dozens of people and there were most likely security cameras hidden somewhere.

"Muthafucka, we not doing this shit here," Strap whispered angrily.

If Ghost was any other nigga, Strap would have stopped fucking with him a long time ago. But since they were blood, he would just make another mental note to school Ghost later because at this rate, he would get them caught up one day.

"Why the fuck not? No time like the present!" Ghost turned his attention back to their prey.

Ghost didn't believe in playing cat and mouse with these niggas. He didn't care who was around, he would merk a nigga in broad daylight if he had to. He felt like

Strap was getting soft, but what he failed to understand was that Strap liked to play it smart. He wasn't trying to get knocked. Let Ghost tell it, he wasn't either, but his careless actions showed otherwise.

"What the fuck y'all niggas want?" Greg asked, stopping in his tracks. He was trying to play hard but inside he was sweating bullets. With their hoods pulled low over their faces, Greg couldn't tell who was following him but he recognized the voice soon enough.

"Nigga, you know what the fuck we here for," Strap spoke up.

"Is this about that bullshit with Cash?" The men were silent, confirming the answer to Greg's question. "I done told that nigga that I ain't had shit to do with him bein' short them grands. He need to be sniffin' around Mike monkey ass instead of stalkin' me over this shit!"

"Shit. Looks like you done made a come up, my nigga." Ghost eyed the Lacoste and Belk bags he carried. "Them crocodile shirts run for damn near a hundred dollars apiece and you got three bags worth. And now you can afford to cop ya bitch a new BMW… From what I understood, you don't be makin' that big of a bank."

"I save money just like the next man," Greg tried to convince them but his fear caused his voice to come out shaky. He was far from believable. Greg had a feeling that they could see through the bullshit but he would be damned if he admitted the truth.

He had been skimming off Cash's money for months, but he thought that he had done a damn good job of setting Mike up to take the fall. He hadn't considered in the least bit that his seemingly overnight come up would draw attention to himself.

"Y'all better back the fuck up," Greg warned as he started to reach for the back of his pants.

Unfortunately for him, Strap had his .380 aimed before Greg could even get a grasp on his heat. "Keep reaching back there and you'll be a dead man. Put ya hands up."

"Shit," Greg cursed, but he did as he was told.

Ghost wasted no time rushing Greg and relieving him of his weapon. "Pussy ass nigga."

Greg looked around, surveying the seemingly deserted parking deck. There were rows of cars but he didn't see anyone nearby. That fact didn't stop him from trying his luck, however. "HELP!"

"Shut the fuck up!" Strap growled, simultaneously hitting him upside the head with the butt of his gun. He was trying to think and Greg was fucking up his concentration.

Strap knew that holding a nigga at gun point at the mall wasn't the smartest thing he'd ever done, but he had been left with no other choice. Now he had to figure out how they were going to manage to get Greg in the back of their truck without drawing any more attention to themselves. Strap knew from past experience that there was no sight that went unseen. Somebody had probably seen what was going on, they were just smart enough not to get involved.

"Damn, nigga. You runnin' round here with this kind of money like muthafuckas won't rob ya ass?" Ghost commented as he helped himself to the knots in Greg's pockets. "You ballin', huh?" He laughed obnoxiously.

"Take all that shit, man. I don't want any problems," Greg begged.

"Nigga, you already got fuckin' problems. You think we would really just take the money and let ya bitch ass live?" Ghost shook his head. "Shit don't work out that way."

Before Greg could say another word, Ghost had shot him in the side of the head causing blood to splatter. Although he'd been using a silencer, the sound of the shot still seemed to echo across the parking deck. A few people screamed and as if on cue, Ghost and Strap took off running. If it hadn't been for the traces of blood staining their hoodies, they could have blended in with the crowd.

"Fuck," Strap cursed with exasperation present in his voice, "Nigga, do you realize what you just did?!"

"What did you want me to do?" Ghost yelled. He seemed unfazed by how much trouble he had potentially gotten them into. He got off on doing reckless shit, loving the adrenaline rush.

"Put the gun down, now!" an officer shouted, cutting them off as they started to bend the corner. He seemed to have appeared out of thin air. His gun was pointed at them but he was slightly trembling. It was evident to them that he was just a rookie trying to be a hero.

Strap and Ghost exchanged glances as they slowed down. The twins slightly nodded at each other in understanding. "Chill out, man," Strap spoke up. "I'll put it down."

The officer's eyes were focused on Strap as he started to lower his gun to the floor, giving Ghost the perfect opportunity to take aim at the officer. Gunshots reverberated in the night air as if indicating the start of a race and both men took off again.

"You ain't kill that nigga did you?" Strap asked as they maneuvered around cars and in-between shoppers.

"Fuck if I know, but that shit don't sound good," Ghost commented as he heard the officer's walkie-talkie going crazy and the pounding of heavy footsteps behind them. "We parked on the other side of the damn mall… How the fuck we gonna pull this shit off?"

Strap wanted to tell him that if he hadn't strayed from the original plans, they wouldn't have had to worry about that. Still, right now wasn't the best time. They were knee deep in some shit and it was up to him to get them out of it. "Go ahead to the car. I'll distract these muthafuckas."

Ghost looked at him skeptically, but the somber look on Strap's face told him not to question him. He didn't know what his brother had planned but he knew it would be in his best interest to do as he was told.

"I'll get up wit' you at the house," Strap told him, although he wasn't so sure. There had to be at least five rent-a-cops behind him and he knew that they couldn't wait to riddle his black ass with bullets even though he hadn't been the one to let off any shots. Strap was ready to go out blazing if he had to.

Just a few more steps to the car, Fallon chanted to herself as she exited the mall. The brief break she had gotten off her feet hadn't given her much relief. The moment she slipped her heels back on, she felt the same fatigue from earlier.

"Freeze!" Fallon heard as she turned to her right. She had been so engrossed with the pain she was in that she didn't notice all the commotion outside. A lot of people were standing to the side, fearful of the chase taking place.

Several security officers were sprinting behind two young men. They looked like blurs due to how fast they were moving. As they got closer, Fallon could see that it was none other than Ghost and Strap. Their hoods were pulled down low so it was hard to see their faces, but she remembered their clothes from earlier.

What the hell? Fallon thought before shaking her head. Shantreis told her that they were always in some shit and they had proved her point without a shadow of a doubt.

Ghost zoomed past her, but Strap pulled her into a sloppy embrace while whispering in her ear, "Forgive me, shawty."

"What?" When she felt the cool steel pressed against the side of her head, she understood.

"I'm not gonna hurt you, but help a nigga out, aiight?" Strap murmured. He didn't give her a chance to respond before turning to the officers, "Y'all betta back the fuck up or I swear I'll merk this bitch!"

"Drop the weapon, son! Now I'm sure you don't really want to hurt this young lady," the officer tried to stall as he took slow footsteps towards them.

"Nah. I *don't* want to hurt her but I will if you don't back the fuck up—NOW!" Strap warned again, briefly taking the gun off Fallon and pointing it towards the officers. He yanked Fallon closer to him and gripped her in a headlock. "Where you parked?" he whispered.

"Right there—that black BMW." Fallon motioned with her head as they hurried in the direction of her car. Strap sat down in the driver's seat and pulled Fallon onto his lap. He tried to stay as low as possible while he struggled to climb over the middle console. It was cramped but he couldn't risk any of the officers getting a shot in. He knew that the moment they saw a chance to take him out, they would.

"What the hell is going on, Damien?" she asked, her tone laced with irritation.

"Just drive, ma, and I promise I'll tell you whatever you wanna know."

Fallon said nothing else as she quickly pulled out of the parking space. A few officers tried to get a shot in but her windows were tinted, making it hard for them. She was doing nearly forty miles per hour in the parking lot, honking her horn as a warning for others to clear out of her way.

Sirens wailed in the distance as she turned left onto Glenwood Avenue. Fallon ignored the fact that the light was red and the lane she was in was for right turns only. All she could think about was evading the police. Her tires screeched as she made another right on Creedmoor Road just before the light changed.

"Got damn, NASCAR," Strap joked as he looked in the rearview mirror.

"Do you wanna get arrested and hauled off to jail or what?" Fallon snapped. She could no longer hear sirens. Other than the sounds of horns from a few disgruntled drivers, it was quiet.

"I think we're straight now." She still didn't let off the gas pedal but that was normal for her. Fallon regularly drove as if she were in the Indy 500 even when she wasn't being chased by police.

"Ay, good lookin' out back there, ma." Noticing her massaging her neck, Strap quickly spoke up, "My bad. Had to make the shit look real."

She nodded her head in understanding, "Now tell me what happened."

Strap sighed as he placed his gun back into the waistline of his jeans. He didn't really want to reveal what had just gone down but figured that he didn't have anything to lose. If she was going to tell the police, she could do that regardless. But deep down Strap knew that she would never do him that way. All she'd ever done was try to look out for him.

Still, he couldn't tell her the complete truth. To Strap's knowledge, Fallon had no idea of what he did now—merking niggas if the price was right—and that was a far cry from the high school kid that sold weed in-between classes that he used to be. Strap knew that Fallon would be shocked and probably disgusted. He had to admit that he never thought his life would pan out this way, but killing was easy for him. Strap realized that after he pulled the trigger for the first time.

"Me and Ghost was supposed to be gettin' back some money that this dude owed Cash but shit got outta hand," he said, only giving her half-truths. "Somebody called the po—"

"*Strap,*" she referred to him by his street name, surprising him. "I know what you do now so you may as well stop giving me the edited version."

He smirked. She had always seen right through him. "Basically, Ghost shot that nigga. Police came and you was my ticket out." Strap shrugged as if he hadn't just committed a crime.

"Ya'll just ain't gonna learn until you get locked up," Fallon said disappointedly.

"I'm tryin' not to! Ghost started that dumb shit. I had to get us out of it. I already know Cash gonna be mad as fuck about the way we handled that shit!"

"He sent y'all on that dummy mission? To *kill* somebody at the mall?" she questioned incredulously.

"I mean… It wasn't all like that," Strap muttered weakly, wanting to defend his older brother's orders.

"You need to stop all that, Damien. Cash doesn't hold a gun to your head and say he'll kill you if you don't do it. The street life is something you need to stay away from. I thought that Cash would have tried to keep you away from it instead of encouraging it." Fallon placed her small, soft hand on the side of his face, "You're smart, baby. Why don't you go to college or something?"

"I forgot you a college girl. You graduated already?" Strap asked, slyly shifting the conversation in a different direction. He wouldn't know what the hell he would do in college. It was a thought that he had seriously never entertained.

"Yes." Fallon smiled proudly. "I have my Bachelor's in Business and I'm thinking about going back to get my

Master's… I haven't decided yet." She looked at him again. "What do you want to do with your life, Damien?"

He shrugged. "I don't really know. Honestly, I never really thought about it. I guess I'll do this until Cash—"

"You can't live your life based on other people's actions. You have to do what *you* want to do because it's what *you* want."

Strap sat there and let her words really marinate. He had to admit that he didn't really want to take over Cash's drug empire when he was retired. Strap also knew that he didn't want to merk niggas for the rest of his life. Having to look over his shoulder everyday wasn't something that he wanted to do long-term. Up until this moment, he had never believed he could do anything else besides slang drugs or murder for hire. There was rapping or playing ball, but Strap had never been good at either.

"There isn't anything you're interested in?" Fallon prompted again.

Strap shrugged again. "I mean, I know I don't wanna be workin' for pennies and runnin' errands for the white man."

Fallon rolled her eyes. "You can be your own boss, Strap. There *are* black business owners in the world, you know."

"I mean, I know that but—"

"But what?" Fallon interrupted, "Believe in yourself, Damien. I do." She smiled. "Whenever you're ready, I'll help you."

Strap nodded. Her words were really having an effect on him. He knew it wouldn't be anytime soon, but he would work on it. "I may take you up on that."

"You should. The streets don't have a 401k…" Tears came to her eyes as she recalled having the same conversation with Cash a year ago. Then the conversation had fallen on deaf ears, but hopefully it would permeate with Strap.

The rest of the ride was quiet with the exception of the radio. Strap pointed the way to his house, which was buried in rural Zebulon. It was a city nearly forty minutes away from Raleigh. Strap liked living in the cut because it was less likely for niggas to sneak up on him. Nobody knew where he laid his head at and he took proper precautions to ensure that it remained that way. The house was small, nothing fancy so as not to rouse any unwanted attention. The inside gave away how lavishly he lived, however.

As they pulled up, Strap smiled slightly. Ghost was sitting on the front porch smoking a blunt. Knowing that his brother was okay eased his mind.

"Uh… You wanna come in?" he asked her nervously.

Fallon looked at him, surprised by the invitation. "No. I better be getting home. I'm sure the police are looking for me and my car… It is a hostage situation, you know." She smiled. "Take care of yourself."

"Alright." He closed the door and started off towards the house. As he did, he couldn't help but wonder if this would be the last time he would see her. He wanted to tell her how he felt—how he *still* felt about her. Fallon dating Cash hadn't done shit except force him to be more discreet about his feelings for her.

Say somethin', nigga, it's now or never! he thought urgently.

Just do it! Fallon's insides screamed. Just as she rolled down the passenger side window, Strap, too, had stopped in footsteps and turned back towards the car.

"Look, Fallon, about you and Cash… I know y'all were together and shit but—"

Say it before you lose your nerve! She inhaled deeply, not even giving him the opportunity to finish his statement.

"Yeah... So can you tell Cash to call me...? Please?"

Feeling deflated, Strap was silent initially but finally picked his face up off the ground. Reluctantly he accepted the slip of paper with her number on it. "Bet."

Chapter 3

How the fuck this nigga gonna tell me to hurry my ass home and he ain't even here? Shantreis thought angrily as she kicked off her flip flops and made herself comfortable on the Italian leather sofa. She had been pissed off ever since she opened the garage door and noticed that Outlaw's Maserati Quattroporte Sport GTS wasn't parked inside. The fact that he wasn't returning any of her calls only added fuel to the flame. She knew that meant one of two things: He was out fucking some ho or out handling business.

With Outlaw's occupation as a general to one of the biggest drug operations in Raleigh, it was possible that something unexpected had come up. There had been many a time that he'd had to head out to ensure that everything was running like clockwork. Cash couldn't have asked for a more thorough nigga on his team. Outlaw liked to pop in on the stash houses to keep niggas on their toes and he always kept himself abreast of everything that was going on in the streets.

It made Shantreis proud to know that she was fucking with a boss, but it had its advantages and disadvantages.

Right now was a perfect example. She didn't know where the hell he was at and Outlaw didn't even bother to check in with her. She dialed his phone number over and over but each time she was sent directly to voice mail.

I know this nigga ain't got his shit off! I know he with a bitch now! Shantreis' nostrils flared angrily as she waited for the beep to indicate that she could leave a message, "You stupid muthafucka. I—"

Shantreis heard her line beeping and glared at the picture ID of Outlaw. She didn't bother to greet him; instead she went ham the moment the line picked up, "Outlaw, where the fuck is you at?"

"I went to go check up on my daughter since you wanted to stay out all damn day!" he retorted, his voice full of agitation.

"I wasn't gone that long!" she insisted. It was true by her logic, but anyone else would disagree. Coming to the mall in the middle of the day and not leaving until thirty minutes before the mall closed at nine *was* all day.

"Yeah? Well, you had that stank ass attitude when I tried to holla at you earlier so I decided to go chill with a girl who's gonna appreciate my company."

"Please. You probably went over there just to see Kaleesha's ass," Shantreis murmured under her breath, referencing to his baby momma.

"What?" Outlaw sucked his teeth. "I wish you would stop sayin' that shit! I told you I don't want that bitch. This shit is *strictly* about Monet! My daughter! I don't care about what the fuck Kaleesha doin'!"

Kaleesha had been the girl he was fucking with off and on before they'd gotten together. Obviously, Outlaw hadn't been ready to leave her alone after he and Shantreis hooked up, because Kaleesha informed him that she was pregnant about six months into their budding relationship.

Outlaw had hoped that she would abort the baby after he bribed her with money but being the trifling female that she was, she kept it. It wasn't because she cared about the life growing inside of her; she just wanted to always have a part of Outlaw—to have a guaranteed spot in his life. Kaleesha was one of those chicks that believed that since she had the baby, she would *always* have the man—no matter how much of a piece that was, she was satisfied.

Each time Shantreis thought about it, she still didn't know what made her stay with Outlaw after that happened. Initially he had denied the accusations. It was only after the blood test proved that he was 99.9% the father, that he had no choice but to tell Shantreis the truth. Most girls would have dumped him, but she stayed with him, blaming love as the reason.

No matter what Outlaw did, Shantreis was stuck to his ass like glue and had been for a little over three years. She loved that nigga without a doubt. They fell out often, but it was more than obvious that she wasn't going anywhere. She knew it and so did Outlaw.

"Whatever, Outlaw." She rolled her eyes, unconvinced.

"Look," Outlaw sighed exasperatedly. Shantreis could imagine him pinching the bridge of his nose as he often did whenever he was mad. "I'm coming home soon. Just let me get Monet situated for bed and I'll be there." He paused for a moment then added, "I love you."

There was a brief period of silence before she finally spoke up, "Love you too."

Outlaw wanted to say something smart but didn't want to give his baby momma anything else to comment on. He knew that she was eavesdropping on his conversation with Shantreis so he tried to keep his voice low.

"Aiight, baby." He disconnected the call before turning back to Kaleesha who was looking at him anxiously.

"The fuck you lookin' at?" Outlaw asked.

Kaleesha shook her head, deviously removing the comforter from her exposed breasts, giving Outlaw an enticing view of what she had to offer. She was hoping for a round two but judging from the look on his face, it probably wasn't going to happen.

"Don't get any ideas." Outlaw reached for his Levi's jeans and started to pull them on.

"Why not? Outlaw, this shit is fucked up and you know it! Me and your daughter need you here but you'd rather be with that gold digging bitch."

Outlaw sighed, hating that he had fucked up and slept with Kaleesha again. He *had* come to see Monet, but as usual, the visit turned into something more.

It was as though his baby mother had some sort of radar—she could tell whenever he and Shantreis were going through rough patches in their relationship. She took full advantage of these moments knowing Outlaw was in a vulnerable position. All it took was a little sweet talk, a little liquor in his system, and brain like she graduated from Harvard Law. After that, Outlaw was more than eager to bend her over.

"Whatever, Kaleesha. I ain't tryna hear that tonight. You weren't thinking about that shit when you fucked that nigga Eric."

Kaleesha sighed, wishing that he would stop throwing the past back up in her face. It was true that she had fucked with his homeboy while they were together, but damn, that shit happened three years ago. She and Outlaw had been together for four years before that. It went without saying that he had done far worse but all it took was her *one* mistake to end everything.

Because Outlaw had cheated on her with Shantreis, sleeping with Eric had been her way of getting back at him—she just hadn't planned for him to know about it. It was supposed to be a secret but after getting sloppy drunk one night, Eric spilled all the beans, breaking up their relationship. Like a typical nigga, Outlaw couldn't take the same shit that he dished out. He gave Shantreis the official title of wifey in less than a day's time after finding out.

Shantreis won, but Kaleesha had a victory every now and again whenever Outlaw would come through and fuck her brains out. It had taken Monet's birth to get Outlaw to even consider dealing with her again. Before, he had avoided her like the AIDS virus, but in coming to visit his daughter, it softened his heart towards Kaleesha. Each time she thought that he could see past her little mishap, Outlaw would snap out of it and brush off her advances. The hold that Shantreis had on Outlaw was strong and Kaleesha couldn't understand why.

"What do you see in her?" Kaleesha asked angrily, trying to change the subject.

Outlaw chuckled, "You real funny, 'leesha. What the fuck you saw in Eric? You coulda picked any muthafucka out here but you picked a nigga from my camp."

Kaleesha was quiet as she watched him pull a wad of money out of his pocket and toss the bills casually on the bed.

"You payin' for the pussy now?" she asked, feeling degraded and hurt.

He shook his head. "I don't trick on *no* bitch."

"You trickin' on that bitch you got at home," Kaleesha muttered under her breath, feeling salty that it wasn't *her* who was being spoiled with monetary gifts anymore.

Outlaw didn't miss a beat. "Watch your fuckin' mouth."

"I'm just sayin'." She shrugged, imitating Kanye West during his infamous disruption at the music awards. "She's just using you for your money."

"Nah. She ain't like that," he responded smoothly. "She ain't like you."

"Outlaw, please. I was with your ass back when you was still regular ass Travaris Robinson," she referred to him by his God-given name. "So miss me with that gold-digging shit because you ain't have shit but ya black ass and a dream back then!"

"Yeah okay." Outlaw wasn't convinced. "If you had stayed down for a nigga then—"

"If you could keep your dick in your pants then shit wouldn't be so fucked up!" Her nostrils flared angrily. "If Shantreis knew that you was cheating on her with me and them other hoes you keep on the side, I'm sure she would change up her tune real quick."

Kaleesha let out a small squeal as Outlaw rushed her, pinning her down on the bed by her throat. "She ain't gonna find out because you ain't gonna say shit about it! Understood?" She didn't respond and he knew that she wasn't able to. His grip was too tight. "And I told ya ass to start mindin' ya own fuckin' business."

Just when Kaleesha thought she was about to black out, he released his hold on her. She gasped, feeling light-headed as oxygen refilled her lungs.

"Shantreis wouldn't believe you anyway. Everybody knows you want me back." He turned to exit the bedroom. "By the way, that money is for Monet. The pussy ain't good enough for me to tip ya ass."

"Fuck you, Outlaw!" Kaleesha yelled as she felt tears welling up in her eyes. She felt stupid for allowing him to make a fool out of her again. She vowed that he wouldn't get another chance to, but that was what she said every time he insulted and hurt her.

Nevertheless, Outlaw had gone too far. She was tired

of him talking shit and putting his hands on her. She could bet that he didn't treat Shantreis like that. Knowing that tore her up inside.

After Kaleesha heard the front door close, she walked over the mirror, inspecting her reflection. She wasn't a bad looking girl but compared to the Lisa-Raye-lookalike that was Shantreis, she couldn't hold a candle to her beauty.

At least, not in Kaleesha's opinion and obviously not Outlaw's either. He had her self-esteem all fucked up.

I'm cute too, she thought to herself, trying hard to convince her reflection. If you squinted your eyes enough, she could have passed for a thicker Kimbella from *Love and Hiphop: New York*. Kaleesha nodded her head in approval, satisfied with that until she noticed the red finger bruises around her neck. They were clear as day on her light-bright skin tone, causing her to grimace.

Outlaw was going to pay for that shit.

Chapter 4

"Twenty-two year old Greg Richards was shot and killed today in the parking lot of Crabtree Valley Mall. Additionally, Officer Ronnie Reynolds was shot but he was taken to Wake Med where he is expected to make a full recovery," news reporter Adam Owens informed. "The Wake County Police Department is looking for two suspects involved in the shooting. Both are black males around six feet tall. They were last spotted wearing black and gray hoodies.

"One of the suspects fled on foot while the other held a female shopper at gunpoint and forced her to be his getaway driver. The victim was unharmed and reported home safe and sound. The suspects are still at large and considered armed and dangerous. Anyone with information about the robbery should contact Raleigh Crime Stoppers at 919-834-4357."

Cash stared at his younger brothers in disbelief. He cut off the television and looked to them for an explanation. He'd come by to find out how everything went, preferring not to discuss sensitive information over the phone. The news report he was greeted with had him pissed. Cash had taught them better than this. He'd always instilled in them to be discreet and here they were, setting in off in front of hundreds of muthafuckas—some that he was sure would be able to identify them in a lineup.

"So who is gonna tell me what the fuck really happened?" his deep baritone was cold and laced with anger. He took a deep pull from his blunt in an attempt to calm himself.

Cash was a boss and made moves as such. He didn't get where he was today by being careless, or having niggas on his team that were. He couldn't risk having anyone fucking shit up. In this game of chess, everyone played by *Cash's* rules. Those that didn't were expendable. Without a doubt, if Strap and Ghost hadn't been his kin, he would have merked them for the stunt they pulled.

Strap was quiet. He hung his head low, expressing his dissatisfaction with the way they'd chosen to handle things.

Ghost smiled, either missing or ignoring the look on his brothers' faces. "Shit. I bust that nigga head open like a fuckin' watermelon!" He laughed raucously. "I should a' killed that fuckin' cop though."

Cash's nostrils flared, unable to contain his anger anymore. Ghost needed a wakeup call. If he didn't tame him now then he would always be out of control. "Nigga, you need to quit bein' so fuckin' reckless! You think this shit is a muthafuckin' game?! This ain't no damn movie where muthafuckas get away with shit. I shouldn't ever see y'all on the fuckin' news!"

Ghost waved him off. "Cash, we gucci. Them niggas ain't seen our faces! And what kind of weak ass description was that?" He shook his head and imitated a news reporter, "Black males about six feet tall." He laughed at Cash's paranoia. "We ain't the only black niggas in the Triangle."

Strap shook his head at his little brother. He was only

older by a couple of minutes, but at times he felt like it was much longer than that. Ghost was a young knucklehead that just wouldn't learn.

At twelve he brought a gun to school and shot another boy after a small classroom argument during recess. Luckily, the boy survived but Ghost was remanded to a juvenile detention center until he turned eighteen. It didn't do any good because when Ghost came out, he was still the same as he'd always been—malicious, unfeeling, and ruthless. Those characteristics made him an exceptional killer but his lack of control and tact would be his downfall. Strap and Cash were trying to mentor him, but their warnings went in one ear and right out the other.

"You gettin' sloppy."

"Whatever." Ghost blew his breath, flashing his brother a vicious look. "Shit. We all know you just gonna have this shit covered up anyway so why the fuck do it matter? They'll never find the videos and they'll never find the fuckin' clothes we wore… It'll be like the shit never happened."

"You can't count on me always bein' able to fix shit, Ghost! Every move you make needs to be thought out first! You shot a fuckin' *cop!*"

"I told him not to do it," Strap spoke up finally.

"Fuck you, Strap!" Ghost spat, hating how he tried to flip everything on him. He snapped his fingers. "Matter fact, that New-New bitch," he referred to Fallon, calling her by Lauren London's character in the movie *ATL* because of their similar appearance. "You talkin' bout I'm careless and shit, but how you figure shawty won't snitch? She knows you by your government and now she knows where the fuck we stay."

"She ain't said shit yet," Strap snapped, hating that Ghost had brought it up in front of Cash.

"That don't mean she won't!"

"I know shawty. She wouldn't do that."

"Whatever, nigga." Ghost shrugged. He wasn't really worried about it. He figured that the bitch wasn't suicidal but he wanted his brothers to realize that he wasn't the only one behaving haphazardly.

"You brought a bitch *here*?" Cash asked in astonishment upon hearing their exchange. "*And* you told her about the shit?"

"Man… It weren't even like that," Strap defended.

"Tell me what the fuck it's like then! To me it sounds like—"

"It was Fallon!" Strap yelled, cutting his brother off.

Cash was quiet. He couldn't believe it. He just knew that his ears were deceiving him. "Fallon?"

"Yeah... She told me to tell you to call her…" He reached into his pocket, revealing her phone number. Strap explained what happened as Cash listened intently.

Fallon had been the last and only female that Cash ever let inside of his cold and carefully guarded heart. He thought of her from time to time but knew that he couldn't be the man that she was looking for. Cash wanted to be but what Fallon required of him—to walk away from the drug game—was something that he couldn't do.

It was something that she had been asking him for years and he would always make her promises that he couldn't keep. Finally she gave him an ultimatum. Cash thought that Fallon was playing, but she was dead ass serious. He'd tried to rationalize it to her, but she wasn't trying to hear it. He could see in her eyes that she was fed up.

Fed up with sleeping alone most nights.

Fed up with worrying about whether he was dead or alive, or hauled off by the alphabet boys.

Fed up with the bitches that were always throwing themselves at him.

It didn't matter that Cash only wanted *her* and thought that he was doing what he felt was necessary to give her the life she deserved and put her through college. He was strictly motivated by the money and the things it could buy them but she only wanted *him.*

Fallon didn't understand that the street life was all that a nigga knew. It was addicting. The allure of the game was something that he couldn't explain. When he couldn't make the decision to walk away from it, Fallon walked away from him. As much as he wanted her to stay, he didn't bother to beg her to stay.

Cash let her leave because he knew that she was right. She deserved so much more than what he could give. She needed to be with some legitimate, white-collar brother, not some hood nigga that was probably destined for the pen. Cash told himself that but it wasn't really what he wanted. He wanted to be the nigga that put the smile on her face. He wanted Fallon to be the woman that he came home to every night.

He'd deemed it impossible, thinking that his chance had slipped out of his grasp that year ago, but since she had reached out to Strap, maybe it was Fallon's way of letting him know that she felt the same way about him. Cash wasn't sure, but he was going to find out.

"Is anybody gonna tell me who she is?" Ghost asked finally, not missing the spaced out look on Cash's face.

"My ole lady… I mean, she used to be," Cash admitted.

"Goddamn. You was hittin' that?!" he asked in awe, remembering her coca-cola shape. "Shit. Shawty was bad as hell. If I was you I would—"

"I'm goin' to bed," Strap interrupted, not caring to hear any more of the conversation. "You had anything else you wanted to talk to us about?"

Strap's latest revelation about Fallon had completely eradicated Cash's thoughts from earlier—that and the blunt that he had been smoking. "Nah. Y'all just watch that shit next time. I'll holla at y'all."

"Ole sucka for love ass nigga," Ghost scoffed as he closed the front door behind Cash. "You seen the way that nigga was looking?"

"Yeah," Strap answered unenthused.

"Better yet…" Ghost smirked. "I seen the way *you* was lookin'. Don't tell me you got feelings for his bitch?"

"What? Don't be crazy, nigga. She bad as hell, but that's it."

"Nah, nigga. If it's one thing I know, it's how to read a muh'fucka. Especially you. You want that bitch too and you better hope Cash don't ever find out *especially* if that's wifey."

Ghost had been in juvie during Cash and Fallon's relationship, hence he never knew about it. When he got out, they were already broken up.

"Niggas don't play bout that shit." Ghost thought of his own girl and shook his head. His feelings for her weren't that deep but he would be damned if he let another nigga try him by hollering at her. Now if she hollered back, that was a different story. 'If you could hit her, you could have her', was his mantra. "Is she feelin' you too…?"

"You trippin', nigga. I told you it ain't shit so drop it!"

Strap couldn't believe that his emotions had been so easy to detect, but then figured it was only because they were twins. They may not have been identical in appearance but their thought process was undeniably in tune with one another. They could read each other like an Ashley & JaQuavis novel.

"Whatever, nigga. Just watch that shit," Ghost warned. "You playin' with fuckin' fire."

Chapter 5

Outlaw frowned as he stumbled in the doorway. He had just gotten home after leaving Durham, where Kaleesha stayed. He'd also made a brief pit stop to check on his three p's—his peoples, his profit, and his product. It was nearly one o' clock in the morning so he knew that Shantreis was pissed, but he had to handle his business.

The house was dark so Outlaw couldn't tell what had caused him to trip up and nearly bust his ass. "You always talkin' bout me leavin' my shit out but—" he stopped when he flipped the light switch and noticed his suitcases packed up by the door. "What the fuck?"

He stormed to their bedroom, muttering obscenities the whole way. "Shantreis, what's up with this shit?"

Shantreis feigned sleep as she rolled over on her side. Outlaw sucked his teeth, "I know you hear me, girl." He removed her sleep mask from her eyes.

Immediately she put on her bitch face and pulled the mask back down, "Get the fuck out of my face, Outlaw. Ya shit is packed up so you can go on back to whatever bitch you came from house."

"What the fuck, man!" he exclaimed, throwing his hands up in the air. "Why is you trippin' again? I told you I was seein' my daughter and you gonna kick me out for that shit?!"

Shantreis couldn't believe that Outlaw had the audacity to play the victim. She pulled her mask up and frowned, "Nigga, that was damn near an hour ago and you want me to believe that bullshit?!"

"Damn. You act like you don't know that a nigga be in the streets. Why the fuck you actin' brand new?"

She laughed as if she was watching Kevin Hart perform standup comedy, "Negro, please. Save that shit for one of them simple bitches that'll believe it."

"I ain't got time for this shit, Shantreis. What the fuck wrong wit' ya ass?"

"This, muthafucka!" she shouted, pulling out her iPhone.

Outlaw looked dumbfounded as he took in the picture that she was showing him. It was Kaleesha, butt ass naked showing off his chain proudly like it belonged around her neck.

"Say somethin', muthafucka!" she barked, jumping in his face and pressing a finger into his chest.

"What the fuck is that supposed to prove? That I'm fuckin' that bitch?" he asked incredulously.

Shantreis rolled her eyes. "You tell me, Outlaw!"

"Why would I fuck with her when I got you at home?" he asked, deciding to go in a different direction. "You know that bitch desperate to break us up and you gonna believe a damn picture?"

Shantreis snickered as she clapped her hands to put

emphasis on every word she spoke, "Why niggas always gotta lie? Tell the truth, my nigga! You was fuckin' that bitch!"

Outlaw sighed. He was trying to be calm but he was heated. He wanted to walk out and beat Kaleesha's ass for that shit, but he knew he couldn't. It wasn't because she was the mother of his child. He could give a fuck about that. He was more concerned about her calling the law and having him locked up over some bullshit.

"Look, when I play with Monet I take my chain off sometimes. The bitch musta picked the shit up then." Outlaw shrugged her off. "You trippin' bout nothing. Like always."

"Whatever!" she huffed. "Tell that bitch to quit playin' on my fuckin' phone! She shouldn't even have my damn number in the first place!"

Outlaw was quiet as he started to get undressed. To argue with Shantreis would be pointless. She wouldn't believe anything he said and even if she did, she wouldn't admit it. Instead, she preferred to argue until he shut her up.

"You hear me, Outlaw?" she asked, trying hard not to stare at his body. He looked like he had come straight out of a sexy men's calendar for women. His ripped body and rugged appeal turned her on. He reminded Shantreis of a more muscular version of the rapper Future. Looking at Outlaw, it was easy to see why bitches went gaga over him, but he belonged to her.

"Yeah, Shantreis. Goddamn! Even the fuckin' neighbors can hear ya loud ass!"

"I don't give a damn!" she shouted. "I dare any one of them muthafuckas to come over here and say shit to me!" She tossed a pillow at his head. "You better gon' 'head and get you a blanket out of the linen closet 'cuz you ain't sleepin' with me tonight. Or you can take ya ass back to where you came from!"

Outlaw stepped closer to her, invading her space. Shantreis frowned as he pushed her back onto the wall. His expression was emotionless and for a quick second she wondered if she had gone too far.

"Well?" she asked finally, fed up with their staring contest.

Shantreis was completely taken off guard when he kissed her passionately, backing her up against the wall. She wanted to be angry but he was caressing her most intimate places. She couldn't suppress the squeal that escaped her lips from the pleasure he was giving her. Feeling his hardened dick against her body only turned her on more.

"Baby, stop trippin'. You know I hate bein' away from you," Outlaw murmured in-between kisses. "You know that right?"

Shantreis couldn't get the words out of her mouth when Outlaw smoothly slid one hand down the front of her boy shorts. She trembled at his touch and her hard demeanor had quickly disappeared. His other hand groped her soft, cantaloupe sized breasts while his mouth continued to rain kisses feverishly on her neck.

"O-Outlaw," she gasped. He dipped his fingers inside of her before placing a finger into her mouth so that she could sample her sweetness.

"Take my pants off," he whispered.

Shantreis didn't waste any time unbuckling his shorts and pulling down his boxers. Slowly he inserted his chocolate wand inside of her love box teasing her at first with the head.

"Baby, please…" she moaned.

Outlaw smiled. He loved to hear her beg. He continued for a few more seconds before he decided he couldn't take it anymore. Shantreis was soaking wet and he couldn't wait to indulge in her tight, warm insides. She let out small moans as Outlaw plunged in and out of her deeply. He wanted to make sure she felt every inch.

"Baby, take it easy," she uttered softly trying to place a hand on his leg to slow him down.

"Nah, cuz you wanna act like I don't miss my pussy and shit while I'm out." He swatted her hand away and placed both of his hands on her shapely hips, allowing himself to go deeper. "I'm bout to show yo lil' ass."

"Unt uh. I'm bout to show you," Shantreis insisted as she held onto his neck and shifted her legs to encircle his waist.

"Damn, girl…"

Utilizing her lower body strength, she bounced up and down on his dick. "That bitch fuck you like this?" she asked seductively.

"Hell no."

"Her pussy as good as mine?"

"You know it ain't," Outlaw uttered, looking her deeply in the eyes.

"Then stop fuckin' with them hoes."

"I swear…" he groaned, loving the way she took control and enjoying the way her titties shook like jello.

"Better not."

Outlaw smirked as he linked his arms under the back of her knees, regaining control. He drilled into her like a jackhammer but that didn't slow Shantreis down. She continued to bounce with him as they stared into each other's eyes intensely, wondering who would succumb to the orgasmic feeling first.

"Baby!" Shantreis squealed when Outlaw surprised her

by slowing up the pace and cramming his full girth into her. She knew that she was about to explode. She kissed his lips ardently before surrendering to the pleasure he was giving her. He gave her two good orgasms in a row before he was finally spent.

"You happy now?" he asked with a smirk. He knew Shantreis' MO. This was their usual routine. She would throw a fit until he gave her some of the magic stick. There was no sex that was better than makeup sex, in her opinion. He agreed so he never failed to oblige her.

"Whatever, nigga." She laughed as she threw a pillow at him. "The dick was good but you still sleepin' ya ass on the couch."

Damn.

Chapter 6

"How y'all doing today? What can I getcha?" the elderly waitress asked, her pen and paper in hand ready to take down the couple's order.

"Let me get a coffee to start with and she'll have a sweet tea. Right, Fallon?"

They were sitting at the Waffle House on Westinghouse Boulevard, where Kevin had invited her out to breakfast. At first Fallon had wanted to decline but then she remembered her friend's words from yesterday. Kevin did have a lot to offer and maybe she wasn't giving him a fair chance. She decided that grabbing a bite to eat wouldn't hurt anything.

"Yeah. That's right," Fallon replied.

"Y'all ready to order?"

They rattled off their orders and the waitress looked at Kevin with an odd expression on her face. "Mind me for staring. It's just you look like someone famous but I can't quite place my finger on it."

Kevin smiled, revealing both rows of his perfect pearly whites. "Terrence Howard, perhaps?"

"Yup." She snapped her finger excitedly as if he had admitted that he was the famous actor. The waitress flashed a gap toothed grin at Fallon. "Y'all make a fine couple. Hold on to that one."

"I will try," Kevin spoke up good-naturedly before glimpsing at her name badge. "Sally, I keep trying to tell her that it's hard to find a good man. I'm one of the last."

There goes that damn cockiness, Fallon thought as she plastered a fake smile on her face. She had to admit that Kevin was good looking and dressed to the nines that morning in an Armani suit. He looked like he'd just stepped out of the pages of a GQ magazine.

"He's right, girlie." Sally nodded. "Don't worry. You all will be fine."

Kevin turned his attention back to Fallon as the waitress trotted off, "I appreciate you coming out to meet me… although I really could have picked you up."

"I have a few other errands to run and I know you have to run to the office a little later. I didn't want to hold you up," she lied, knowing damn good and well that she just didn't want Kevin to know where she stayed. He'd been trying—and to no avail—to invite himself over but each time she found an excuse. Now was no different.

"Are you embarrassed about where you live?"

"What?" Fallon asked, raising an eyebrow, slightly offended by his suggestion.

"I'm serious. We've been dating for nearly five months and I still don't know where you live, Fallon. You don't find that a bit odd?"

"I don't see what the big deal is."

"I've invited you over to my house but you never

come... Even if I offer to pick you up from your house, you insist on meeting me."

Fallon sighed. "Honestly, Kevin, I just think things are moving too fast. When the time is right I'll let you know but for now, let's just take things slow."

Before Kevin could say another word, the waitress had come back. She sat their respective plates before them and proceeded to ask if they needed anything else.

"We're fine. Thank you."

"Okay, sugar. Y'all just holler if you need me." As the bells jingled signifying a new customer, Sally shouted out, "Welcome to Waffle House!"

"Fallon, we've been moving slowly enough as it is," Kevin spoke in a hushed tone. "Any other woman would be dying to come over to my house. I'm starting to think that you're not interested. That or you're a lesbian."

"Excuse me?" She sat her fork down on her plate, not believing she'd heard him correctly. "That's really how you feel?!"

"Well got damn, if it ain't muthafuckin' New-New!" a boisterous voice yelled, causing a few customers to look up in annoyance.

Kevin looked up and frowned at the young man that had seemed to appear out of thin air. He was standing next to their table and appeared to be talking to Fallon. He could tell that the boy was some sort of wannabe thug from his baggy attire and thick dreads.

"Hey... uh... Ghost, right?" Fallon asked nervously, trying to avoid another encounter like when they'd first met.

"Yeah. What's good witcha, lil' momma?" he questioned as if she was sitting alone. He pulled up a chair and sat his *Waffle House To Go* bag next to her. "I'm glad you ain't actin' all saditty and shit today."

"Fallon, do you know him?" Kevin gave Ghost another onceover and shot him a disapproving glare.

"Don't it sound like it?" Ghost asked, returning his glare. He turned back to Fallon. "The fuck is this Uncle Tom muthafucka you sittin' with? You ain't got love for my brother no more?"

"I don't know who your brother is but she's with me," Kevin responded gruffly.

Ghost snickered. "My nigga, you have no fuckin' idea of who you talkin' to. I suggest you take that muthafuckin' bass out ya voice when you speak to me."

"I'm not afraid of anyone. Especially not some fake Little Wayne looking—"

That was all that it took for Ghost to set it off. He pulled his heat from the front of his pants and placed it under Kevin's chin. "Still talkin' that rah-rah shit now, muthafucka?"

A few people in the restaurant shrieked and somebody yelled, "I'm callin' the law!"

"Stop!" Fallon told Ghost, not missing the murderous glare in his eyes. "Please put the gun down."

He looked Kevin in the eyes, shoving the glock roughly into his skin. He held his gaze until Kevin finally looked away. Ghost grinned, satisfied when he saw fear in his eyes. "Pussy ass nigga." Calmly he placed his firearm back into his pants and laughed loudly. "How you gonna be with a nigga that can't even protect ya ass if some shit go down?"

Not waiting for a response, and knowing that things were sure to get hot if he didn't leave soon, Ghost threw Fallon the deuces as if nothing had happened. "I'll holla at you, New-New."

Fallon watched as he strolled casually out of the door, tossed his food onto the passenger seat of a candy apple red

Chevy Caprice and skidded off.

"Who the hell was that?" Kevin asked, embarrassed by the turn of events.

Fallon shook her head. She didn't know what to say.

"And what did he mean by his brother? You're cheating on me?"

"First of all, Kevin, we're not together but no, I'm not seeing anyone else."

"Then I would really like to know how you know that thug."

"It's none of your business, honestly." She stood up, grabbing her Versace bag. "Maybe I'll talk to you later. I can't do this right now."

"Wait, Fallon." He grabbed her by the wrist, twisting it inadvertently. "You owe me some sort of an explanation."

"Will you let go of me before you start another scene?" Fallon warned. She was still pissed about his earlier allegations.

Reluctantly he released his grip. "Thank you." As Fallon marched out of the restaurant, she felt everyone's eyes on her but she didn't care what any of them thought. And she for damn sure didn't care about Kevin thought.

Kevin sighed. He just couldn't win with Fallon. He didn't understand what the hell he was doing wrong. In his opinion, he treated her the way a woman wanted to be treated. He took her out more than a little bit—at least he offered to, but most times she would decline his invitation.

They had met back in Greensboro, when she was going to A&T. Every morning she stopped by the Starbucks on Battleground Avenue to get a cappuccino, while he came for his morning coffee. He saw her every day like clockwork and finally built up the nerve to approach her. Things started out platonically enough but the more he got to know her, the more he wanted her. He thought that he'd lost his chance when his job relocated him to Raleigh, but when he ran into her at the Starbucks in Triangle Shopping Center; he figured that it was fate.

They caught up with one another, exchanged numbers, and here they were today. He was trying desperately to build something with Fallon, but it was clear to him that she wasn't ready for that yet. Still, Kevin just couldn't leave her alone. He was convinced that he could change her mind.

"You okay, baby?" Sally the waitress asked, still glancing over her shoulder every ten seconds as though she expected Ghost to come back blazing.

"Yes, ma'am." He flashed a smile, but when he thought about the way that young punk had pulled a gun out on him, he grew pissed off. He had made Kevin look like a punk. It hurt his male pride in the worst way. "If I could get the check, however."

"Sure thing, baby."

Bzzz... Bzz...

Fallon, Kevin thought as he pulled out his cell phone eagerly. Confusion washed over his face as he saw that his phone still displayed his normal background but the vibrating continued. Standing up, he noticed Fallon's phone in her seat.

Unable to mask his nosiness, he stared at the number. *919-555-5244.* As he opened the text message, his jaw dropped in shock.

Fallon, my brother gave me your number yesterday. He said you was askin' bout me... I know you probably been thinking that I ain't give a shit about you but that's not true. You been on my mind real heavy, shawty. I miss you and I want shit to go back to how it used to be. Let me know somethin'. I'm tryna get up wit' you. --Cash

No one else, my ass, Kevin thought furiously. He tossed a twenty dollar bill on the table as he stormed out of Waffle

House. The waitress was calling after him but he ignored her as he hopped into his Cadillac. Starting up the engine, he dialed the number back. He was going to break things off with Cash right now.

Kevin barely heard the phone ring before Cash picked up the phone. "Fallon? What's up, baby?"

"Try again. This is Kevin, Fallon's *man*. Stop texting my lady. Whatever you two had in the past is just that—*the past*. So I would appreciate it if you would show us some respect, and delete her number out of your phone."

Cash laughed at the man's insecurity. "Respect? Listen here, potnah, if shit was like you claim, then Fallon wouldn't have given me the number, now would she? Y'all may have had some shit going on, but I assure you that it's a wrap now. I'm back and I'm not letting her go this time."

Kevin huffed. "I'd like to see you try. Fallon had a slight lapse in judgment but it won't happen again. She's mine, *homeboy. Feel me?*" he asked, trying to match Cash's street lingo.

"I'll believe that when *she* tells me. Not some crab ass nigga that goes through his female's phone checkin' for shit." He didn't give Kevin a chance to respond before continuing, "Tell Fallon I'll holla at her later."

"Stay away from her!"

Cash snickered again, finding the conversation amusing. He was really getting a kick out of fucking with the man. "Tell her I love her and I miss that pussy too. Tell her that *He* misses her too. She'll know who I'm talking about."

Kevin didn't miss the reference and felt sick to his stomach. Fallon hadn't allowed him to sample any of her goodies and he couldn't stop the envy he felt towards Cash. Who was he to Fallon? And why was he so damn cocky and sure of himself?

"I'm not telling her shit, you fucking bastard!" Kevin

continued to yell obscenities, nearly foaming at the mouth. Noticing that Cash was quiet, he looked back at the phone and saw that he'd been talking to himself. Kevin debated calling him back but knew that there was no point. Fallon was choosing and he would be damned if he wasn't the chosen one.

He deleted Cash's text message as well as the outbound call, before slipping the phone in his pocket and pulling out of the parking lot. Making a left on Capital Boulevard as the light finally turned green, he smiled, noticing Fallon pulling out of the Dunkin Donuts a few cars ahead of him. He guessed that she had gone there for a makeshift breakfast after theirs was spoiled.

Kevin wasn't sure where she was going but he was going to find out. Ensuring that he kept a lengthy distance between them, he followed her onto I-440. He attempted to gather his thoughts, wondering what he was going to say to her when they finally reached her destination. He wanted to ask her about Cash, but didn't want it to be known that he'd gone through her phone. He knew that he wouldn't be able to score points with her that way.

Normally he wouldn't even want to be bothered with a female after this point but his male pride was once again bruised. This was like a competition to him and there was no way that he was going to let Cash win. Kevin vowed to win Fallon over and then dump her ass. He wasn't anybody's fool.

After traveling on the highway for several minutes, she finally got off on exit 7B towards Crabtree. Kevin continued behind her, being cautious to ensure that she didn't notice him. He doubted that Fallon would check her rearview and spot him, but he wasn't taking any chances. When she finally turned into Colonial Grand apartments, Kevin was smiling like a Cheshire cat. He parked a few spots away from her and watched her get out of her BMW and trot to an apartment on the second floor.

Got you, Fallon. Kevin wouldn't strike now, but he would use this piece of information to his advantage later. He had an appointment to attend and he was already fifteen minutes late—but it was well worth it.

Chapter 7

"What the fuck was that shit, Kaleesha?" Outlaw barked, pulling the cell phone receiver closer to his mouth. He wanted to ensure that she could hear him clearly.

"What are you talkin' about?" she asked nonchalantly, ignoring how loud he was yelling in her ear.

"You sendin' that picture to my ole lady."

"I don't know what you're talking about."

"Bitch! Do I need to send you the muthafuckin' picture? Ya ass was wearin' my damn ace of spades chain!"

"Oh yea…" Kaleesha responded dryly. It was clear to Outlaw that she didn't give a fuck and it was pissing him off.

"You lucky I don't beat ya ass for that shit!"

"Whatever, Outlaw, you ain't gonna do shit or I'm a' give ya ole lady some better shit to confront ya ass about. That picture wasn't shit. I got plenty of dirt on ya ass. You done put ya hands on me for the last time, muthafucka."

"Bitch, you think it's a fuckin' game?! I've killed niggas

for less than that shit!" He was quiet as he listened to what sounded like Kaleesha covering up the receiver and speaking to someone. "What? Who that talkin' in the background? You got a nigga over there?"

"Hey, baby," Shantreis sang as she entered the house. She headed over to where Outlaw sat on the sofa and wrapped her arms around him, getting ready to give him a kiss but he moved back from her and raised his index finger to signify that she needed to be quiet.

Well fuck you too, Shantreis thought as she sat on the loveseat furthest from him.

"What do it matter if I do or not?" Kaleesha responded finally. "You ain't my nigga so you shouldn't be worried about it. What I do with my pussy is none of your concern."

"I knew you was a fuckin' ho!" Outlaw roared.

Shantreis raised her eyebrows at the conversation. She already knew that he was talking to Kaleesha and frowned. *What the hell this bitch done did this time?*

"I don't give a fuck about what you do but you ain't gonna have niggas in and out of the house where *my* daughter live! Besides that, I pay the bills in that muthafucka!" Outlaw continued to rant.

"And you gonna keep payin' 'em because your daughter is here," Kaleesha retorted with a smile in her voice. She was enjoying how pissed off Outlaw was getting.

"Bitch, I oughta—" Before he could finish his threat, he heard the line go quiet and knew that she had hung up. Outlaw turned to Shantreis, "Can you believe that bitch got a fuckin' nigga around my daughter?"

Shantreis rolled her eyes. "What's this really about, Outlaw? Is it really about your daughter or something else?"

"The fuck you mean?" he asked incredulously, "There you go with that bullshit!"

She shrugged, not giving a damn about his outburst. "I mean, the bitch been single for what—damn near three years now? It's about time she find a nigga to settle down with. If she had her own man then maybe she would leave mine alone. Unless…" her voice trailed off, "Y'all got some shit goin' on and that's what you so salty 'bout."

"I need to meet that nigga first!" Outlaw yelled, ignoring much of what Shantreis had said.

"You ain't Kaleesha daddy. She don't need ya approval."

"I'm Monet's daddy and I got a right to know who the fuck gon' be around her! It ain't many but there's a few muthafuckas that would love to do some shit to fuck with me. You don't think my daughter would be the first person they would go after? And that stupid bitch Kaleesha wouldn't even realize it!"

Shantreis nodded, realizing his point. Immediately she felt foolish in her accusations but she wasn't about to let Outlaw know that. "So what you gonna do about it?" She arose from the other sofa and sat next to him. She placed her soft hands on his shoulders, giving him a massage.

Outlaw sighed. "I wanna go over there but that bitch ain't stupid. I know that nigga will be ghost by the time I get there. I'll deal with the shit later."

She kissed his cheek. "Well, me and Fallon are going out tonight."

"Going out?" He raised an eyebrow. "Where?"

"Wouldn't you like to know?" she teased. Seeing the serious expression on his face, she changed her answer, "To the club."

"Damn. When was you gonna ask me?"

"*Ask you?* Negro, you ain't my daddy."

"But I'm still ya nigga. I coulda had some shit

planned."

"Be for real. You know damn well you ain't had nothin' planned. Besides, I ain't had a girls' night out in a long ass time. I'm tired of sittin' in the house all the damn time."

Outlaw scowled. "Hell nah, Shantreis. I ain't wit' that shit. My ole lady ain't bout to be at no damn club shakin' her ass for niggas to look at. What the fuck you wanna go out for anyway? You lookin' for another nigga?"

"Why it gotta be all that?"

"Because muthafuckas only go to the damn club to find somebody to fuck so ya ass ain't got no business in there."

"You be goin' to the clubs!"

"I handle *business* in the club!" he snapped. "You a female."

Outlaw continued to lecture her but Shantreis had tuned him out. She had made up her mind already. Nothing he said would change that. She was a grown ass woman!

"You hear me, Shantreis?" Outlaw asked. "The only time you need to be up in a club is if I'm there."

"I got you, baby," she replied in a syrupy sweet tone although she was inwardly rolling her eyes. She knew that the easiest way to end the conversation would be to agree with him. Shantreis knew that he had a business meeting to attend that night so he wouldn't be home to babysit her anyway. She was going out and she would be damned if he thought that he was going to keep her in the house.

"Only you, bitch," Shantreis commented with a smile as Fallon relayed the story back to her. "That's one wild lil' nigga!"

"I know right?" Fallon shook her head as she continued to rifle through the many rows of clothes in her closet.

"I bet Kevin's ass was embarrassed."

"I could see it on his face but if he hadn't tried to be 'macho man', it wouldn't have happened. I'm sure of that." She shrugged. "I'm surprised he hasn't texted me yet."

They were at Fallon's house, putting the last touches on their makeup and hair before they headed out to the club. It was almost midnight but they wanted to ensure that they made a fashionably late appearance. They certainly didn't want to appear as though they needed to rush while the bar and the doors were still free.

"Oh and, bitch, I texted you earlier."

"I didn't get it." Fallon walked over to her purse and dug her hand inside, feeling for her phone. After several unsuccessful tries, she finally dumped everything out of it. "It's not in here."

"Damn. Damn. Damn," she joked, mocking Florida Evans from *Good Times*. "You think Kevin got it?"

"It's probably just in the car…"

"Yeah. You'll be all right." Shantreis shrugged. "You got a phone lock right? Or that lil' GPS shit that tells you where your phone is?"

"Nah… But what the hell can Kevin do with my phone anyway? I don't have anything in there." Then her mind raced back to Cash. What if he tried to call her? Fallon shook her head, dismissing that notion immediately. Cash hadn't tried to get in touch with her yet. She was apparently the only one that wanted that old thing back.

"Then quit trippin'." Shantreis smiled at her reflection in the mirror and blew herself a kiss. She was flawless.

"She ain't nothin' but a hoochie mama," Fallon teased

as Shantreis stepped out of the bathroom. "I can't believe Outlaw let you out of the house looking like that."

Shantreis wore a tight, Herve Leger dress that barely left anything to the imagination. Her breasts were threatening to spill right out of her top and the material hugged her ghetto booty snugly, causing it to appear larger than it was. Because of her apple bottom, the dress stopped directly under the brown of her ass. Her Christian Louboutin heels matched perfectly but in Fallon's opinion, Shantreis was dressed more like an overpriced hooker than a chick going out with her girl to a club.

"He didn't," she replied casually. "But he's never gonna know because he has some business meeting with some niggas and blah blah." She waved her hand dismissively. "I'll just change my clothes before I get back home." Shantreis pointed towards her overnight bag. "That nigga gonna be all right. Besides, he should want his bitch to look fly when she steps out."

"Yeah and when Outlaw beat that ass…" Fallon joked before she looked at her own ensemble. She wore a peasant blouse that hung off her shoulders and exposed her flat stomach. She matched it with a pair of short black shorts and her own red bottom pumps.

Shantreis frowned. "Fuck you, bitch. My game is tight. I'm good." She jingled her car keys. "You ready or what?"

The two women stepped out of the house looking like video vixens. Shantreis knew that all eyes would be on them and she couldn't wait.

Chapter 8

"Ghost, can't we go somewhere a little more... *private?*" Ri-Ri whispered in his ear, ensuring that he could hear her over the noise in the packed club. Lightly she licked the outline of his ear, in an attempt to convince him that with her was where he needed to be.

"Shit... You ain't said shit but a word." Ghost grinned as he walked towards his brothers. "I'm a' holla at y'all." He nodded towards the redbone requesting his company for the night.

Ri-Ri was the closest thing he had to having a real relationship with a female. He had broken shawty off a few times but didn't hit her up as often as she would have liked. Ghost knew that because she was always texting him and shit, begging for him to come through. It wasn't that he wasn't interested, but he had more important things to handle besides checking in with a bitch on the daily. Tonight however, he would make the exception. Ghost hadn't had some good pussy in days and knew that a night with Ri-Ri was just what he needed.

"Aiight then." Cash nodded his head, giving him the okay.

"Maybe we could too?" Ri-Ri's homegirl asked Strap. Strap had barely noticed her but she had been trying to get his attention all night. She thought that he was cute and she was dying to fuck with hood royalty.

Everybody knew of the Hardy Boys, which was what most people referred to them collectively, calling them by their last name. They were three of the most elite hood niggas that a female would want to fuck with and without a doubt, ole girl wanted a piece of the pie—the privilege of having one night with a member of their camp.

"I don't know about that, lil' momma." Strap didn't make it a habit to fuck with random females because he didn't trust them. Ever cautious, he always thought things through. He wasn't trying to get caught slipping—be it by a male or female.

"Why not?" Ghost asked with raucous laughter. "You scared of the pussy?"

"Never that," he responded coolly.

"Then what's the hold up?" Ghost lowered his tone so that Cash couldn't hear him. "It'll take your mind off O.P.P." Again he erupted into laughter at his tasteless joke.

"Fuck you, nigga!" Strap yelled. Determined to prove his brother wrong, he turned to the female. "Let's go, shawty."

Cash laughed to himself as he watched them walk away. He didn't know what their exchange had been about but watching the two of them interact was always amusing. They were like day and night but still so similar.

"My nigga, you straight?" Cash asked Outlaw. The answer was obvious judging from the Buffie the Body lookalike that was giving him a lap dance.

"Fo' sho." He smiled. "Thanks for hookin' a nigga up."

"Hell nah. You ain't puttin' that shit on me! Shantreis ain't 'bout to blame me for it. You know how ya ole lady get."

Outlaw chuckled. It was true that Shantreis didn't play when it came to him, but what she didn't know wouldn't hurt her. Besides that, he already knew that she was going out to the club tonight. When he had called her earlier, she was keeping up the innocent act, but he knew better. In order to avoid a headache from coming home to an empty house, he decided that he would just stay out.

"She'll be straight. She knows I'm at a business meeting."

Cash shook his head, knowing that if Shantreis were to see him, she would never believe it. "Yeah, aiight."

"Shit. Am I lying? We had the meeting. I just had time to chill too."

"Whatever, nigga. That's on you."

No sooner than the words left Cash's mouth, had Shantreis and Fallon entered the club. Outlaw didn't notice and neither had Shantreis—yet.

"This shit jumpin'!" Shantreis yelled as she rocked back and forth to the beat, leading her girl to the bar.

Fallon nodded her head in approval singing along with Nicki Minaj, *'I'll do anything that you say, anything cuz you the boss…'*

Shantreis ordered a Blue Motorcycle and sipped it slowly as she scanned the dance floor. She was starting out slow but she intended on getting fucked up tonight. She knew that she probably wouldn't get another opportunity to come out so she wanted to make sure that the night was one not to be forgotten.

They sauntered back to the dance floor, drawing plenty

of stares from the men in the room. Just as Shantreis had predicted, they were the baddest in the building. While that rang true, her provocative dancing also had a lot to do with it. She was gyrating more than the females in those old BET Uncut music videos.

"Damn, lil' momma," one man commented, admiring Shantreis.

"I got a man," Fallon told one of the hopefuls that approached her. Quite a few men had tugged on her, requesting a dance but she wasn't interested.

She was more reserved. She rocked back and forth half-heartedly, starting to regret her decision to come with Shantreis to the club. It just wasn't her scene anymore. Hell, she hadn't been to the club since she was a teenager. Fallon felt out of place and awkward even though she didn't look it.

"Hey, Fallon," Shantreis leaned over to whisper in her ear, "I'm gonna—"

"What?" she asked with a frown, wondering why she'd stopped abruptly. She pointed behind her.

"There goes Cash."

Fallon felt like the air had been knocked out of her. Suddenly she could no longer hear the sound of the music and she couldn't see anyone else but him.

Decked out in a pair of True Religion jeans, a fresh wifebeater, and enough ice to cool off a desert, Cash was *that* nigga. He was dressed simply but his demeanor … That was something different all together. His swagger made anything that adorned his 6'4, 210 pound frame look fly as hell. To Fallon, he was the finest man she'd ever seen. She loved his ebony-colored skin-tone and the way his dreads stopped in the middle of his back. Even after a year Cash still looked like the same guy that she had fallen in love with. He hadn't changed a bit.

"You gonna say something to him?" Shantreis asked, breaking Fallon out of her thoughts.

"I can't..." she whispered finally. Her eyes stayed trained on him, but she couldn't will her feet to move towards him.

"Girl, you better say somethin' to that nigga or *I* will. You know how I get down."

Without a doubt, Fallon knew. Shantreis would get all loud and hood as hell, embarrassing Fallon in the process. She would rather that she did it on her own terms.

"What do I say?" Fallon felt like she was back in high school, unsure of herself when it came to her crush. She didn't know if she wanted to yell at him, cry, ignore him, or run from him. Waves of different emotions were flooding her brain.

"Just say hello. Damn, Fallon. You actin' like you weren't with the man for three years."

"So much time has passed... He may have a girl already."

"Oh well! You'll never know unless you say something to him!" Without another word, Shantreis pushed her gently in his direction.

Fallon stumbled slightly, but quickly found her footing and made her way through the busy crowd. Cash was still standing at the bar, waiting for his drink. She sucked in a deep breath as she stood next to him. She could already smell the tantalizing scent of his Giorgio Armani cologne. "Hey, Damontrez," she squeaked.

Surprised by hearing his God-given name, he looked towards the low voice. He blinked twice, as though his eyes were deceiving him. "Fallon? Damn, I missed you, shawty." Without another word he wrapped his arms around her, holding her tightly. She returned the embrace wholeheartedly. She felt secure. It was a sensation that she hadn't felt in a long time.

Cash pulled back, grabbing her left wrist. He smiled noticing that she still had the tattoo she'd gotten back when she turned nineteen. It read 'First Love' along with the date they officially hooked up: September 16, 2008.

"You never covered it," he stated in awe.

"Why would I?" She smiled. "It's true." Fallon brushed his dreads away from his neck, revealing a tattoo of her red, heart-shaped lips. Her name was signed underneath in a way that resembled lipstick. That had been her way of branding him and his way of showing his love for her. Although his body was covered in tattoos, that one was always easy to make out. "And you didn't either. I know your girlfriend has to be mad."

"Nah. No girlfriend. I'm solo dolo…"

"I never—" She stopped, noticing the intense look in his eyes. "What?"

Cash pulled her into him, kissing her passionately. The first feel of his tongue against hers caused Fallon's panties to soak with cream. The taste of liquor and weed entered her mouth but she didn't mind it. If anything, she invited it. She'd missed him, every little thing about him.

Just as she felt his dick harden against her stomach, Cash pulled back from her. It was as though he remembered that they were in a public place. "Can we talk…? Somewhere else?"

Fallon nodded. "I came with Shantreis… I'll have to let her know… I'll be back."

She pushed her way through the crowd. As the lights came back on and DJ Unk stopped warning females not to hide the pussy, she looked around confused. *Is it over already?* Fallon glanced at her watch. It was only one thirty. She knew the club didn't close until at least two thirty or three. *What's the deal?* She didn't have to wonder for long because she could see why everyone had gathered into a small semi-circle.

"Nigga, you don't know that's my fuckin' bitch?!" Outlaw hollered at another dude. The man appeared to be unfazed by his threats while Shantreis stood on the sidelines with wide eyes.

What's Outlaw doing here? Fallon wondered, watching the scene unfold.

"Shit. We was just havin' a good time, my nigga. Nothing serious," the man replied in a nonchalant manner, his hands shoved deep into the pockets of his baggy jeans. He was small compared to Outlaw's thick, muscular frame but the man didn't seem to be intimidated in the least.

"Nigga, I'll show ya ass a good time… You must not know who the fuck I am!"

"Should I?" he asked, unimpressed.

Outlaw snickered. "If you don't, you will soon. 'Lemme holla atcha outside."

"You ain't said shit but a word."

"Stop!" Shantreis begged as she grabbed for Outlaw, who was already heading out the door.

"Get the fuck off me, Shantreis!" He snatched away from her violently, nearly causing her to fall to the floor. "I told ya ass to stay at home but you never wanna listen to a nigga! Then I catch ya ass grindin' on another nigga dick and shit! Get the fuck outta here!"

"Fuck you, Outlaw! I saw you with that big booty bitch in VIP too so save that shit!" Shantreis continued to follow after him, tugging on his Polo shirt. "Thought you was at a business meeting, you lyin' muthafucka!"

Outlaw ignored her as he finally made it outside, surprised to see that ole buddy was waiting for him. He didn't show any signs of backing down. Outlaw would enjoy knocking this nigga down to size. It wasn't as though he wasn't little enough. The dude reminded him of the rapper T.I., he was just as yellow and just as scrawny. He couldn't be much taller than 5'10 and 160 pounds soaking wet.

A small crowd had gathered, but most were smart enough to get in their cars and bounce. They didn't want to get caught up in the crossfire if bullets started flying.

"Just leave, Blaze!" Shantreis pleaded, speaking to the T.I. lookalike.

"Fuck that shit. I'm a man about mines."

Outlaw raised his eyebrow at their exchange. She seemed too friendly with him and he immediately wondered if she knew him before tonight's encounter. "What's good, my nigga?" Outlaw pulled out his chrome to let him know that he was serious.

"Ay. Chill," Cash demanded, coming in-between the pair. He had stood silently long enough. It was time to break things up. "Y'all makin' my shit hot."

Cash owned the club and made plenty of illegal transactions there. The last thing he needed was an investigation after they started shooting shit up. There were too many witnesses around and he had enough legal woes. He would be damned if some shit that didn't involve him fucked up his operation.

"If y'all got some shit to handle, handle your business. But not in front of *my* business," Cash added in an authoritative tone. "Take that shit elsewhere."

Blaze nodded his head, respecting Cash's wishes. "I can respect that." He looked Outlaw in the eyes, a murderous glint present. "For now."

Outlaw only smirked. "Bet."

"I'll see you around, shawty," Blaze said, winking at Shantreis. He did it solely to piss Outlaw off, but he meant it too.

Shantreis stood there looking stuck-on-stupid as she watched Blaze hop into a black Yukon Denali. Bumping a Pastor Troy throwback '*Pussy Ass Nigga*', his tires screeched as he bent the corner and disappeared from sight.

"Get in the fuckin' car!" Outlaw shouted from where he stood near his Maserati. As Shantreis made her way towards him, he suddenly shook his head, changing his mind. "Matter fact, carry ya ass on home. You better hope you make it there before I do. I want ya ass out of my fuckin' house!"

"Fuck you, Outlaw! I ain't leavin' shit! That muthafuckin' condo is in my goddamn name! Try me, muthafucka! I dare you!"

He nodded his head with a slick look on his face. He was embarrassed, but he kept his cool. "Keep talkin' that shit for muthafuckas to hear! It'll be World War III off in this bitch!"

"You ain't crazy enough to put ya hands on me!" Shantreis continued to yell after him as she walked towards her Jaguar. In the midst of all the chaos, she had completely forgotten about her girl. All that was on her mind was what was going to happen when she got home.

She knew she had fucked up royally but she was tired of Outlaw thinking he could do shit and get away with it. Shantreis decided to give him a dose of his own medicine when she spotted him with Big Booty Judy in VIP. Even when she finally managed to catch his eye, that didn't stop her show. She continued to bump and grind on Blaze and now here they were—having a shouting match for everybody to gossip about.

"What happened?" Fallon asked in disbelief to no one in particular.

"All I remember is Outlaw coming over and snatchin'

that girl up like a rag doll after he seen her dancin' with buddy… I think you pretty much caught everything else," a clubgoer commented.

Fallon shook her head, hoping that Outlaw would have calmed down by the time he got home. He looked mad as hell and she wanted to be sure that he wouldn't take it out on her friend.

Cash walked over to her and as if reading her mind, he spoke, "He ain't gonna do nothin'."

"I hope not… But Shantreis left me and I rode with her so you'll have to take me home."

He grinned, tossing her his keys. "Aiight. You drivin' though."

"You really want me to drive?"

Cash shrugged. "Why not? Didn't I always used to let you push my shit?"

"Yeah but…"

"Honestly, I'm a lil' fucked up so if you don't wanna die tonight, I suggest you drive."

She giggled as she punched his arm lightly. "You so silly."

Chapter 9

"You said you talked to *my* man?" Fallon asked, perplexed as they glided down the streets of downtown Raleigh in Cash's silver Bentley Continental GTC. Her hair whipped back and forth from the wind since she had the top down. They garnered stares whenever they stopped at any red lights from people attempting to get a better look at the car that cost as much—if not more than their own house.

"Yeah. Earlier today," Cash replied.

"I don't have a man."

"Well the nigga answered *your* phone, tellin' me to stop callin' you and shit."

"Aw hell… You must mean Kevin. He's not my man though," she tried to quickly explain. The last thing she wanted was for Cash to get the wrong idea. "We—"

"Ssh," Cash quieted her. "Fuck all that shit. I don't give a damn about no shit you had with another nigga. As long as the shit over with, that's all that matters."

"Like I told you, he's *not* my man," Fallon stated again, wanting to be clear. "And never was."

He shrugged, not fully believing her. "Yeah okay. But it still don't make no difference to me either way." Cash took a pull of his blunt. "How you been though?"

"I've been good. You know I got my degree a few months ago."

He smiled widely, happy to hear the news. "Congratulations, baby. I always knew you would. You smart as hell. I wouldn't expect anything less from Fallon Cherisse Hall."

"Thank you," she blushed. "And thanks again for paying my tuition *and* my rent. You know you didn't have to… especially after we broke up and all."

Cash shook his head. "Yes I did. Don't worry about it. That lil' money they was askin' for ain't shit to me."

She sighed, knowing it was solely due to his dirty money. "Yeah. You still hustlin' huh?"

"Don't do this, Fallon." He blew a thick cloud of smoke as he positioned his chair from its reclining position. Cash knew that shit was about to get serious.

"Do what?" She shrugged as she pulled into her apartment complex. "I'm just saying."

"Baby, you got to understand… This shit is all I know! What the fuck else you want me to do?" Cash extended both of his arms for emphasis. "You see this car? This is a two hundred thousand dollar car, Fallon! You can't tell me you don't like this shit!"

Fallon frowned. "It's a nice car, but so what?"

"I like to have nice shit! That's the point. I gotta do what the hell I gotta do to *keep* having nice shit! Think about it. *Hustlin'* is what got you through school! *Hustlin'* paid for the apartment you stayed in so you could stack your own paper—so you could focus more on them books instead of stressin' 'bout havin' to pay some crackas back on a fuckin' loan." He pointed at her BMW. "*Hustlin'* is what got you that 7-series Beemer. C'mon, shawty, how can you really fault me?"

"Don't get it twisted, Cash! I could have paid for my own things!"

"But you didn't! You let *me* take care of it. That's what I'm supposed to do. I'm ya man! You can't tell a man how to provide for his family!"

"You can't take care of anything locked up, Cash! Didn't you always used to tell me that empires fall when niggas get greedy? That niggas need to learn when to pull out of the game? You don't think it applies to you too?"

She could feel herself getting too emotional and sprang up from the driver's seat and towards her apartment. She was embarrassed by the tears that she knew were coming soon. Things weren't going anything like Fallon thought it would, but then again, she didn't know what she'd expected. Thinking that Cash was just going to offer to pull out of the game was farfetched and she felt stupid for having her mind set on that.

Fallon reached inside her purse clumsily, fumbling for her house keys. No sooner than she had the key inside of lock, Cash had caught up with her. He grabbed her gently by the arm just as she pushed the door open. "I know you don't believe me, but nothin' is gonna happen. I'm good right now. I got a year—maybe two and I'll retire. Pass this shit on to my lil' brother or—"

"I was just talking to Strap about that. I told him to strive for more than the drug game. At least push your brothers to find a legal hustle! There are only two outcomes, Cash, death or jail." She freed herself from his grasp and walked inside of her apartment with him close on her heels.

"That won't be me," he tried to convince her. In all honesty, he knew the odds. Cash knew that the game didn't love anyone and that shit could change in the blink of an eye, but he didn't want Fallon thinking negatively. He knew that the moment he fed into her beliefs, it would only make things worse. "I'm tellin' you, baby. I been doing this since I was fifteen. Trust me, I'm good."

"You can't be this dense!" she exclaimed. Fallon may not have been raised in the streets, but she had a little bit of street smarts. Most importantly, she had common sense. She knew well enough to know that Cash was feeding her some bullshit.

"I know you can't possibly believe the shit coming out of your mouth! Just be real with me, Cash!"

"What you want me to say?" he shouted back, throwing his arms up in defeat. "Yeah, I know this shit dangerous! Yeah I know I could get locked up! In life, everybody has to take risks. Niggas who risk the most see the most profits!"

"I guess that's why you risked me…" she added softly.

"What?" Cash asked, not believing that he heard her correctly. "Why I risked you? Baby, what are you talking about?"

Fallon's eyes welled with tears as she stared at him. She couldn't respond. Her voice was caught in her throat and she knew that if she tried to speak, everything would come out garbled. She swore that she had cried her last tears for Cash last year when they broke up, but here she was once again crying over him.

As the tears finally fell, Cash kissed them away softly. "That's not true. I mean, yeah I have money but what is it worth without you?" He pulled her into his arms. "It wasn't about puttin' money before you. Honestly, I just stopped being selfish. It wasn't right for me to think you'd be cool wit' me leaving you at home alone and shit while I handle business. A nigga tried, Fallon, but I knew you deserved more."

"So basically, nothing's changed huh?" Fallon asked bitterly.

Cash sighed. It was a question that he still wasn't sure he could answer. He wanted to balance both of the things that mattered most to him but he knew that Fallon wanted all of him or none of him.

"For what it's worth, I love you. And although I tried to move on, I always feel like I'm missing something and that's you." He kissed her on the forehead and whispered in her ear, "If you can just give me some time, lil' momma, I promise it'll be just me and you. I'll be out of the game for good."

"How much time?" Fallon found herself asking, despite willing the words not to come out. She didn't want to get caught up with Cash again. At least that's what she kept trying to convince herself.

She'd never wanted to be the wifey of a kingpin. Fallon had read enough books in high school about the dangers and heartbreak of dealing with a nigga in the streets to know that she didn't want any parts of it.

All that changed when she met Cash. He immediately swept her off her feet with his personality and charm. It also helped that he had been able to conceal his lifestyle from her. That didn't last long but by the time she discovered the truth, she was in too deep.

She was in love.

"You tell me, shawty. Whenever you want."

Fallon shook her head in disbelief, "You don't mean that..."

Cash couldn't believe that he'd said it his damn self but

he knew what was most important to him, and that was having her in his life. Besides that, his legitimate businesses made more than enough for his kids and his great-grandkids to be straight, so her request wasn't as implausible as he'd made it seem throughout the years.

"Give me a date and that's it. I'll be out. I'll tie up my loose ends and focus on my legal hustles. But you gotta gimme something too… In exchange for me walking away from the game."

Fallon raised her eyebrows. "What's that?"

"Your heart."

She smiled as she kissed his lips. "Deal. You have three months."

Cash looked at her surprised. He opened his mouth to speak but she interrupted.

"I'm giving you that long because when you're out, I want it to be for good. No excuses that you didn't have sufficient time, okay?"

"Aiight, shawty." Cash kissed her again, this time deepening the kiss. Their tongues wrestled in a passionate dance of love. Smoothly he pulled off Fallon's shirt and unbuttoned her shorts.

"Oooh," she moaned. "Cash…"

"You want me to stop?" he asked, removing his hands from her body.

"No… Please don't."

Obeying her request, he slid off her thong and glided his fingers inside her most private place. She was wetter than a hurricane. "Damn, baby."

Fallon felt her legs trembling as he guided her to the sofa, urging her to have a seat. Spreading her legs wide, he got down on his knees, lapping at her juices like a kitten would its milk. "You taste so good," he complimented in-between slurps.

She was at a loss for words as she grinded her love box closer to his mouth, enjoying the feeling of ecstasy he was giving her. Her legs started to shake again and Cash knew as well as she did that she was about to reach her peak.

"Cassshhhh," she squealed as she came. Her chest was heaving and her body shuddered slightly from the aftershocks. "Oh my God..."

Cash smiled, expecting her reaction. There was no shame in his game. He was good at what he did and it was a privilege reserved only for her.

He started to unbuckle his pants, eager to feel her walls contracting against his dick. He was harder than a brick and after seeing how wet she was, he knew that he was in for a treat. Fallon's pussy had always seemed molded precisely for him, fitting like a glove.

"I missed *him* so much, baby," Fallon moaned in anticipation as she watched him release the foot long anaconda he was hiding in his pants. She couldn't wait to have him inside of her.

Bzzz... Bzzz...

"You ain't give my pussy away did you?"

"No. I wouldn't ever," Fallon answered, looking him directly in the eyes. She hoped that he could see the sincerity in her eyes—in her voice. Cash always turned her into a junkie for his sex and after they'd broken up, she'd been going through withdrawals. Still, she couldn't see herself with anyone else. Her fingers had taken the place of a man and while the feeling couldn't compare to Cash, it appeased her.

Bzzz... Bzzz...

"You let me know if it feels like another man has been

inside of me. I promise you it's tight."

"Damn," Cash could feel his dick getting harder with every word that she spoke. "I'll call ya bluff, lil' momma," he teased, but he already knew that Fallon was telling the truth. Call him a sucker, but he knew his girl. That was the difference between her and other females. She was loyal to him, no matter what. That was also the reason why he chose her—and always would.

Bzzz… Bzzz…

"Is that your phone, Cash?"

"Yeah." He sighed exasperatedly as he saw Ghost's name on the caller ID. He pushed 'ignore' and tossed the phone back on the sofa. Pulling his body closer to hers, he reached in to kiss her lips. While she was focused on their lip lock, he pushed himself inside of her.

Fallon gasped, no longer used to his girth.

"Take it, baby. It's almost in."

Bzzz… Bzzz…

"Lord have mercy…" she cried out, gripping at the cushion—gripping for anything to help her withstand the pain. "Damn, Cash!"

"You can do it. Take this dick…"

"I am!"

"That's my girl," he kissed her again in appreciation.

"Nigga, you fuckin' a bitch so you can't pick up the phone?!"

What the fuck? Cash thought, looking around. Eyeing the sofa seat, he saw that Fallon had accidentally pushed a button on his phone, answering the call.

He picked up the phone unwillingly, unable to mask the annoyance in his tone, "Whassup, Ghost?"

"Fuckin' shiesty ass bitch!" he yelled. Cash could hear a female crying in the background. "Shut the fuck up, ho!"

"Nigga, what the fuck is going on?!" he urged.

"Ay… We at… Shit. Meet us at the Super 8 off Capital."

Cash raised his eyebrows. "Ghost, this better not be no bullshit."

"Whatever, nigga." Ghost sucked his teeth. "You know I never call ya ass for shit. I know how I wanna handle it but Strap said to call you and see what you say. I'll fill you in when you get here."

"Aiight. I'll be there in like twenty minutes."

"Damn, nigga, where the fuck you at?"

"Round Briar Creek. I'm on the way. Oh and Ghost?"

"What's up?"

"You better watch the way you talk to me. Check ya tone, nigga. We blood so I let some shit slide, but I'm still ya fuckin' boss. You gon' show me some respect. Don't let us have to have this conversation again. Understood?"

The line was quiet so Cash prompted him again. "I said, do you understand me?"

"Yeah," Ghost mumbled.

Cash hung up, satisfied with his response. He knew that had been hard for Ghost. He was one of those rebellious types. He hated taking orders but Cash didn't give a damn. Ghost could act any way he wanted with anybody else, but Cash wasn't the one.

Although he knew that business came first, any nigga would be pissed off about having to slide out of some good pussy to handle somebody else's shit. Cash had to force himself to get dressed.

"What's wrong?" Fallon asked fearfully, noticing his

vexed expression.

"Fuck if I know. I'll bet it ain't shit good though." He pulled his pants back on. "Ghost and Strap always into some shit lately. I done told them niggas!"

"Be careful."

"You know I will." Cash tucked his .45 back into the waistline of his jeans. "This shouldn't take long… You want me to swing back through or…?"

"Well, I'm sure you have some business or something to take care of in the morning."

"Nah. You good. I'll be back when I finish up with my brothers." He kissed her quickly on the lips. "I love you."

"I love you too." She blushed. She hadn't said it in a long time but it felt good to say again.

"I'll hit you up when I'm on the way back."

"I don't have my phone… I lost it earlier."

Cash chuckled. "That nigga probably got it since he was playing on ya phone and shit."

Fallon sighed. "I hope not but I'll figure something out tomorrow." She hugged him tightly. "Make it back in one piece."

"I told you I will." He kissed her on the forehead.

Fallon locked the door behind him and walked back to her bedroom, slipping her satin robe on. She padded back into the living room with a smile on her face. The room still smelled like him. *Three more months,* she thought.

Knock knock!

That was quick. She looked around the floor to see what he could've possibly left behind but she didn't see anything. "Ghost changed his mind?" Fallon giggled as she opened the front door.

Her smile instantly faded when she noticed Kevin on her doorstep. "What the hell? What are you doing here? It's two thirty in the morning!"

Kevin didn't reply, only sticking his hand inside of his pocket, revealing her cell phone.

She eyed him strangely, removing the phone from Kevin's grasp. His head was down, staring at the tops of his shoes. He was creeping her out. "Thanks…" She moved to close the door but he stuck his foot between the door jamb.

"You're not going to invite me in, Fallon? Where's your hospitality?"

"What the hell is wrong with you? It's too late for company." Fallon attempted to close the door again, but Kevin used his hand to assist in his entry. "STOP!!"

"I'll be damned." With one strong push, Kevin rammed the door open. He used his other hand to push her back, knocking her onto the floor. He closed the door behind him, making sure to lock it.

Chapter 10

"Who the fuck was that nigga?" Outlaw roared, spit flying from his mouth. "You fuckin' him?"

"No!" Shantreis denied, not feeling the corner he'd backed her in—literally. She had started off dodging his questions but soon realized that Outlaw was serious. Tonight's altercation was different from their usual break up to make up sessions. The reason was most likely due to the fact that Shantreis was normally the shit starter, but now the tables had been turned.

Outlaw eyed her suspiciously. "Yeah right. What's up with this shit you got on?" He tugged at her form-fitting dress, bringing her attention to how short it was in the back. Shantreis had felt so sexy in it earlier, but now she felt cheap. "You ain't think you was gonna see me out tonight! You dressin' for other niggas and shit?!"

Shantreis swallowed the lump in her throat. She didn't know what to say. Outlaw was going hard and didn't seem like he was going to let up any time soon. She figured she would try to ride out Hurricane Outlaw by keeping quiet.

There was only so much arguing he could do by himself, right?

"Say somethin', Shantreis! You got so much shit to talk any other muthafuckin' time! Now you quiet as fuck!"

"I always dress like this!" she defended finally. "So don't act brand new now, Outlaw!"

"I be got damn if I've *ever* seen you—or let you—leave out of my muthafuckin' crib in some ho shit like this!" he snarled. "This ain't how I let my ole lady dress! Like some fuckin' ho! Bitch, get your mind right!"

"Don't call me no bitch, Outlaw!"

"Whatever, *bitch*."

Shantreis had had it. If it was one word that she couldn't stand being called, it was bitch. Ironically, it was fine when joking with friends, but in a disrespectful manner—and from a man, no less—she couldn't go for that. She pushed Outlaw with both hands and while he only went back two steps, it was two steps too far. He snapped, shoving her back against the corner.

"Don't put ya fuckin' hands on me, Shantreis!" Outlaw cautioned.

"Or what?!" she shrieked, dusting herself off. "You gonna put ya hands on me, Outlaw?! Just like a pussy ass nigga!"

He blew his breath loudly, in an effort to calm down. She was right; he wouldn't put his hands on her. At least, he didn't want to. Outlaw had slapped plenty of females around before, namely his baby mother, but never Shantreis. He didn't want to start, but he knew that if she continued like this, he would probably end up doing something to her. Outlaw was already fucking up by pushing her.

"Let's talk about you and that bitch at the club!"

Shantreis continued. The menacing look on his face scared her, but the tenacity in her wouldn't allow her to back down. *Stand your ground and let this nigga know,* she thought. *He ain't bout to just turn the tables on me when* his *ass was in the wrong first!*

"Fuck that bitch! You would come up in Cash's club on some ho shit?!"

"I ain't know it was Cash's club!" she defended. *If I had, I wouldn't have brought my black ass up in there,* she thought.

Ignoring her explanation, Outlaw persisted, "How the fuck you know Blaze? Ain't that that muthafucka name?"

"He just told me at the club tonight!" Shantreis lied, not missing a beat.

"Yeah right," he replied unconvinced. "You seem a lil' too familiar with that nigga. If it's some shit going down, best believe I'm a' find out. Won't *no* bitch try to fuckin' play me!"

"Fuck you, Outlaw! If you was at home takin' care of business then you wouldn't have to worry about no other nigga stepping up to the plate!"

"What the fuck did you say?" he asked quietly with his head lowered.

Shantreis could see his fists tightening. Outlaw seemed to be fighting his own emotions but she didn't care. "I said if you was takin' care—"

Suddenly he lunged for her. His fist was raised in midair and headed straight for her face, but he stopped abruptly as he gained control of his senses. Outlaw stood there, his chest heaving in and out deeply. After a minute, he spun around and stalked out of the bedroom. Shantreis could hear his car keys jingling and rushed after him.

"Where are you going?"

He ignored her as he opened the garage door.

"Outlaw, you don't hear me?"

"Somewhere away from ya ass." He hopped inside of his car and sped out of the garage, nearly denting her Jaguar in the process.

I can't believe that bitch, Outlaw thought angrily as he changed gears. He didn't know whether or not to believe her when it came to Blaze, but he knew that he was gunning for that nigga regardless. Nobody insulted him and got away with that shit. Every time he blinked, he could see the smirk on Blaze's face when they stood in the parking lot.

"Fuck boy," he mumbled before turning on his music and sparking a blunt.

"*Fuck em, I'm screamin' fuck em!*" Rick Ross' boomed through his speakers. Outlaw bobbed his head to the beat, rapping along with the new mixtape. Shantreis was blowing his phone up but he still refused to answer. He powered his phone off and tossed it in the back.

Several minutes later, he'd pulled up at Kaleesha's apartment at Addington Farms. He hadn't spoken to her since their last encounter, when he'd confronted her about the picture, but he knew that his dropping by wouldn't be an issue. He was always welcome at her house. Besides that, he paid the bills *and* had a key so he would be damned if she ever tried to tell him otherwise.

Taking the stairs two steps at a time, Outlaw reached the front door. He didn't bother to knock, choosing instead to let himself in. The house was dark, blinding him momentarily until his eyes adjusted. He started towards his daughter's bedroom when Kaleesha's door opened.

"Nigga, what the fuck?" Outlaw exclaimed, seeing a man exit out of her bedroom wearing only a pair of boxers. "Who you?"

"Outlaw!" he could hear Kaleesha from inside the room. "Wait!"

"Nigga, who the fuck is you?" Outlaw repeated.

"My name Filthy…" the man mumbled warily as he tried to back into Kaleesha's room. He was wishing that he'd kept his ass in the room instead of trying to be Superman and find out the source of the noise.

"You better get ya filthy ass out of my daughter's fuckin' house!"

"He's my company," Kaleesha spoke up, finally coming out into the hallway.

"Right now really ain't the time, Kaleesha. I'm already pissed the fuck off and you makin' shit worse. You got this clown ass nigga walkin' 'round this bitch with no fuckin' clothes on! I don't need my daughter seein' that shit!"

"Outlaw, it's three in the morning! Monet is asleep."

"Whatever, man." He waved her off. "What I told you about having niggas up in here?"

She blew her breath. "What I'm supposed to do? Wait for you to come around and gimme some dick? Nigga, please."

Filthy exited the bedroom, fully clothed this time. He eyed Outlaw up and down before turning back to Kaleesha. "I'll holla at you next time, Ma."

"Nigga, you won't holla at shit." Outlaw lost it. All he saw was red as he attacked Filthy mercilessly. He had a lot of pent up aggression that he was glad to release. He didn't feel bad about it either. As far as he was concerned, Filthy had coerced it. If he hadn't been there, he would have been spared. Wrong place, wrong time.

"Stop it, Outlaw!" Kaleesha screeched. He was like a crazed madman. He couldn't hear Kaleesha's pleads and his fury gave him superhuman like strength. Filthy didn't stand a chance even on his best day. Outlaw continued to stomp him out before Kaleesha finally snapped him out of it.

"Outlaw, you better go or I'm callin' the police!"

"Call the law! I'll tell them what this shit really is. A muthafuckin' intruder in my fuckin' house!" Outlaw was co-signer on the lease so he knew that his story would hold up pretty well. He hated the police but he knew how to flip things in his favor if need be.

"Just go, Filthy!" she yelled again, helping him up. Looking at Filthy, she could tell that he was in pain. His face seemed to have sustained the most damage and he clutched his chest. His body was shaking with anger. Then again, it could have been out of fear. Kaleesha wasn't sure but she didn't want things to get any more out of hand. She was just glad that he was able to walk out of the door. "You're a monster, Outlaw!"

He ignored her cries as he walked back to Monet's room. It was a pale shade of pink and a white, canopy bed stood in the middle of the floor. Everything in her room was pink and to say that it was fit for a princess was an understatement. Outlaw spared no expense when it came to his daughter.

Monet sat upright in the bed, frightfully. A small elephant with her name embroidered on the ear was cradled in her small hands.

"Daddy... What was that noise?" she sobbed. "Was it a monster? I heard Mommy say it was a monster!"

"It was, but Daddy got the bad monster." Outlaw sat down on the edge of the bed and pulled her into his lap.

"Are you sure?"

"Yup. But just in case, I'm gonna stay in here with you to make sure he doesn't come back. Cool?"

She grinned, mimicking him, "Cool."

"Aiight then." He kissed her forehead and tucked her back in. "Daddy loves you, Monet."

"I love you too, Daddy."

Outlaw smiled. No matter what kind of day he was having, those simple words from his princess could light up his whole world. His daughter was the only person in the world that he loved wholeheartedly and unselfishly. He would always put her first.

He laid down on the floor with his hands beneath his head, glancing at his daughter who stared back at him with a smile.

"Night-night, Daddy."

"Goodnight, baby."

And just like that, Outlaw had temporarily forgotten about all the bullshit he'd endured earlier. All was right in the world. Even if only for the night.

"Just calm down or I'll give you a reason to be scared!" Kevin threatened as he stood in front of the door. "I'd just like to talk. Find out where I stand."

"Kevin, you couldn't just talk to me in the morning?" Fallon asked, trying to do as he'd suggested. He was like a ticking time bomb. The deranged look in his eyes and the liquor that reeked from his rumpled suit let her know that she wasn't dealing with a man in his right mind.

A thousand thoughts were running through her mind as she tried to figure out her next move. Her first thought was to run in the kitchen and grab a knife but she'd have to pass in front of Kevin to do so. Her cell phone was dead and she didn't have a house phone either.

Keep calm and maybe he will too, she thought. *If all else fails, kick him in the nuts.*

"I just so happened to be around the neighborhood. I

figured, why put off in the morning what I can tend to now?" he replied. "Who the hell was that, Fallon?"

"What are you talking about?" she asked nervously.

"That thug nigger that you thought I was when you answered the door."

"What does it matter, Kevin?"

"Why? WHY?!" In one split second he had rushed Fallon, pinning her against the wall. "Because I treat you like a Queen, Fallon! I want you but you keep brushing me off! And this is how you treat me. Giving your number out to other men…"

Kevin stopped and stared straight at her. His gaze was as penetrating as a bullet. "Is he the one you want?"

"Please stop, Kevin… You're hurting me."

"Oh no. I'm not hurting you *yet*," he scoffed.

Fallon's eyes widened and her heart was racing out of her chest as she kneed him in the groin and took off running. Without giving it a second thought, she rushed out of the front door. She was barefoot and only wearing a robe but she figured she would be safer out in the open rather than in the confines of her second floor apartment.

"Help!" Fallon yelled, running down the stairs. She could hear Kevin behind her and she didn't know where to go but she screamed until her voice became hoarse. She knocked frantically on a few doors but nobody answered.

It was times like these that she despised her bourgeois neighbors. Everyone was tucked into their warm beds and not a soul was outside. She saw a few lights cut on, but nobody opened the door and offered any help.

"Stop causing a scene, Fallon, people are going to think you're crazy," Kevin responded evenly.

With her attire and wild hair from her romp with Cash,

she reasoned that he was probably right, but Kevin didn't look much better than she did. They both stuck out like sore thumbs. Fallon was fairly new to the complex and rarely fraternized with her neighbors, so no one knew her personally to feel the need to assist her either.

When she heard a gun cock back, Fallon trembled and stopped in her tracks. *This crazy nigga has a gun!*

"What the fuck is going on?"

The voice resembled Cash's but Fallon couldn't believe it. He'd gotten off the call with Ghost only minutes prior and she knew that he'd left because she'd heard his car leave. He wasn't supposed to be there but she was glad that he was. Other than that, she was glad that the gun had been Cash's and not Kevin's.

Kevin held his hands up in mock surrender and said sarcastically, "Relax, *homie,* I don't want any problems."

Cash was livid but he knew that he couldn't behave impulsively. Although it seemed that the neighbors were reluctant to help, he had no doubts that they had already called the boys in blue. He couldn't afford to get caught up in some shit.

"Bounce, nigga, or we really gonna have some fuckin' problems." Cash kept his firearm on Kevin, watching him intensely as he backpedaled towards his Cadillac.

"Good night, Fallon," Kevin said with a smug look on his face. He got into his car and pulled off.

Cash turned back towards Fallon, embracing her in his strong arms, "You okay?"

She was still a little shaken up over what happened but having him there made everything feel so much better. "Yeah. I'm good. What are you doing here though?"

"I saw that grimy muthafucka gettin' out of his car when I was leaving. He was muggin' the shit out of me..."

He shook his head, remembering their encounter. "And some shit just wasn't sittin' right with me. Tried to brush that shit off but I ain't get where I am today by not trusting my instincts. Decided to double back and I'm glad I did."

"Me too," she exhaled a sigh of relief.

"I'll handle that shit with Kevin later, but for now go put on some shoes and pack ya shit. You comin' wit' me," he stated firmly, letting Fallon know that it wasn't a request, rather a command. He had let her get away from him once before but he would be damned if he let it happen again—especially at the hands of another nigga.

Chapter 11

"It's a damn shame muh'fuckas can't even go out and get some pussy without havin' to kill a bitch," Ghost commented as he sat down on the bed, smoking a blunt with some of the best ganja he'd ever had. He deserved it after the night's events.

Ri-Ri sat adjacent to him on the bed, bawling her eyes out. She was damn near hysterical and it was pissing Ghost off.

"Didn't I tell you to shut the fuck up?!"

"You ain't lyin'," Strap cosigned, shaking his head. He eyed Ri-Ri's homegirl, Vanessa. She was knocked out—literally.

He had been weary of her since the club, but went along with Ghost's suggestion to fuck with her anyway. They had just gotten into the hotel room when Vanessa insisted that she freshen up. Strap couldn't say that he blamed her. He was sure that she had worked up a sweat from dancing most of the night. That wasn't the issue.

Strap went to the mirror, located next to the bathroom,

and overheard her whispering on the phone to some niggas about setting him and Ghost up. Hearing that, he sent Ghost a text, advising him to contact Cash. They were in enough hot water with their brother so Strap wanted to make sure they handled things exactly as he would have wanted.

Vanessa was one hell of an actress. Strap had to give it to her. She'd flushed the toilet as though she'd really taken a piss and was smiling in his face, gushing about how much she was feeling him. If Strap had never thought it before, he would now: *Bitches ain't shit.* She acted as though she hadn't just been plotting on them.

After Vanessa discovered that the jig was up, he gave her an ultimatum. She could save the lives of the niggas she just dialed by calling them back and warning them to back off *or* she could let them come and he and Ghost would start blazing on niggas. Vanessa opted for option one, not wanting her baby's father to be hurt. Her actions didn't go without repercussions, though.

As soon as Ghost came over to their room, he spazzed out. Viciously he began raining blows on the girl. Hearing the commotion, Ri-Ri came over, screaming at the sight of her fucked up girlfriend. She wanted to help but knew better than to interfere with Ghost when he got like that. Finally, he let up after Strap convinced him that she'd had enough.

So here they were now, waiting on Cash's arrival.

"You ain't had to fuck her up like that," Ri-Ri sobbed. She had always known what kind of nigga Ghost was, but she had never personally witnessed anything.

"Bitch, you serious? Ya bitchass homegirl tryna take us out and I'm just supposed to let her do it? Fuck outta here." He gave Ri-Ri the side eye. "Shit, you lucky I don't beat ya ass offa GP. You had to known ya girl was shiesty as fuck."

Ri-Ri howled even louder. Snot dripped from her nose and her eyes were puffy. "I-I ain't had s-shit to do with it, Ghost!"

"Then shut the FUCK up!"

Knock knock!

"Bout time," Strap muttered as he peered through the peephole. "What's up?" He opened the door, but left the security latch on so the visitor couldn't see inside of the room.

The portly, balding manager looked at Strap with a frown. "I'm afraid that I've been hearing complaints about noise from this room." He pushed his glasses up his nose. "Some of the staff has already asked you to keep it down but the noise level *still* hasn't. I'm going to have to ask you to leave immediately or I'll be forced to contact the authorities."

"Chill, Pops. We'll leave," Ghost spoke up as he put out his blunt. "Ay, c'mon, Ri-Ri," he coached her towards Strap. "I'll get shawty."

Strap guided Ri-Ri out and the manager looked at her tear-stricken face. He couldn't help but ask, "Are you okay, Miss?"

Strap nudged her after she hesitated to respond, "Y-yes."

The manager didn't believe her for a moment, but he wasn't going to interfere. As long as they got the hell off his property, whatever happened was their business. Their baggy, thuggish attire already made him feel uncomfortable so he quickly moved to the side as the party of four exited the hotel room.

Ghost held Vanessa bridal style as he eased out of the doorway. She was still unconscious but he was glad he'd allowed Ri-Ri to clean up Vanessa's face earlier. The caked blood had been wiped away and now she looked as though she was sleeping peacefully.

"She had a lil' too much to drink," Ghost smiled impishly.

The manager watched them intensely as they walked down the corridor and out of his sight.

"What are y'all gonna do to her?" Ri-Ri asked, sniffling slightly.

"The less you know, the better," Strap replied although he knew that it was already too late for her. In the game, the motto was 'no witnesses'. He didn't doubt that Ri-Ri had nothing to do with it, but the sheer fact that she was with them made her murder necessary. Strap would leave that up to Ghost though, since that was technically his girl. He knew one thing though, the way that she was carrying on showed that she wasn't built for the kind of lifestyle they led. Without a doubt, Ri-Ri would get loose lips.

The light illuminating the parking lot was out, making it easy for Ghost to slip Vanessa in the trunk of his Chevy unnoticed. "You too, sweetheart," he sneered, motioning to Ri-Ri.

"Wha? Why, Ghost? I'm not gonna say shit! I'm not laying back there!" Ri-ri insisted, her eyes wide with fear.

"You don't have a choice," Ghost snickered.

Ri-Ri opened her mouth to scream, but Strap quickly knocked her out with the butt of his gun. He laid her next to Vanessa and Ghost slammed the trunk down.

Doubting that anyone noticed the encounter, but still preferring to play it safe, Ghost jumped inside of his Caprice and hightailed it out of the parking lot.

"What about Cash?" Strap asked, "Didn't you tell him to meet us at the hotel?"

"Man, fuck that nigga. He takin' too damn long. I don't know why you wanted me to call his ass in the first place!

We know what the fuck we doing!"

I do, but you don't, Strap thought. He knew that his brother barely listened to him, but if he called on Cash, Ghost would have no choice but to fall in line with whatever was being asked of him.

"Man, call that nigga before he be pissed and shit."

"You call his ass." Ghost pulled into the Handee Hugo gas station, stopping at a pump. His tank was near empty and if he didn't get gas now, they'd be stuck on the side of the road.

Strap called Cash, advising him of where they were before hanging up. "He said he on Capital now. What's up with you though?"

"Fuck you mean? Ain't shit wrong with me!" he exploded. "You need to talk to *your* brother. Cash was trying to handle me like I'm a lil' nigga or some shit earlier." Ghost shook his head. "I don't play that disrespect shit."

Strap was quiet. There was no use in saying anything because he knew how his brother was. Ghost and Cash beefing was nothing new. They had butted heads ever since Ghost was released a year ago.

Ghost always had a problem with following orders. He wanted to do things his way regardless of whether or not it was the best way. He loved power and control. Strap thought that those two reasons alone were why Ghost liked merking niggas. It was sick and maybe even twisted, but he had power and control then—he held their life in his hands.

"There he go," Strap said, noticing Cash's headlights behind them at the pump.

"Took that nigga long enough," Ghost muttered under his breath as he bopped to the store.

Strap walked towards the luxury vehicle, greeting Cash on the driver's side. He started to explain what had went down but spotting Fallon in the passenger seat caught him off guard.

"Hey, Damien," Fallon greeted drowsily.

"W-what's up?" Fallon's earlier advice to Strap about staying out of trouble echoed in his mind. "Ay, can I holla at you… outside?"

Strap told himself that he was only asking because Cash had always stressed to them the importance of only talking business to those in the circle, but he knew that it was really because he didn't want Fallon to be disappointed in him.

Strap briefed him on the details and Cash nodded his head in understanding before asking, "Where Ghost at?"

No sooner than Cash had posed the question, Ghost came out of the store with a brown paper bag in hand. He didn't bother to speak to Cash as he sat his drink down and proceeded to fill the car with gas.

Cash shook his head. He knew that Ghost was still salty about earlier but he didn't give a fuck. He was going to continue to put him in his place until he stayed there. "Call the cleaners. Have 'em meet y'all somewhere with the van… Y'all don't need to be ridin' round like that."

He eyed the trunk that was starting to jump. Evidently one of the girls, if not both, had regained consciousness and wanted out. Their voices couldn't be heard over the music, but if anyone looked that way, they would be able to notice.

Ghost cursed under his breath. He started his car and turned up his subwoofers. It quickly masked any efforts the girls were making to get help.

"Why wouldn't y'all tie them bitches up?" Cash asked heatedly. "I swear y'all niggas just askin' to get knocked." He shook his head, knowing that it didn't do any good to complain about it now. "I'll tell Woo to meet y'all at the spot off New Bern."

"Aiight," Strap nodded his head. "You and Fallon back together?"

The mention of his woman brought a smile to Cash's face. "Yeah. Saw her at the club… We had a run in with some pussy ass nigga earlier so that's why I'm late but shit's straight now. We on our way back to the crib."

"Oh… Aiight then, Cash. I'll holla." Strap started back for the Chevy and sat down. He looked in the rearview mirror, admiring the peaceful look on Fallon's face on the sly. He wished that he was the one she was going home with but he knew that shit wasn't happening.

"What that nigga say?" Ghost asked, slamming the door in his customary manner.

"We gotta meet Woo nem on New Bern."

He nodded. "Why you sound like that? All down and shit." He pulled out of the parking lot, directly behind Cash. Noticing Fallon in the passenger seat, he grinned. "That damn New-New again. She must got some good ass pussy the way you trippin' over that bitch."

"I ain't trippin' over her!" he yelled defensively before adding, "And nah. I ain't never fucked her."

"Then I don't know why the fuck you stuck on her. But you know what they say, if you want somethin', go get it."

Strap shook his head. "She Cash shawty now."

"She always been his shawty but you still be checkin' for her."

"Man, she was mine first."

Ghost's eyes bugged out of its sockets. "For real, nigga? You was with that bitch and Cash knew? But he still fucked with her?" He laughed. "Real nigga shit, I'd a' spazzed on him *and* that bitch. That was some grimy ass shit!"

"Nah. Nah… It wasn't all like that. I been tryna get with Fallon since I was a youngin'… She never took me serious though."

"Well… You should a' been said somethin'." He ran his hands through his thick dreads. "Either you do somethin' bout that shit or sit back and let that nigga fuck the pussy you should be gettin' every night."

"Nigga, please. What the fuck would you do?" Strap asked, trying to mask his curiosity.

Ghost grinned mischievously. "Nigga, don't ask if you too pussy to actually do it."

"Fuck you, Ghost…" He waved his brother off and threw his hood over his head. "Ain't nobody 'pussy' but I ain't disloyal like that either."

"I'm just fuckin' wit' you but really, nigga, you already disloyal for thinkin' shit bout his bitch in the first place. You tryna beef with blood over pussy that don't belong to you! Fuck outta here!"

Strap didn't respond as he stared out of the window. He knew that Ghost was right so he wasn't even going to argue.

Chapter 12

Shantreis felt around the nightstand for her phone, refusing to remove her eye mask and look for it. It was early and she was still groggy from going to bed at damn near two in the morning. She'd left Outlaw countless voicemails but he never returned any of her calls. As she shifted around in the bed, she realized that Outlaw still hadn't come back.

Bout time he called. I knew this nigga couldn't stay away for long, she thought confidently as she pressed the button to answer the call. "Nigga, you better be on your way home!"

"Shit… You ain't said nothin' but a word," an unfamiliar male voice said.

"Blaze?" she asked.

"Damn, you tryna flex on a nigga now like you don't know my voice?" He chuckled. "Yeah this me."

"How you know my nigga ain't here?"

"Shit. That was evident from your greeting, wouldn't you say?"

Shantreis sat up in the bed and removed her eye mask. She sighed. "You the reason for all this bullshit."

Blaze sucked his teeth. "The hell if I am. If he'd a' been takin' care of home, a nigga like me wouldn't a' had room to slide in, ya dig?"

"What's up, Blaze?" she asked impatiently, wanting him to get to the point.

"I was just callin' to see if you wanted to chill or some shit."

"I don't know about all that... Outlaw will probably be back soon apologizin' and shit..." Shantreis doubted it, but she wanted to believe it. "Besides that, you know you askin' for a death sentence fuckin' with me."

"Man, fuck that nigga. He ain't gonna do shit to me," Blaze replied confidently. "Why you actin' brand new? It ain't never been a problem before."

Shantreis was quiet. Blaze had a point. She'd known him from back in the day in Virginia. He'd lived in her neighborhood and they had hooked up on more than a few occasions. Things changed when she moved and he was locked up after committing a robbery with some dudes around the way.

They reunited a few months ago after he spotted her at the gas station. He was in North Carolina visiting his cousin, trying to get back on his feet after being released. Shantreis tried to resist temptation but eventually gave in. Outlaw was busy fucking around on her so what was the difference? She wasn't sloppy with her shit and Blaze didn't run his mouth. They had kept their dirt hidden so well that not even Fallon knew about it. Shantreis knew she would judge her so it was a secret she kept to herself.

"Now what's good? Come chill wit' a nigga for a few."

"All right," she relented. "Gimme bout an hour."

"So you can put on all that makeup and shit? Hell no. Come like you is."

"Negro, please. I *needs* my makeup."

Blaze chuckled. "Let me find out you only a dime because of that gunk on ya face."

Now Shantreis had to laugh. "Whatever, nigga. You like it though. But I'm a five star bitch with or without it. I'll hit you up when I'm on the way."

"Aiight."

Shantreis knew that most would consider her wrong, but she had never given a damn about how other people felt about the way she lived her life. Outlaw not coming home or even bothering to call her was an indication to her that he didn't give a damn. So for the rest of the day, she wasn't going to either.

Outlaw stuffed another mouthful of pancakes in his mouth and gulped down his cup of orange juice. "Damn this shit good as fu—I mean…" Remembering his impressionable daughter was there, hanging on his every word, he tried to clean up his speech but it was too late.

"Oooh, Daddy, you said a bad word!" Monet giggled as she munched on a piece of bacon.

"Your woman don't feed you this good at home?" Kaleesha asked with a smirk.

Outlaw didn't respond. He wasn't about to play into Kaleesha's antics this early in the morning but she was right. Shantreis didn't cook breakfast for him anymore, yet if he thought about it, he realized that he was always rushing off to take care of something. He wouldn't have time for it even if she did.

"Daddy, I wish you ate breakfast with me and Mommy every morning."

"Me too," Kaleesha added.

Outlaw gave her the look of death before turning back to Monet, "I wish I could eat breakfast with you every morning too." He gave her a kiss on the cheek before rising from the table.

"You're leaving?" she asked with a disappointed look on her face.

"Nah. I'm gonna take a shower right quick."

Kaleesha sighed wistfully. She knew that she had done some fucked up things in the past, and yesterday's encounter with Filthy probably didn't look any better in his eyes but she and Outlaw belonged together. She knew it, so why couldn't Outlaw see that?

That bitch he with can't be all that if he over here, Kaleesha thought with a sneer, slightly proud of the fact that he always ran back to her. *Now if I could just get that nigga to stay here.*

"Are you done, Monet?" She didn't miss the way her daughter was merely pushing her food around on her plate. It was Kaleesha's fault. She knew that Monet preferred to eat cereal, but since Outlaw was over, she wanted to go all out. She cooked a full breakfast that morning: pancakes, bacon, grits, toast, and scrambled eggs.

"Yes, Mommy." She took a sip of her juice. "Can I go watch *The Backyardigans* until Daddy gets out the shower?"

"Go ahead." Kaleesha cleared the plates from the table and threw them in the dishwasher quickly. Outlaw normally took showers that were damn near an hour but she wasn't about to take any chances. She had already gone out of her way to get all dolled up *and* have breakfast prepared, but now she had to really give Outlaw a reason not to go back home.

Kaleesha stalked into her bedroom quietly, shutting the door gently behind her. She locked the door to avoid any interruptions from Monet. After dabbing *Chance* by *Chanel* perfume between her thighs and neck, she gave herself another onceover in her floor-length mirror.

Shantreis who? Kaleesha asked herself with a smirk.

She knew that she needed to leave Outlaw alone and after their last altercation, she fully intended on doing so, but it was hard to resist him when he was right in front of her. Each time he interacted with their daughter, she couldn't help but think about how badly she wanted a family. Not with just any ole Joe Schmo, but with her baby's father.

Kaleesha had a soft spot in her heart for Outlaw. It was like no matter how fucked up he treated her, she just couldn't get rid of him. She knew that Monet was the main reason, but the other was the fact that she'd never had a man do her like Outlaw did. He used to spoil her and treat her like a Queen. Things had only changed when Shantreis came into the picture. He started treating her like yesterday's trash then—the whole situation with Eric only made it worse.

Oh well. The past was the past and she was trying to build a new future with Outlaw.

Hearing the bathroom door open snapped Kaleesha out of her thoughts as she looked up at Outlaw with a sexy expression on her face. She sat on the bed with her legs spread like an eagle, inviting him to partake in her treasure chest, but he only looked at her with a frown.

Ignoring her, Outlaw walked over the walk-in closet with only a towel wrapped around his waist as he searched for something to wear. He kept a sizeable amount of his things there, just for moments like this when he was beefing with Shantreis. Picking out a pair of jeans and a Lacoste button up, he started out but Kaleesha blocked his exit.

"Watch out," Outlaw warned.

"You just gonna get dressed?" she asked, smacking her lips.

"Yeah," he said in a matter-of-fact way. "What you expect me to do? Fuck you?"

"Why not? I know you like pussy in the morning." Kaleesha reached for his towel but he pulled back from her.

"I'm good on that, 'leesha. What makes you think I would wanna stick my dick in a bitch that just got done fuckin' some nigga named *Filthy?*" He laughed. "Where the fuck you find these niggas?"

Trying to mask her hurt, she trudged out of the closet. "Whatever, Outlaw. I know you ain't talkin' when you got that smut Shantreis at home."

"Fuck her ass too."

Kaleesha's ears perked up at his words. "Y'all broke up?"

"Wouldn't you like to know?"

"She was fuckin' wit' another nigga wasn't she?" she prodded.

"Mind ya business, 'leesha. The only one you need to be worried about is yourself." Outlaw snapped his fingers as if remembering something. "Matter fact, let's talk about that fly shit you was poppin' off about the other day."

"What are you talkin' about?" Kaleesha asked, suddenly developing a case of amnesia.

"Bout you havin' dirt on me and shit. Talkin about how I'm a' keep payin' the bills in this bitch cuz you got my daughter. *That* fly shit."

"So what?" she asked with attitude. Outlaw could hear the fear in her voice despite her bravado.

"Don't threaten me with no shit like that, Kaleesha, or

I'm a' really beat ya ass." The stern look on his face indicated that he wasn't playing and his tone didn't hold an ounce of humor. "Don't have that Filthy nigga over here no damn more either unless he gonna pay all the bills in this muthafucka. Got it?"

"Got it…" she mumbled.

Outlaw finished buttoning his shirt and checked his appearance in the mirror. "Now… I'm takin' my daughter out. We'll be back later."

"I can't go too?"

"For what, Kaleesha? You ain't my ole lady."

"*For what*?" she asked incredulously. "I'm still the mother of your child."

Outlaw shrugged. "You should know that don't matter. I ain't one of these sucka ass niggas that'll wife a bitch up just cuz she has my seed. Fuck outta here." He strolled out the bedroom door, calling for Monet.

"You ready to chill with Daddy?" Kaleesha could hear him say from the living room.

"Yay!!!" Then there was a pause. "Mommy's not going?"

"Nope. Just me and you today, Princess."

"Bye, Mommy! I love you," Monet shouted as the door closed behind them.

Kaleesha didn't respond, instead collapsing in a heap of her own tears. She was tired of all the hurtful things Outlaw said to her on a daily basis. More than that, she was tired of depending on him financially. She couldn't say that she wanted to find a job because the only ones she was qualified for made minimum wage. She wouldn't be able to afford the pricey apartment they currently stayed in and she didn't want to downgrade her lifestyle either.

She loved Outlaw, and probably always would, but he'd made it more than evident that a reunion between the two wasn't in the cards, so Kaleesha had no choice but to accept it.

Her ringing cell phone brought her back to reality and she answered it unenthusiastically, "Hello?"

"Ya baby daddy still over there?" Filthy asked vehemently.

"No. He just left... But I think you better keep your distance."

"Fuck that! This shit ain't over with! He only got the best of me because I was fucked up."

Kaleesha rolled her eyes, knowing that wasn't true, but she wasn't going to be the one to burst his bubble. "Well look, it's only gonna get me in more shit with him so don't call here no more."

"Fuck that. I'm tired of havin' to sneak around that nigga schedule. You be actin' like that nigga own you and shit." He paused for dramatic effect. "I thought you was really feelin' a nigga, but you gonna let what we have go down the drain because of Outlaw? I can take care of you."

They had been talking off and on for a year, but honestly, Filthy was nothing more than a cutty buddy. His dick game was decent, and his head game was fire, but besides the sex, he didn't have anything else going for himself.

"Huh," she scoffed. "How you gonna do that, Filthy? You still stay with ya momma."

"She stay with me!" he reminded her, hating that she'd brought it up.

"Yeah, you could take care of me..." she started as an idea sprang to mind. "If you had as much money as Outlaw does."

"You shot out for that shit, Kaleesha," he spat, offended by her statement. He was broke, living at home with his momma, and had no job. Filthy was the exact type of dude that women normally stayed away from.

"No, baby, I don't mean it that way," she said attempting to butter him up. "You can get there and I'm gonna help you. Matter fact, me *and* Outlaw are gonna help you."

"With Outlaw's help? You crazy as fuck. That nigga don't like me and I can't stand his bitch ass."

"Just hear me out, okay?" Kaleesha pleaded.

Filthy tried to front, but his interest was piqued. "I'm listening…"

Chapter 13

"Ay, why you so stuck on that nigga?" Blaze asked finally, fed up with the way Shantreis was constantly checking her cell phone.

Embarrassed that he'd caught her, Shantreis quickly tossed her phone into her Prada bag. "Ain't nobody stuck on him!" she lied. She was pissed because Outlaw hadn't bothered to call her or even send a text.

"The fuck if you ain't. I swear you females so damn backwards. You tell me that this nigga is always cheatin' on you but all you can do is think about him," he said good-naturedly, finding the whole thing comical. "Can't fault niggas for the shit they do when females just gonna stick by 'em regardless. Niggas only do what you allow them to."

Shantreis knew that everything Blaze was saying was true, but she couldn't bring herself to agree with him—at least not aloud. "I ain't say he was cheatin' on me," she mumbled, snatching up her fork and digging into her Lemon Raspberry Cream Cheesecake violently.

Blaze was treating her out to lunch at *The Cheesecake Factory*, which just so happened to be her favorite restaurant. Things had been going well, save for Shantreis looking at her phone every thirty seconds. They'd finished up the main course but she was still babysitting that damn cheesecake. Blaze didn't mind though because he still enjoyed her company.

"Damn, girl. You tearin' that shit up. Is it good?"

"Yup." Just as he opened his mouth, she cut him off with a smile, "And nah, you can't have none."

"Quit playin', girl," Blaze commanded, meeting her flirtatious tone.

"Just a lil' bit or you gonna have to buy me another one." She carved a piece for him and guided it into his mouth with her fork. "You like it?"

"It's straight." He nodded. "I know something that tastes better though."

"Whatever, nigga." Shantreis giggled, not missing the lustful glance he gave her.

Blaze took a sip of his beer before resuming their original conversation, "What I'm sayin' though is it's amusing that females will hold on to a sorry ass nigga when they got a good nigga right up under they nose! I know my paper ain't as long…"

"Hold up now, Negro," she cut him off and raised her hand to mimic a stop sign. "I ain't no gold digger."

He shrugged nonchalantly. "Then what do you do? To me, it sounds like that nigga buyin' you. You ain't got no 9 to 5, you do whatever the hell you want and spend that nigga money."

Shantreis' eyes narrowed as she sat her fork down on her plate, ready to school Blaze. "It's a man's job to take care of his woman, first and foremost. But if you think I'm some sort of gold diggin' bitch, why you out with me?"

"Chill out." Blaze grabbed her hand just as she started to stand up. "I'm just fuckin' with you."

"Whatever." She pulled away from him and folded her arms against her chest.

Blaze looked her directly in the eyes. "A nigga been feelin' you for a long time. And I know that you *think* you in love with that nigga, but that shit ain't love, baby girl. Open ya eyes."

Blaze knew that Shantreis wouldn't have anything to say and he didn't want to hear any more excuses, so he decided to end the conversation his way. He reached into his wallet and tossed a hundred dollar bill on the table.

"You ready?"

Shantreis nodded as she stood up, following his lead. She knew that everything Blaze was saying was true, but she wasn't yet ready to let go of Outlaw. He was her man… Yeah, he pissed her off and they fussed and fought a lot, but what couple didn't? She had come to accept the fact that every man cheated. It was something that she didn't agree with and didn't understand, but it was what it was.

Blaze looked like a knight in shining armor now; but she knew that if she gave it a few months, he would be the same as every other nigga. He would stop appreciating her, start staying out late, and start straying from home. Shit was always gravy in the beginning. Shantreis tried to convince herself of that, but there was something in Blaze's eyes that told her otherwise. She was just afraid to find out.

The last thing Shantreis wanted to do was leave one bad situation for another. It was better to be stuck with Outlaw. He did a lot of messed up things, but Blaze was right in his assumption: Outlaw was paid. Shantreis no longer knew how to be independent, she needed someone to finance her lifestyle and truthfully, Blaze wasn't yet up to par. Sad but true, money helped to influence her decision.

"Shantreis?"

She looked up at the sound of her name being called.

Shantreis had been so in tune with her thoughts that she wasn't even paying attention to the couple that had just walked past her.

"Hey, Fallon…" she greeted timidly as she turned around. Shantreis wouldn't have been so nervous if it wasn't for Cash standing next to her, staring at her suspiciously.

"You didn't uh…" Fallon cleared her throat, looking back and forth from Shantreis to Blaze with a confused expression. "Call me back last night and let me know you were okay."

"Yeah well. I'm fine… I'll call you later," Shantreis said ending the conversation as she pulled Blaze out the door with her.

Fallon and Cash exchanged glances as they sat down at the table their server guided them to.

"Guess she really is fuckin' round on my nigga." Cash shook his head disdainfully.

"Please don't tell Outlaw," Fallon begged, realizing that Shantreis was probably worried that Cash would say something. She wished that she could have spoken with her before they left. She needed to know what was going on.

"I'll mind my business but that's some fucked up shit."

"Well, he cheats on Shantreis, so how is it any different?"

"It's *way* different. Fallon, get real, you know that women can't do the same shit as a man. We're held by two completely different standards."

"And that's so wrong."

"No, it's not," Cash defended. "When women cheat they're emotionally involved—nine times out of ten. When men cheat there are no strings attached, it's nothing more than a fuck. Niggas don't give a fuck about all that other shit. Females gotta be feelin' a nigga to even open her legs unless she a ho… From what I've seen of ya girl, she ain't like that. So I know it's somethin' deeper than what you probably think it is. Shit, you see it! They out eatin' like they a fuckin' couple or some shit."

Fallon smiled as she looked over the expansive menu, "You said you were gonna mind your business, Cash."

He chuckled. "I am. I'm just telling you."

"Yes. I know all about you men and your crazy logic," she joked.

"It ain't crazy, girl. It's the truth."

"Anyways, it's been nice spending the day with you, Cash. I missed our conversations about things like that. Our heated debates," she giggled as if remembering something humorous.

"Yeah. I missed them too. I missed everything about you."

"You mean it?" Fallon asked curiously.

"Hell yeah. I missed my nerd," Cash teased, referring to the name he used to call her. It was a reference to how booksmart she was. He loved that about her and truth be told, it was one of the many things he admired about her.

Noticing the solemn expression on her face, he sobered up, "What's wrong?"

"Just wondering if you're really gonna keep your promise… I wanna make sure that you weren't just caught up in the moment or something."

"How many times have I ever not kept my word?" Cash asked seriously. "Especially when it comes to you? I've never lied to you and I ain't gonna start now. Word is bond, shawty."

Fallon smiled, loving that about him. The last thing he would ever do is let her down.

"Now I'm a' keep it real wit'cha. I do have a few loose strings to tie up, but nothing I can't handle in three months."

"I'm trusting you then."

Cash nodded. "That's all I ask. Have faith in ya man."

"Wasn't that ya boy's nigga?" Blaze asked Shantreis as they headed to his car.

"Yeah and I bet he's probably gonna tell Outlaw too," she added pitifully, shaking her head. She pulled her oversized Chanel shades off the top of her head and onto her eyes, hoping that would be a good enough disguise in case anyone else spotted her.

In Raleigh, there weren't too many people that didn't know Outlaw but luckily, she wasn't as recognizable. Shantreis didn't mingle with too many females and Outlaw never paraded her around his niggas either. When she thought about it, the only people that would have realized something was amiss would be the employees at her favorite stores or at *The Cheesecake Factory*. She hadn't considered that when she and Blaze walked in there like some sort of couple.

At least Letitia wasn't there, Shantreis thought, referring to their usual server at the restaurant. *Fuck 'em. Me and Outlaw don't go out much anymore. By time we come back and show our faces, they'll have forgotten Blaze.*

"I ain't worried about that shit." Blaze shrugged. If anything, he wished that Outlaw *would* find out. Maybe if he heard about Shantreis parlaying around with another man, he'd clean up his act. Even better, he might even dump her. A female cheating on her nigga was like one of the deadly sins, except no forgiveness could be found in that.

"Hold up. That's my cuz," he told her as he waved at a lanky, Snoop Dogg lookalike.

"Let me get the keys. I ain't tryna stand out here in the sun while y'all catch up."

"Be easy." Blaze reached down and tossed her the keys just as his cousin walked over.

His cousin eyed Shantreis hungrily as she sauntered off, not even bothering to respect the fact that she was with Blaze.

"Watch your eyes, nigga," Blaze warned.

"Who that?" his cousin asked, stopping his gaze only after she disappeared from his sight. "She bad, nigga. Ain't seen you with that bitch before."

"Shawty I know from Virginia named Shantreis."

He shook his head. "She ain't too friendly."

Blaze sucked his teeth in response. "She too busy trippin' bout some clown nigga named Outlaw."

"Outlaw? Aw shit… She still fuck with that nigga?"

He shrugged. "I'm tryna change that." Blaze stared at his cousin intently. "What's up, Filthy? You actin' like you know shawty."

"Nah but I know her nigga… I'm fuckin' with his baby momma." Filthy screwed up his face remembering the beatdown Outlaw had given him. His eye was a little fucked up, but the dollar store shades he'd purchased did a good job of covering it up. His body was a little sore but other than that, he was good. "Bitch made nigga…"

"You right about that shit." Blaze smirked. "Well listen, cuz, I'll holla at you."

"Alright, cuz. I got some shit I wanna holla at you 'bout later too." Filthy gave him a pound and they both headed their separate ways. *Ain't that some shit?* he thought with a devious grin, already plotting on what he could do with the information he'd just discovered. *Shit comin' together like a puzzle.*

Chapter 14

Outlaw opened the door to Kaleesha's apartment quietly. It was only eight o' clock at night, but Monet was knocked out. He had taken her everywhere her little heart desired: Chuck E. Cheese, Marbles Kids Museum, and even Monkey Joes. A trip to Cary to go to Toys R Us wasn't out of the question either.

"Hey," Kaleesha whispered. She was sitting in the living room, watching a movie. The lights were out and she munched noisily on her bag of popcorn.

Outlaw nodded his head in acknowledgement before heading back to Monet's room. He nudged the door open with his free shoulder and laid her gently on her bed. He removed her shoes and pulled her pink Hello Kitty comforter over her. Kissing her softly, he whispered, "Daddy loves you." He turned on her night light before closing the door slightly.

"Y'all had fun?" Kaleesha asked as he took a seat on the sofa adjacent to her.

"Hell yeah. I'm bout as tired as she is."

"You gonna sleep here or…?"

"Probably. Why?" Outlaw asked, eyeing her warily.

"I was just gonna say that I think you need to go home and make up with Shantreis."

"Fuck outta here!" He couldn't believe his ears.

"I'm serious…"

Outlaw raised his eyebrow. "So let me guess, you tryna get me to leave so that other nigga can come through, right?"

"Damn, nigga, why everything gotta have some kind of ulterior motive?" An offended expression flashed on her face.

"Because I know you. And I know you can't stand Shantreis…"

Kaleesha shrugged. "She ain't for me to like though. I know you love that girl and I know you miss her. Hell, you been with the girl for a long ass time! You might as well quit playin' and take ya ass home."

Outlaw was quiet, seriously mulling over what she was saying. He had to admit that he'd missed Shantreis and had been slightly curious about what she'd done that day. She hadn't called him and that bothered him. He was so accustomed to her blowing up his phone that he didn't know how to act. Twice he'd thought about calling, but each time he built up the nerve he disconnected the call.

"Just go, boy. If shit don't work out, you welcome to come back here and sleep on my couch," she joked. "But if you keep bein' stubborn as hell, you're gonna lose her. Do you wanna see her with another dude? If you don't, then you better go home. Quit doin' stupid shit cuz you get mad."

"Damn…" He knew that Kaleesha had a point. Outlaw had always been one to hold grudges, even when he knew that he should let go. Now was a prime example. It would kill him if she was with another nigga. If he didn't go home and settle things with Shantreis, he was sure that it wouldn't take her long to find a replacement.

Blaze's face popped up in his mental rolodex and he frowned. In Outlaw's heart of hearts he knew that Shantreis could never be that grimy to fuck with another nigga, regardless of how he treated her but he would never find out for certain if he didn't go back home and ask her.

"'Preciate it," Outlaw thanked Kaleesha as he pulled her into an uncustomary hug. She was taken aback by his gesture but accepted it wholeheartedly. "I don't know why you doing this, but I 'preciate it."

Kaleesha shrugged. "I just been thinking about some shit today. It's time for me to grow up and move on. And it's time for you to stop playin' games. Nigga, you twenty-five years old." She smiled at him.

"Yeah, you right." He kissed her on the cheek before heading out the door. Never did he believe that he would get any words of wisdom from his baby momma but he was glad that he did.

Kaleesha peered out the blinds inconspicuously as she watched Outlaw drive off. She sighed as she placed a hand on the cheek where his lips had only been moments prior. It hurt like hell that he was going back to Shantreis but she'd get over it.

The kind way that he'd treated her almost made her want to change her mind about what she was going to do next, but she knew firsthand how quickly Outlaw could change up. It wouldn't be long before he'd push this encounter to the back of his mind and resume the bullshit.

She pulled out her Blackberry and pushed speed dial number 2. Filthy answered on the first ring. "It's done. He's going back."

Shantreis sprang up from the bed as she heard the front door open. She held her .22 behind her back, prepared if any shit was to pop off. She didn't know who would be so bold as to rob Outlaw, but she was pissed that he wasn't home to protect her like he was supposed to. With her back pressed against the hallway, she leaped out with her gun raised.

"Put ya fuckin' hands up!"

"Ay, chill!" Outlaw yelled, raising his hands in the air for surrender. "Put that shit down." Then he laughed, "Didn't I teach you to shoot first and ask questions last?"

Shantreis breathed a sigh of relief as she tossed her gun on the end table. She wanted to jump into his arms and rain kisses all over his face but like Outlaw, her stubbornness wouldn't allow her to. She had to get a feel on him first. Right now he seemed to be in a pretty good mood, but Outlaw could be unpredictable at times.

"You'd be dead if I listened to that logic," she retorted. "Why didn't you go in through the garage?"

"Can't find my garage door opener," he answered simply before stalking past her, heading to their bedroom.

"So…" She cleared her throat and threw her hands on her hips as she stood in the doorway. "Where you been?"

"Please don't start that shit with me just yet, Shantreis. I'm in a good ass mood."

Shantreis looked at him curiously before taking a seat on the bed next to him.

Outlaw took a deep breath as Kaleesha's words echoed in his head: *If you keep bein' stubborn as hell, you gonna miss out on what you want.* That gave him the push to get out the words. "My fault about yesterday. I was a lil' drunk and seein' you grindin' on that other nigga and shit…" His hand curled into a fist with anger. "That shit was fuckin' with me."

"How do you think I—"

He raised his hand to silence her. "Look, Shantreis, I love you… And I want you… But I gotta know this first, did you fuck that nigga? Did you know him before the other night?" Outlaw looked her in her eyes, searching for the truth.

Staring right back at Outlaw, she replied, "No. I met him that night. He tried to holla but I turned him down. It was just dancin', Outlaw. I was tryna make you jealous."

The lie rolled off the tip of her tongue easily and she held his gaze to further prove her "honesty". There was no way that she could tell him what she'd really done—not if she wanted to be with him. Shantreis knew that when it came to a nigga—a street nigga especially—once you fucked another man, there was no coming back from that.

Outlaw nodded, satisfied with what he thought he saw. "Don't fuck with me like that no mo', Shantreis. I swear I'll body a nigga over you and that ain't good." He pulled her into him, savoring the scent of her *Guilty Gucci* perfume.

"I know, baby, and I'm sorry. I was just…" She bit her lip as she tried to regain her composure, but it was an impossible feat. The tears started rolling down her cheeks one by one like soldiers marching for war. "I'm tired of you fuckin' around on me, Outlaw. I hear the rumors! I always dismissed the shit as bitter bitches gossipin' but when I see the shit, Outlaw… It fuckin' hurts."

Seeing Shantreis tear up like that was killing him softly because her tears were always hidden from him. She usually kept up such a hard shell. It was impenetrable. He never got to hear her vulnerability, only her anger. In so many ways they were alike. Both were afraid to put down their guard. It was as though they were always at war with one another and neither was willing to show their fears, their weaknesses. Not doing so had been detrimental to their relationship and caused it to be as unhealthy as it had been.

"I'm sorry, baby. I swear I'm not gonna fuck up no mo'." Outlaw held her tighter. "You know I ain't love them bitches…" He continued to apologize as he kissed her body all over, slipping her out of her silk La Perla robe. "You hear me, baby?"

Shantreis couldn't respond, she was still choked up with her own emotions. All she could do was nod and hope that this time Outlaw meant it. He was always full of empty promises and while he'd sworn a million times before to do right by her, this time actually felt genuine. Only time would tell.

Chapter 15

"What's so urgent that we couldn't have spoken over the phone?" Strap asked, looking at his brother curiously. His tone wasn't disrespectful, but showed his concern.

They were sitting in Cash's study at his mansion in Wakefield. Cash stated the need to discuss some business with him but asked him to come over to his house. That was unusual along with the fact that he asked Strap not to bring Ghost.

"Well, you know how Fallon feels about hustlin' so..." Cash exhaled the smoke from his blunt before offering it to Strap, who declined. "I'm gettin' out of the game. The plan is to retire in three months but I wanna aim for a little sooner."

"Okay...?" Strap didn't quite understand what he was getting at.

"This is where you come in, Strap. My empire is yours... if you want it," Cash informed.

"What?" He wasn't sure that he'd heard his brother correctly. Cash wanted to pass his damn near billion dollar empire to him?

Cash chuckled at the bewildered expression on his brother's face. "I know it's a little overwhelming but, Strap, you've got it in you. With a little bit more guidance, I know that I could mold you into—"

"Thank you, Cash, but I can't. Just like you have a woman that feels strongly about you gettin' out of the game, so do I."

Fallon's words to him had really stuck with him. He was determined to get off the wrong end of the law. "I can't let her down… I'm lookin' into a legal hustle. I've already spoken with a few franchises to see about setting a few things up. I'm tryna be a law abiding citizen," Strap joked with a smile.

"Oh yeah?" Cash nodded his head in approval, proud of Strap. "Let me know if you need *anything*. I'll help you out in any way that I can."

"Preciate it."

Cash stood up, signaling the end of their talk. He gave him a hoodshake before pulling him into an embrace. "When you got a female like that, that's pushing you out of the game instead of headfirst into it, don't let her go. You know you got a good one."

Strap nodded although the irony was that they were in love with the same woman. "I'll try, man."

"Listen, don't mention this to Ghost… What we discussed…" Noticing the perplexed look on his face, he continued, "I'm telling everyone at the meeting on Friday, aiight?"

"Yeah aiight." Strap didn't know why Cash bothered to tell him a lie. He knew that Ghost was the only person that he didn't want to know. It was most likely because he had no intentions of offering the position to him. Strap couldn't say that he blamed Cash in fact, he understood him completely. Unfortunately, the one person that needed to understand wouldn't. Ghost didn't believe anything negative that anyone said about him.

Strap knew that the meeting was bound to be entertaining, to say the least.

"Tell Fallon I said 'what's up'," Strap called as he walked out the door.

"Aiight." After locking the door behind his brother, Cash headed back up the stairs to lay down with his Queen. Fallon was dressed casually in a pair of basketball shorts and a sports bra. Her long hair was still wrapped up but she looked sexy as hell to him. "Strap said what's up."

Fallon looked up at him, still partially engrossed with watching some program on VH1. "I didn't know he was stopping by. I would've said 'hello'." Then she felt her tied up hair, "Well, if I wasn't looking a hot mess."

"Shit, girl, you look sexy as fuck to me." He grabbed her and planted a kiss on her exposed stomach.

"Whatever, boy." She hit him playfully with a pillow. "Now tell me about Strap."

"We was discussing some business… I offered to pass the throne to him but he don't want it." Cash chucked. "I would a' killed for that kind of offer when I was his age…"

Noticing that he didn't have her full attention, he turned off the TV despite her protests, "We got DVR," he responded simply, pulling her close for a kiss. "Your man missed you today."

"I missed you too, baby." Fallon gave him another kiss, following their usual pattern of two. "But you know I had to work."

"Yeah…" his voice trailed off. He admired the fact that Fallon still wanted to work despite the fact that he had more than enough money to take care of her.

"And I know you had to handle your business too," Fallon added. "I'm just glad you're not comin' home late like you used to."

Cash chuckled. "Yeah. I set my own hours now. I don't miss that block for shit…" He remembered how he would grind from sunup to sundown. Cash had always been about the almighty dollar and didn't let anything—not even his own discomfort, stop him from getting it.

"Me either…"

Fallon had plenty of times in the past where she had feared for his safety. She dreaded watching the news reports on WRAL, fearful that she may hear something about Cash. Whenever there were reports about some sort of drug bust, she wouldn't waste any time calling him, only to have her calls unreturned. He would come home late as hell and she could smell the work on him every time, mixed with gunpowder and weed. It was Cash's usual scent especially after having to bust a cap in a few niggas' asses.

She would stress out if he even came home with so much as a scratch. Fallon treated it as though he'd suffered a gunshot wound so Cash would start exercising more caution so that he wouldn't have to hear her mouth. He'd tell her not to expect the worst, but she couldn't help but to. Fallon had known girls in high school whose boyfriends worked the block and police were hauling them off to jail on a damn near daily basis. She couldn't understand what would make Cash exempt from that kind of treatment.

Seeing the worry on her face, Cash kissed her lips. "Whatchu thinkin' about?"

"The past…"

"Don't. We've come a long way since then and it'll never be like that again…"

"Yeah because now a bunch of swat agents and the DEA and whoever else will kick down the door now…"

"Would you hold me down if they did?" Cash asked seriously.

Fallon stared at him incredulously, "What kind of question is that?"

"A real one. Every nigga needs to know they ole lady would hold 'em down if some shit popped off."

"I would…" she answered softly. "But I shouldn't have to be put in that kind of situation."

"You won't, baby, I promise…" Cash murmured huskily as he started sucking on her neck and easing his hand down the front of her basketball shorts. He inserted two fingers in and out of her honey pot, loving how wet she was.

"Stop playin' with me…" she moaned, wanting to feel him inside of her, blessing her with his twelve inches.

Obliging her request, he removed his pants and Fallon smiled at his erection. She tugged off his boxers and wasted no time guiding his tool into her warm mouth.

"Damn," Cash cursed as he placed a hand on her head.

She bobbed up and down then slurped him in a circular pattern. Fallon made sure to pay equal attention to his nuts, massaging them with her free hand like Chinese stress balls. Feeling him about to tense up, she removed her mouth. Getting down on her hands and knees, she showed Cash exactly how she wanted it.

Unable to contain himself, he pushed himself deep into her sugar walls. They contracted against his girth, and Cash loved how tight she was.

"Shit, Cash," Fallon shrieked as she tried to crawl away from him.

"Unt uh. Stop running…" he urged as he pulled her back. "Take this dick. Take it for me…"

"I will." She gripped the sheets and bit down on her lower lip as she tried to endure the pounding he was putting on her little kitty cat. It felt so good that she could've sworn that she blacked out a few times. It had been a long time since she'd felt anything like this and she knew she would be sore in the morning.

"Damn, this pussy tight," Cash murmured, knowing that he was about to tap out at any moment. He had given Fallon nearly four orgasms already so he knew it wouldn't be an issue if he stopped. He just called himself making up for the year that he had gone without her. Cash had had more than his fair share of different women, but Fallon by far, had the best pussy.

"Shit, girl," he groaned as he gave one last, hard thrust before shooting a thick load of semen inside of her.

Cash laid on top of Fallon, both of their breathing hard and sporadic. *A nigga could get used to this again,* he thought before dozing off in her arms.

"So what the hell have I missed?" Fallon and Shantreis asked in unison before bursting out in laughter. They were sitting at T.G.I. Fridays as they did every Friday. Lately the girls had all been caught up with their own respective lives, but they always made time to go out to eat and catch up.

"Shantreis, you're the one with the most going on," Fallon said, putting the spotlight on her homegirl. "Every time I call you I can't ever reach you. And who was that dude you was with at *The Cheesecake Factory*? Wasn't that the same dude from the club that Outlaw was about to fight?"

"Girl…" Shantreis sighed. "It's a long story…" She paused. "You told Cash not to tell, right?"

"Yeah but who is he?"

"His name Blaze and I know him from Richmond... I saw him at the gas station down here and next thing I knew, I was givin' the nigga the panties... Shit just got out of hand. He be tryna romance a bitch," Shantreis referred to herself, "and I like that shit but... I mean, he nice and all... But his pockets just ain't deep enough. A bitch got expensive tastes and shit."

"You're hung up on how much money he got *but* he treats you good?" Fallon blurted out, perplexed by her friend's logic.

"I mean every relationship is gravy in the beginning but—" Shantreis started.

"Me and Cash haven't ever had any problems like you and Outlaw, honestly. You can't group all men in that clique, Shantreis. Blaze sounds like a good dude."

Shantreis rolled her eyes, regretting her decision to tell Fallon about her secret affair with Blaze. More importantly, Shantreis hated that she told her whenever Outlaw fucked around on her. Fallon throwing that shit up in her face had her jumping on the defensive.

"Fallon, you don't know what the hell ya nigga be doing behind your back. Some niggas just better at coverin' that shit up. You can look at Cash and tell that that nigga be gettin' pussy! It ain't no secret that he gettin' money. With money comes hoes! Besides that, y'all ain't been together but for a week or whatever! You don't know what the hell Cash be doin'!"

"Girl, please," Fallon scoffed, feeling her blood pressure rising.

This was why she hated keeping it real with Shantreis. She would become so defensive about everything that it was hard to tell her the truth. She knew this, but yet and still Fallon would offer her honest advice. Give or take, it always ended this way—in a shouting match, but today it seemed like Shantreis had gone too far off the deep end.

"Cash is making money but he's *always* back home on time. That's more than we can say about Outlaw; his ass is out chasing anything with a pussy!"

"Please," Shantreis sneered, "Outlaw ain't even much like that no more."

Fallon laughed condescendingly, "He's cleaned up his act in less than a week?"

"You ain't heard shit negative about him have you?!"

"If Outlaw was all that then you wouldn't be cheating on him with Blaze!!" Fallon shouted in her squeaky voice.

The girls' conversation could be heard throughout the restaurant, despite how loud and crowded it already was. A few patrons had even stopped their conversations to listen in on the scene unfolding.

Shantreis arose from her spot at the table. "I'll holla at you later. Outlaw is takin' me out to the movies later tonight after his meeting anyway."

"Excuse me, but I'm going to have to ask you all to leave," their server said, walking up with a flustered expression on his face.

"I was leavin' any damn way!" Shantreis yelled as she stomped out of the restaurant in her Giuseppe heels.

Fallon tried to play it off but Shantreis' words had really gotten under her skin. She and Cash had only reconciled within that week and they hadn't spoken much on his year without her. Who was to say that there wasn't some woman that he had on the side?

Chapter 16

Cash sat at the head of the table in his warehouse located in Youngsville. He had assembled everyone there to give his big announcement, as well as to get caught up on the happenings in the streets. Only the highest ranking members of his organization were there, the rest were still on duty in the streets. The information from the meeting would be passed on to them via the lieutenants of their respective blocks.

"Look," Cash started solemnly, briefly making eye contact with his men, "I know we have business to discuss and we'll get to that, but first, I just wanted to let you all know that I'm gettin' out of the game."

Everyone looked at him anxiously, no doubt wondering how his decision would affect them. No one spoke, awaiting his next words, "You'll still keep your jobs and shit will be like it always has, but Outlaw will now be running shit. He practically does now anyway." Cash grinned as a few men clapped and gave Outlaw handshakes.

Outlaw beamed proudly, loving how openly everyone

accepted it. It wasn't as though he'd expected anything different, however. Cash hadn't been lying, Outlaw did practically run things. He was the one constantly in the streets making sure that shit was running smoothly. He ensured that there was enough snow to create a blizzard in Raleigh and he guaranteed that the money was right. Hustling and slanging ran all through Outlaw's veins. It was to no surprise. Outlaw had been hustling since he was thirteen and his hard work hadn't gone unnoticed.

He and Cash had already discussed his "promotion" but he still reacted humbly at the meeting as if he hadn't expected the announcement. Initially Outlaw had been so high off the news; he didn't know how to act. Being the head of a multimillion dollar empire was every hustler's dream.

Solidifying the deal in stone, they were flying to Miami on Saturday so that he could be introduced to the connect and negotiate a few prices. As soon as the new bricks came in, Outlaw would take the official spot as the H.N.I.C., or head nigga in charge.

"Shit, my nigga, we gotta celebrate though!" Quon, one of his lieutenants, piped up.

Cash shook his head, dismissing the notion. "Nah."

"Why not?" he persisted, looking to the other men in the room for support. "It would be the party of the muthafuckin' year. An unofficial inauguration for Outlaw and a celebration of your reign in the game… Farewell party and shit!"

Everyone chimed in, liking the idea. Hell, anything dealing with liquor, weed, and females they were down for. Finally Cash gave in. "All right. We can have the party but right now let's get back to business."

The meeting lasted for another fifteen minutes and then everyone was filing out, headed back to their whips.

"Ay, Cash. Let me holla at you," Ghost said, approaching him before he exited the warehouse.

"What's up?" Cash had barely noticed Ghost's presence. He had been quiet the entire time which was extremely uncharacteristic of his usual raucous behavior.

"You puttin' Outlaw in charge?" Ghost asked in disbelief, as though he hadn't heard the announcement with his own ears.

"Yeah. That's what I said, wasn't it?"

Ghost narrowed his eyes, not appreciating his sarcasm. "That's real fucked up, Cash! You gonna let some other nigga that ain't even blood handle some shit that should be passed down in the family?!"

Cash took a step back inside the warehouse, not wanting anyone else to overhear their exchange. "And who would you have suggested I pass it down to? You, Ghost?"

"Shit. I don't see why the fuck not! I done put work in but you act like you don't see that!"

"Yeah, you do, Ghost! I'll give you that!" He nodded his head in agreement. "But you put your *murder game* down! What the fuck do you know about the drug game?" Cash answered the question for him, "Not shit! Passing down my legacy to you would be some shit that you wouldn't be able to handle. I can't school you on that shit in three months' time!"

"Nigga please. Strap don't know shit bout the drug game like talkin' bout either! But you still asked his ass!"

Cash looked at him tentatively, no doubt wondering how he had known about his proposition to Strap. *Didn't I tell his ass not to tell Ghost?*

Ghost nodded knowingly. Really he didn't know shit, but the look on Cash's face confirmed it. He would bullshit in an instant. Nine times out of ten, Ghost always ended up figuring out things that were none of his business.

Cash shrugged his brother off. "Even if you did know the business, you too hot-headed. You don't think before you act… Strap is more calm and collected. He knows a little more than you're giving him credit for."

"Nah, muthafucka, *I* know more than *you* givin' me credit for!" he yelled hostilely and pointing a finger at his brother.

"Get the fuck outta my face with that bullshit, Ghost!" Cash warned, not appreciating the way his brother raised his voice.

"What the fuck you gonna do?" Ghost challenged, ready to get into some shit.

Cash snickered. Other niggas in the streets may have been afraid of Ghost, but he wasn't. Everything that he knew, it was because Cash had taught him. Therefore Cash had no fear. He could see that Ghost was starting to forget that fact, but it would be his pleasure to remind him.

"What the hell is takin' you so long?" Strap asked, interrupting the quarrel. He had been waiting for Ghost outside in the car but realizing that neither Ghost nor Cash had left, he suspected some foul shit was going on.

Strap looked to each of his brothers, awaiting an answer but he didn't get one. Both were still glaring at each other, wearing a similarly murderous expression.

"That's what's wrong with you young niggas," Cash said, ignoring Strap's presence. "Too fuckin' brazen and reckless for your own fuckin' good. I'm a' give you one last warning, Ghost, and you know I don't do that too often. Get out of my fuckin' face."

After they stared each other down for what felt like five minutes to Strap, Ghost finally nodded and outstretched his hand for a shake. Cash looked at it, but didn't return the gesture.

Good-naturedly, Ghost ignored the diss and placed his hand in his pocket. "My bad, bruh. I was shot out for that shit. It won't happen again."

Cash stared at him, but didn't reply.

"Let's go, Strap," Ghost turned to his brother as he swaggered out the door.

"What was that?" Strap asked as they got into his new Dodge Charger.

"Weren't shit. We was just talkin'." He shrugged his shoulders. "Nothin' too serious."

"Like hell if it wasn't. You mad about Outlaw ain't you?"

Ghost looked at Strap solemnly, "Why you ain't tell me that Cash asked you about taking over?"

Now it was Strap's turn to shrug his shoulders and play dumb. "Didn't think it was a big deal… I didn't accept, as you can tell."

"You was trying to keep that shit from me. Don't lie, Strap. We brothers, nigga. Deeper than that, we twins. If I can't count on you to have my fuckin' back, then who can I count on?" His tone was serious, a stark contrast to his usual loud and aggressive demeanor.

"Ghost, c'mon, we all know how you get! This the first time you talkin' like you got some muthafuckin' sense!" Strap sighed. "Anyway, me and Cash both have your back. That's without a fuckin' doubt! You know he gonna make sure we both straight."

Ghost waved him off. "Fuck all that shit you talkin'. I ain't come up in this world alone but I'm goin' out alone."

"Nigga, what is you talkin' about?"

He didn't answer, instead turning up the radio. Future's "Tony Montana" blared from the speakers and the fifteen inch subwoofers vibrated the car.

"Disloyal ass nigga," Ghost thought aloud. Strap didn't hear him over the music but he didn't give a fuck if he did. *Fuck Cash,* he thought bitterly. *I should've popped his ass.*

They usually had a love-hate relationship because although neither one would admit it, they were very similar. Cash had once been Ghost, but with time comes wisdom, and he learned how to become less foolhardy. Ghost still had a lot of growing up to do but he was wild and harder to tame. Realistically, it was probably too late for Ghost. He would never change because he didn't want to. He didn't find anything to be wrong with himself, just other people.

"You want me to be the bad guy? Okay it's on then," he sang along with a sinister smirk. He and Cash had bumped heads for the last time. Shit was about to get real in the fuckin' streets. Ghost would see to it personally.

Outlaw wrapped his arms around Shantreis and kissed her on the forehead. They were sitting on the sofa watching a movie. The plan had been to go out but the meeting ended a little later than expected so they missed the showtime. Shantreis wasn't mad surprisingly enough and was oddly agreeable when Outlaw suggested they watch a movie at home.

As the credits started to roll, indicating the end of the movie, Outlaw figured now would be a good time to tell her the news. "Don't be mad, baby, but I gotta go out of town with Cash tomorrow."

"Where y'all going?" she asked, raising her eyebrow slightly.

"Miami. I gotta meet the connect."

Shantreis smiled. "You nervous?"

"Hell no," he replied confidently. "I'm ready for that shit. You fuckin' with a boss now, baby." Outlaw kissed her glossed lips before pinching her ass, causing her to squeal in surprise.

"Oow, nigga, you play too damn much."

"You like it though." He grinned. "But ay, I'm 'bout to go to the store and get me a Dutch, you want somethin?"

"Nah. I'm good."

It had been a week but Outlaw was keeping his promise to her. He wasn't staying out late, she hadn't heard of him fraternizing with hoes, and most importantly, he was spending more time with her. His whole persona had taken a change for the better. Shantreis didn't know what had gotten into him, but she liked it.

At least she'd thought so.

Maybe if Outlaw had cleaned up his act a year ago, Shantreis would have been more ecstatic. Better yet, if she had never fucked around and let her emotions get caught up with Blaze. She thought that it would be simple to leave him alone after Outlaw got on the straight and narrow, but she couldn't get him out of her head.

With Outlaw being around more often, it made it harder to get up with Blaze, but she found ways around it. After her big blow up with Fallon, she'd called Blaze and they'd snuck off to a hotel nearby. He wasn't the best lover she'd had, but there was some sort of spark that he ignited inside of her whenever they made love. He made her feel beautiful, like she was the only woman he ever wanted to be inside of. It was something that Shantreis couldn't describe, but she loved the feeling.

Just thinking about his touch was making her antsy. Peering out the blinds discreetly, she waited until Outlaw backed out of the driveway before she pulled out her cell phone.

"Hello?" Blaze asked exasperatedly after the fourth ring.

"Damn. What's wrong with you?"

Blaze chuckled mockingly, "You, girl. You got my head all fucked up. Quit playin' with a nigga."

"Huh? Ain't nobody playin' with you, Blaze," Shantreis denied.

"The fuck if you ain't. You come over here talkin' bout how you miss a nigga and shit, but you still run back to Outlaw ass."

"I mean… He's always home now…"

"If he treatin' you right then why the fuck you keep callin' me? What the hell do you really want from me? You want a fuck buddy?"

Shantreis was quiet. She didn't know how to answer that. Originally she fucked with Blaze as her own little form of get back at Outlaw for his indiscretions. She never thought that she would start catching feelings again. She could tell that he wanted something serious with her but she couldn't say that she could be what he wanted just yet. Her ties to Outlaw were too deeply rooted for her to just pack up and leave. But on the other hand, her feelings for Blaze couldn't be denied. Shantreis was an emotional wreck.

"Quit fightin' it, girl. You know you should be with me and that's the fucked up part about it."

"You think you got it all figured out huh?"

"I do. You gonna have to choose, shawty. I ain't with this sneakin' around shit and I ain't never been one to share a bitch," Blaze confessed. "If it's still about you wondering if I can take care of you, I got you. I might can't buy you an $83,000 Jaguar or take you on shopping sprees to Saks every fuckin' day, but I can promise you that you won't ever go without.

"There'll be food on the fuckin' table and we can still go out and shit like we been doing. Think about it, have I ever asked you to reach in your purse for shit?"

"No," she admitted.

"Aiight then. So don't play me, shawty. I might not be some kind of fuckin' millionaire right now, but that don't mean I won't get there. I ain't hurtin' for shit."

Shantreis' silence gave Blaze all the answers he was looking for. She just couldn't look past his financial situation. He hated that about her—her greed. He could admit that he was going out on a limb asking her to give up everything for him but foolishly he'd even believed that she felt the same way he did about her.

"The timing just ain't right, Blaze…" she said, trying to avoid hurting him.

"Yeah. Aiight." He nodded his head, already expecting the rejection. "I'll holla at you, Shantreis."

"You ain't gotta get off the phone, Blaze!"

"Why not? Ain't shit else to talk about. You chose that nigga so I'm just gonna fall back. I can't even disrespect that man like that no more."

"Blaze, you are really overreacting! I thought females were supposed to be the ones catching feelings and you trippin' on me like this! Really?" Shantreis pulled the phone away from her face, surprised to see that he'd hung up in her face.

Fuck.

Shantreis wanted to talk to someone about it but she had no one to run to. She'd shown her ass to Fallon at the restaurant and she didn't want to give her the opportunity to gloat or say "I told you so." For now, this would be a burden that she had to bear by herself.

When Shantreis heard the door opening, she knew that

Outlaw had returned. "Ay, you gonna spark this shit with me?" he asked, pulling out a bag of green and a pack of Dutch cigarillos he'd gotten from the store.

"Yeah." She needed something to take her mind off the stress. Outlaw couldn't have brought it at a better time. Like an expert, she emptied the "guts" out of the vanilla Dutch and began to fill it with the Kush weed. Her full lips licked the sides of the paper just enough to create a good seal and rolled it, making sure not to roll it too tightly.

Outlaw lit the blunt for her and she inhaled it deeply. Shantreis had never been a big weedhead, but she was known to indulge every once in a while.

"What's up, Shantreis? You lookin' stressed and shit."

"Me and Fallon ain't talkin'," she admitted, only telling him half of the story. "I blew up on her at the restaurant earlier because she was actin' like all niggas don't cheat."

Outlaw removed the blunt from her hand and took a toke. "There you go with that shit, Shantreis. I know I fucked up but you gotta quit holdin' that shit over a nigga head."

"I'm not," she defended. "But don't you think that most niggas do?"

He shrugged, not wanting to think about it. The last thing he wanted to do while he was getting high was to try and have a serious conversation with her about infidelity.

"Fuck that shit." Outlaw took a hit of the weed, holding the smoke in his mouth as he pressed his lips on Shantreis'. She greedily sucked in the smoke, before blowing it out slowly.

It didn't take long before she was higher than a kite. The troubles that had plagued her mind were now nonexistent. Shantreis didn't give a damn about Blaze or Fallon. Honestly, she didn't give a damn about anything at that moment. She just wanted to keep floating on Cloud 9.

Chapter 17

"Baby, let me call you right back, aiight?" Cash asked, signaling the end of his and Fallon's already short conversation.

Fallon sighed, hearing all the noise in his background. "Okay. Bye." She hung up out without giving him a chance to say anything else.

Cash was out of town on a business trip, or so he said. Ever since her conversation with Shantreis on Friday, it had her second guessing every little thing that he did and said. Shantreis had really struck a chord with her. If Cash did have other females then Fallon would probably never know for sure. He was too smooth to get caught out there the way Outlaw did, and she never had proof of whether or not he was actually handling business.

Cash had always been sure to shelter Fallon away from his lifestyle. He never mentioned any details of his illegal dabbling to her, convincing her that she would be better off not knowing. Fallon had agreed with him up until this point. Now she wondered if he was being sneaky. Maybe there *was* some female that he was putting in time with. She hated to doubt him but she had to know for certain.

Reluctantly she picked up the phone and dialed Shantreis. If anything was going on, she would be sure to know about it. Outlaw told her damn near everything when it came to his business. Despite their argument, Fallon knew that there would be no beef. Their falling outs never lasted long.

"Hello?" Shantreis asked drowsily.

Fallon pulled the phone away from her ear and checked the time. It was nearly twelve in the afternoon. "Girl, why you still sleep?"

"Went to bed late… What's up?"

"Uh…" She took a deep breath, hating that she felt like she was sneaking behind Cash's back. "Do you know anything about Cash having a meeting or something to go to today?"

"Why the hell would I know what your nigga got going on?"

"I thought maybe Outlaw would've said something to you."

"Yeah." Shantreis yawned loudly. "They went to Miami to meet Cash's business partner... He didn't tell you?"

"Well, not exactly… So I was just wondering…"

"Wondering what? You think that nigga cheatin' or something?"

"I was just asking!" Fallon said defensively.

"Well don't. You know that nigga love you. I guarantee he ain't foolin' around on you."

"You was the one talkin' 'bout—"

"I know," Shantreis cut her off. "I was mad but… I mean, it's true that some niggas is slick but Cash ain't one of them. I ain't even really see him with no females when ya'll broke up." Shantreis sighed. "Fallon, stop actin' all insecure and shit. You don't have anything to worry about, I'm positive."

"You're probably right," Fallon nodded, feeling slightly better about it. "Thanks, girl." Hearing her line beep, she quickly got Shantreis off the line.

"Hello?"

"Whassup, baby?" Cash's smooth baritone greeted. "My bad about earlier. Shit was real loud cuz some niggas was actin' up in the parkin' lot and shit."

"I thought this was supposed to be a business trip, Cash. You're talking like you're at the mall or something."

He chuckled. "Chill. It is. Just wanted to pick my girl up a few things, is that okay with you?"

"Cash, why didn't you tell me you were going to Miami?"

"Who told you that?"

"Shantreis did! Why? Is it supposed to be some sort of secret or what?" Just that quickly Fallon doubted him again. The way he answered sounded as though he had something to hide.

Cash sighed exasperatedly. "No… It's not a secret."

"Then why didn't you tell me?" she persisted.

"Some shit you just better off not knowing, baby."

"So it's okay for Shantreis to know but not me?"

"How Outlaw handles his ole lady is that man's business. We do shit differently. You and Shantreis ain't built the same way…"

"What the hell does that mean, Cash?!" she asked, raising her tone.

"Fallon, baby, please don't act like this. There ain't no

need for you to trip. You actin' like I'm out with another female or some shit."

"You could be!"

"Man, it's just me and Outlaw." Cash shook his head. "And even *he* ain't holla at no bitches since we got here... What's up though? What's the real reason you actin' like this?"

Fallon was quiet, feeling foolish about the way she'd came at him. He had always kept it real with her and she couldn't even think of one instance that he'd lied to her.

"Hello?" he asked.

"I'm still here," she said softly.

"Look, baby, if you don't trust me then we don't need to be together. I ain't done shit for you not to be able to trust me. I call and give you updates and shit... Hell, I spend too much time with you to be able to juggle another chick. Shit. If I did have a mistress or somethin' she'd be mad as hell because I'd never have time to come through." Cash laughed at the thought. "I love you, Fallon. I wouldn't do that to you so quit actin' like that. I don't know who been fillin' your head up with that shit but—"

"I know, Cash, and I'm sorry. I just..." Fallon sighed. "I don't know."

"Quit over thinkin' shit, baby. I'll hit you up later though, aight?"

"Okay and Cash?"

"What's up?"

"If I ever, *ever* catch yo ass fuckin' around I'm a' cut yo muthafuckin' dick off..." she joked, reciting a line from Biggie's 'Me and My Bitch'. It was one of their favorite songs so she knew that he would find humor in her statement.

Cash laughed. "Aiight. I love you, girl."

"Love you too, boy."

Outlaw waited until Cash disconnected the call before speaking up. "Ya girl was trippin'?" he asked, amused by his conversation.

Cash nodded his head. "Hell yeah. Ya ole lady be gossipin'. She told Fallon we was in Miami."

Outlaw laughed. "That shit funny as hell. You don't tell that girl nothin'."

"Hell nah… I keep Fallon away from this shit." Cash turned his attention back on the ten carat ring the sales clerk was packaging for him.

"You sure you really wanna go through with it?" Outlaw asked, meeting his gaze.

"Yeah. I'm sure. If it ain't gonna be Fallon, it ain't gonna be nobody else. Real talk. There ain't no other female like her."

"I know what you mean," he nodded in agreement before adding, "I don't think I'm ready to propose to Shantreis though…"

"Why not, nigga?" Cash asked, screwing his face up. "That girl done held ya ass down for damn near three years ain't it?" As quickly as the words came out his mouth, he wished that he could take them back. Remembering Shantreis strolling out of the restaurant with that nigga from the club left a bad taste in his mouth. *Fuck.*

"Yeah." Outlaw scratched his dreads with a frown. "Commitment… Marriage… Them some scary ass words."

Cash laughed, trying to lighten up the conversation, "You'll know when the time comes, man. Don't rush that shit."

"Nah I ain't." He placed his hands in his pocket as he

looked at some other rings in the display case. "But then again, I mean… You right. She has put up with my bullshit and baby momma drama. I know Shantreis do some stupid ass shit…" Outlaw thought about the club scenario with Blaze. He still hadn't been able to get up with that nigga but he knew that whenever he did, he was going to body him on sight.

"But she wouldn't fuck around on a nigga. I know that!" Outlaw said convincingly. He nodded his head. "Maybe you right, Cash." Outlaw turned to the sales rep pointing to a princess cut diamond ring, "Ay, can I see this ring right here?"

"Ay, my nigga, you sure?" Cash asked, slightly alarmed. He didn't know if Shantreis was still seeing that other nigga but he knew that things could get real ugly if she was. He knew it would fuck Outlaw up if he knew the truth. Hell, it would fuck any nigga up to hear that their ole lady was cheating. Cash knew how he would feel if it their roles were reversed. It was also because of that same reason that he couldn't bring himself to tell Outlaw.

He would be ready to damn near kill both of them.

Outlaw shrugged. "We ain't gettin' no younger, we might as well do it," he joked, reciting a line from Jagged Edge's old song *Let's Get Married.*

Cash didn't say anything else, but he decided that he would have a talk with Shantreis when they got back to North Carolina. He needed some answers.

He knew that Outlaw had cheated plenty of times and while Cash wasn't saying it was right, he definitely acknowledged and agreed with the double standard. He would give Shantreis a chance to explain herself and he prayed that it was a misunderstanding. If not, it would be in her best interest to bounce because Cash wouldn't have a choice but to tell Outlaw.

Chapter 18

"Filthy, what the fuck is goin' on?! You talked all that shit but ain't nothin' happen yet! I'm startin' to think you just bullshittin'!" Kaleesha yelled at him over the phone. Filthy had been dodging her calls for the past few days and she was surprised that she was finally able to get in contact with him. Now that she had, she wanted an update.

"Chill, Kaleesha. Just because I ain't told you nothin' don't mean I ain't plottin'!"

"Well don't you think you should've been gotten up with me? I'm helpin' ya ass, nigga! I'm the one that got Outlaw to go back to Shantreis. If it wasn't for my lil' pep talk then he'd be with me right now," she huffed.

Filthy narrowed his eyes. "You talkin' like you wanna be with that muthafucka!"

"I'm not sayin' that, I'm just sayin'..." Kaleesha said, trying to fix her slip-up.

She liked Filthy but it wasn't serious by any means. For now she would play her position and have him believe that she was feeling him just as much as he was her. "He would've still been tryna sleep over my house if it wasn't for me and there would've been no guarantees that he would've reconciled with that bitch."

"Yeah okay," he replied, unconvinced. "Anyway, I found out that Shantreis been cheatin' on Outlaw with my cousin Blaze. He from Richmond."

"Shit! That's where Shantreis from!"

"I know. They used to fuck around back in the day, and evidently now too."

"Outlaw don't know about it?" Kaleesha gasped as she placed a hand over her mouth in shock.

"No," Filthy said as if the answer should've been common knowledge. "Do you think he'd still be with that bitch if he knew? Anyway, nobody's gonna tell his ass either—that means you, Kaleesha. I ain't even wanna tell you about it."

She sucked her teeth. "Whatever, nigga. I can keep a damn secret. Anyway, what the hell do Blaze got to do with it? He gonna help you rob Outlaw?"

"Nah. He's actually gonna bring Shantreis to me… It's a change of plans, I wanna kidnap Shantreis."

Kaleesha rolled her eyes. That was his big plan? "Really, Filthy?" she asked unenthused. "That shit ain't gonna work." She had originally come up with the plan to rob Outlaw but Filthy was the one that insisted he come up with the particulars since he was going to be the one to carry it out.

"Hear me out. Most niggas don't keep much where they lay they head at and shit could go awry if we had to hold that nigga at gunpoint and have him lead us to the stash," Filthy stated, matching her tone. "It'll be better this way, trust me, baby. We kidnap his bitch and tell him how much we want for her. He'll drop it off; we'll get the money and boom! We paid out the ass!"

"Be for real. Outlaw ain't gonna pay that much for that

bitch," Kaleesha said with jealousy lacing her tone.

"He loves that girl." Filthy smirked. "Even you know that. And if you don't think it'll work with Shantreis, then we could kidnap ya daughter instead. Less risk involved and—"

"Fuck that, Filthy. Leave my damn daughter out of this. Outlaw would really go ape shit then!" Kaleesha was all about her paper, but she wasn't willing to sacrifice Monet for it. She wasn't that shiesty. "We'll stick with ya plan but if you get caught, I ain't had nothin' to do with it."

"Yeah. I got you. I'll holla at you then."

"I'm just tryna make sure you won't fuck this shit up!" Kaleesha snapped. "We can't afford to get caught slipping. Them Hardy Boys havin' a big ass party Saturday night at Club C.R.E.A.M. so I know Outlaw and Shantreis gonna be there. That might be a good time to nab that bitch."

"Nah. She'll probably be glued to Outlaw the whole night and it'll probably be security up the ass. Look, Kaleesha, just let me figure the shit out. I'll holla at you, aiight?"

"You better," she warned but it fell upon deaf ears. Filthy had already disconnected the call.

Kaleesha groaned before tossing her Blackberry on the sofa. It seemed as though Filthy had everything mapped out. He had done his research and she was semi-impressed. Still, she couldn't believe that she was setting up her own baby daddy.

Then again, yes she could. Outlaw could be a good dude sometimes, but most times he treated her like shit. He had fucked up her self-esteem as well as bruised her emotionally and physically. Whenever she forced herself to think about the bad times, she felt justified about the decision she had made. Besides, nobody was going to get hurt. So what was the harm?

Outlaw had stacks on deck as far as she saw it. This little robbery wouldn't do shit to his already fat pockets. Kaleesha didn't know how much Filthy intended on asking for ransom but knew whatever the amount, Outlaw had it and she needed it.

Shantreis looked at her phone, not recognizing the incoming caller's number. Normally she didn't pick up for numbers that she didn't know but thinking that it could possibly be Blaze, she picked up.

"Hey, Shantreis, this Cash. Is Outlaw there?"

"He actually left bout thirty minutes ago. He said he was goin' to go check on some things around New Bern. You can't get in touch with him?" she asked, wondering if Outlaw had cut off his phone or if he'd simply lied to her about his whereabouts.

"Nah. I wasn't callin' for Outlaw. I wanted to holla at you about something."

Aah, shit, she thought, already having an inkling about what Cash wanted to discuss. Then again, it had been nearly a week and he hadn't said anything to her about it before, so why would he do it now? "What's up? This about the party Saturday?"

"Actually it's about you and that nigga from the club and the restaurant…" Cash replied smoothly. "You still seein' him?"

"No," Shantreis replied quickly. She wasn't lying though. She had tried to get in touch with Blaze but he never answered any of her phone calls or returned them. She knew that she was asking for too much expecting Blaze to be satisfied with sharing her, but she still didn't know what the hell she wanted.

"Good. I know Outlaw done some fucked up shit in the past but don't hurt that man like that. He tryna do right, believe me. He loves you… The nigga talkin' 'bout makin' you his wife. On some real shit."

Shantreis' breath nearly caught in her throat. "Are you serious?"

"Yeah. So if you still got somethin' goin' on with that other nigga, you better dead that shit or make sure he's what you want, shawty… I'm only extending you this courtesy since you my ole lady's best friend, but if you wasn't, I would a' been let that nigga know."

"Thanks, Cash."

"Aiight."

Click.

Shantreis was in disbelief. Outlaw actually wanted to propose and marry her… She never thought that she would see the day. Any feelings she had for Blaze would have to be suppressed. That wouldn't be too hard for her to do since he wasn't really fucking with her anymore. She could admit that she missed Blaze but she would get over it eventually.

The ringing of her phone interrupted her thoughts and her heart beat out of her chest seeing *'Fallon Home'* on the caller ID. She had saved Blaze's number under Fallon's name so as not to draw any suspicion if Outlaw was to ever see her phone. Shantreis knew how to be sneaky. Hell, she'd learned from the best—Outlaw himself.

"Hello?"

"What's up?"

Shantreis grunted, hating how casually he'd greeted her. He spoke as though he hadn't been ignoring her for days. "I should be askin' you, nigga!"

"Shit. I ain't ya nigga so why it matter? I do what the fuck I want. Or have *you* forgotten?"

"Don't call me on that bullshit, Blaze," she snapped, hating the fact that he was right. "What's up?"

"Nothin'. I was just thinkin' bout you."

"Yeah right."

"What you mean? I called didn't I?" Blaze said with a smile present in his voice.

Shantreis smiled, loving his witty humor. "I guess you did…"

"Listen, I wanted to get up with you since ya nigga done left you home alone."

"How you figure?" she asked teasingly.

"You talkin' to me and you ain't whisperin' and shit, so I know he gotta be gone. What's good though? You gonna meet me or what?"

Cash's warning echoed in Shantreis' head: *So make sure he's want you want.* She smiled, taking it as a sign to meet up with Blaze just one last time. It would help her decide where she needed to be. Then she would either leave him or Outlaw alone for good.

"Yeah. I'll be there. Gimme like five minutes."

Shantreis grabbed her car keys and started for the garage with a smile on her face. It wasn't until she started to pull out of the driveway that her smile faded. Outlaw was pulling up alongside the street. Her first thought was to press on the gas but she knew that wouldn't be a good look. He, without a doubt, would want to know where she was rushing off to. Quickly her mind searched for an excuse as Outlaw got out of his Maserati and tapped on her window.

"Ay, baby, where you going?" he asked, giving her a quick kiss on the lips.

"Uh… To the McDonald's… I got hungry. You want something?" she asked, her words coming out nearly jumbled.

"You know I hate McDonalds... But look, I already brought you back something." Outlaw nodded his head towards his car. "Bought you back some of that shit from Popeyes. That shrimp box you like..."

"For real?" Her eyes lit up at the thought. The shrimp tackle box was only available during certain times of the year and Outlaw remembering what she liked spoke volumes. It was small things like this that meant the most to Shantreis. It was rare that he was ever thoughtful like that and she was impressed. Temporarily she'd even forgotten that she was supposed to be heading out to see Blaze.

"Yeah. Since you always actin' like I don't think about you and shit while I'm out, I decided to pick it up." Outlaw shrugged.

"Thanks, baby."

"C'mon then. Move ya car so I can pull in."

"Well... I wanted one of them parfaits from McDonalds. I got a craving for one."

"A craving?" Outlaw asked, raising his eyebrow. "Lemme find out you pregnant with my seed."

Shantreis laughed. "I ain't pregnant, nigga. I just ain't had none in a long time..."

"Shit. I'll ride with you then."

Damn it. She plastered a smile on her face. "Okay."

"Let me get the food out the car real quick."

Seizing the opportunity, Shantreis swiftly texted Blaze back telling him she wasn't going to be able to make it before deleting any traces of their conversation. *Some other time I guess.*

Chapter 19

"Baby, I am so excited for you!" Fallon exclaimed as she adjusted Cash's Armani silk tie. He looked dapper in his suit and he wore his dreads tied up in the back. Although she loved his everyday street attire, there was something so sexy about the sophisticated look he was rocking that night.

It was Saturday night—the night of his retirement celebration. Fallon was giddy and honestly, Cash thought that she was more excited about it than he was. She had barely been able to talk about anything else that day or even that week since he'd first told her about it.

"Yeah. It's gonna be a big night," he stated nonchalantly.

"I know!" Fallon chattered on animatedly, prancing over to the mirror to finish her makeup. "I am *so* proud of you, baby."

"Oh yeah?" Cash asked, admiring how Fallon looked in her cocktail dress. It consisted of light pink sequins and a plunging neckline that was tasteful, but still sexy. The dress fit her like a glove and stopped mid-thigh length. The sight of her made his dick hard when she bent over to pick up a brush that had fallen on the floor.

As soon as she rose, he was directly behind her with his hands on her waist. Fallon could feel the bulge in his pants pressed against her backside.

"How proud?" Cash prompted.

She smiled. "Real proud but you're still not getting any. It's almost midnight, Cash! We're already late."

He shrugged. "Shit. It's my party, right? I can go whenever."

"Bae, you ain't bout to sweat out my hair. I can't go in there lookin' any kind of way. Your groupies would love to see me a hot mess."

"Who gives a fuck what they think?" Cash kissed her neck softly, hoping to persuade her in his favor.

"Cash…" she protested with a moan, although she didn't move away.

"Excuse me, but should I tell the chauffeur you'll need a few additional minutes?" his butler Roger asked.

"No," Fallon answered quickly pulling away from Cash's embrace. "We're ready now." She grabbed for her Christian Louboutin clutch and hurried towards the doorway.

"Great timing, Roger," Cash joked to the older black man resembling Redd Foxx. He had given him a job about three years ago when he was down on his luck. Cash knew him since back when he was a teenager. Roger and his wife lived next door to him.

Due to the poor economy, Roger ended up getting laid off from his job and collecting unemployment checks. After the money ran out and his wife died from breast cancer,

Roger had been so close to ending everything. His home was going into foreclosure and nobody would hire him. Death seemed like the answer to solve all his problems.

Cash stopped his act of desperation and offered to help him out, but Roger still had a shred of pride and refused to take a handout. He actually came up with the idea to act as a butler and although Cash couldn't imagine having the man that he had come to look at as a father figure working for him, Roger wouldn't have it any other way. Because of that, he was paid handsomely and had his own quarters in the house.

Roger shrugged with a slight grin. "It's your night, son. Enjoy it."

Cash nodded before walking out behind Fallon. Waiting was a Rolls Royce Phantom. He'd arranged to have one pick up each person in his immediate circle. He normally wasn't so over the top, but it was a celebration, as he'd been reminded several times before. He had to ensure that he went all out and arrived in style.

This shit should be for me, not Outlaw's ass. Ghost looked around the plush club bitterly, watching Outlaw pop bottles out of the corner of his eye. A bad bitch was draped on Outlaw's arm and all Ghost could do was hate.

Cash doesn't deserve this shit either. His older brother hadn't yet arrived but he knew that motherfuckers were gonna go crazy when he did. Honestly, Ghost hadn't even wanted to come but after Strap's insistence, he showed up. He was going to keep his distance from his brother as best he could though. Ghost didn't give a damn that it was his celebration. He had to give his props however; Cash had showed his ass with this party.

Tickets were damn near in the triple digits, but everyone was breaking their neck to gain entry into what had been coined one of the hottest parties in Raleigh. Ladies knew that men with fat pockets would be there and they had dreams of snagging a baller. Those women considered going to Cash's party an investment in their future.

Men knew that the baddest females in the city would be in attendance and besides that, it was sure to be a good time. Most importantly, people wanted to be able to say that they'd attended. Everyone always expected something big whenever Cash made a guest appearance and tonight would be no different.

The crowd was jumping and the deejay had been playing nothing but hits all night. Strap had yet to see his older brother but knew he would be arriving soon. The two stood in VIP with other members of Cash's crew. The liquor was flowing and the hoes were flocking.

The dress code was 'grown and sexy' and even Ghost had managed to adhere, although loosely. He wore a Ralph Lauren Black Label suit that was one size too big. The button down shirt he wore was opened and his sleeves were rolled up. His black wifebeater was exposed and his chain glistened against the lights in the club.

"This shit is nice," Strap commented to his brother, ignoring the scowl on his face. "They went all out."

"It's still fucked up what Cash did," Ghost said, still unable to let go of what he'd viewed as betrayal.

"I think Outlaw deserved it though. He knows what he's doing and he been Cash's right-hand for as long as I can remember."

"Blood's thicker than water," Ghost muttered, barely audible due to the blaring sounds of Drake's new single. He looked in Outlaw's direction again. He looked like he was having the time of his fucking life. "Nowadays blood ain't shit though." Ghost leaned towards his twin brother, "Cash is grimy, Strap. First he takes ya bitch and then he overlooks my ass."

Strap wasn't sure of what to say, so he didn't bother to speak. He wasn't going to go there with his brother right now. Ghost had done nothing but complain anytime Cash's name was mentioned so Strap would steer clear of those conversations. Honestly, he was surprised that Ghost had even wanted to come to the party tonight but he'd insisted.

"It'd be real fucked up if some shit popped off tonight, huh? On his big day," Ghost added.

"You wouldn't?!" Strap looked at his brother in disbelief, not missing the devilish look in his eyes.

Ghost grinned widely before bursting into laugher, "Nah." He slapped his knee as if he'd heard the funniest joke. "See the look on your face?! I ain't even strapped tonight so chill out."

Strap raised his eyebrow, finding that hard to believe. Whether or not Ghost was toting fire, he knew that he was. It was like his American Express card: He never left home without it.

"Real nigga shit. I wouldn't disrespect my brother like that. I just wanna drink and have a good time."

"Whatever, Ghost." He tried to read his brother but he wore a poker face. His mood switched back and forth easily, making it hard for Strap to figure out what Ghost's true aim was. Knowing his brother, there was certainly some animosity but whether or not he would act on it was up in the air. Strap would play him close tonight, just in case.

"What's up, Cash?"

"What's good with that VIP, my nigga?"

Cameras flashed and people were calling out to Cash as he and Fallon strolled down the red carpet towards the entrance of his club downtown. She was nervous but tried not to show it. A few females were bold enough to look at Cash suggestively but he paid them no mind. He was already with the baddest female there, even the groupies knew it. That was evident from the way some either admired or envied her.

"You good, baby?" Cash whispered to Fallon, pulling her closer to him.

"Yeah," she nodded. She had to admit that she wasn't expecting all this. It was bigger than she could have imagined. Every few seconds they were stopping to take a picture or Cash was speaking to an associate. Fallon had never been to a party like this and it was pretty obvious that many of the clubgoers hadn't either. Most looked just as mesmerized as she did.

"Aw shit! The man of the muthafuckin' hour is here! What's good, Cash?" the deejay shouted over the loud speaker giving him a salute.

Cash nodded his head and returned the gesture as he and Fallon headed up to the VIP section. The club was designed with two different levels. Upstairs, overlooking the dance floor, was VIP. Plush round booths were available and they had a perfect view of the huge screen displaying music videos of the popular hits the deejay was spinning. There was an open bar and every five minutes the female dancers were rushing up to VIP with Ace of Spades and other expensive drinks with sparklers on top, attracting attention.

"Ooh, baby, there goes Shantreis," Fallon said, happy to see her girl in the sea of strangers.

Cash smiled. "Do you, baby girl. I'm a' holla at my brothers real quick."

"Strap and Ghost are here?" she asked. "I'll come with you to say 'hello'."

The two of them headed in the twins' direction. Cash gave each brother a hoodshake although he didn't miss Ghost's initial reluctance. He gave his younger brother a look but didn't speak on it.

"Damien, you look so nice," Fallon fussed over Strap in a sisterly way, admiring how mature he looked in his suit. She reached over to give him a hug and kiss on the cheek.

"Thanks. You lookin' good too," Strap complimented, holding the embrace a little longer than he should have. He inhaled deeply, loving her scent. He was unable to keep his eyes off her, but fought his hardest to. Luckily Cash hadn't been paying attention or he would have surely checked him. Strap made a mental reminder to watch himself so as not to cause any issues later.

"Hey, Ghost," Fallon greeted, also giving him a quick hug.

"What's up, New-New?!" he asked, surprising everyone when he kissed her on the cheek.

Cash may have missed Strap's lingering embrace but his eyes were fixed on Ghost's display of affection. "You aiight?"

"Yeah. I'm straight. Did I do somethin' wrong?" Ghost asked innocently with a slight smirk.

"You better keep your lips to ya'self, nigga."

"Nigga, please, I don't want ya bitch." Ghost laughed. "You got it all fuckin' wrong. I'm not the one you should be worried about." With that said, he brushed past them, headed towards the bar.

"What the hell he mean?" Cash asked Strap confused.

Strap shrugged, mad at the subtle way his brother had put him on blast. "Who the hell ever knows what *your* brother be talkin' bout?"

"That's *your* brother," Cash joked back.

"Cash!! What's up, nigga?" Outlaw yelled, tipsy as he approached his former boss.

Taking that as an opportunity to slip off, Fallon headed in the direction of her girlfriend. "Hey, Shantreis!"

"Hey, Fallon!" Shantreis said, taking a sip from her glass. "Bout time y'all asses arrived. I thought y'all weren't—"

Shantreis couldn't finish her sentence before vomit spewed from her mouth. Everyone jumped back while Fallon raced to the bar to get some napkins. Handing them to her friend, they headed in the direction of the bathroom.

"You okay?" Fallon asked concerned, shooing the other females out so that Shantreis could have some privacy.

Shantreis nodded. "Yeah. I just been…" Feeling the urge again, she hurried into a bathroom stall.

"You aren't pregnant, are you?" Fallon half-joked.

"Oh God…" Shantreis moaned as she sat on the floor. The color was drained from her already light complexion and her breathing was ragged. "No… I can't be. I take birth control."

"Well, if you are I'm sure Outlaw will be happy. You know he can take care of y'all," Fallon suggested brightly, cleaning her friend up.

"What's going on?" Outlaw asked, entering the women's bathroom without knocking. As soon as he realized that it was Shantreis that everyone was talking about, he wasted no time trying to get to her. "Baby, you alright?" He kneeled on the floor beside her.

"Yeah," she responded, holding her head with her hand.

"C'mon, let's go home."

"No… It's your night, baby. I don't wanna ruin it," Shantreis insisted, wanting to be alone.

"You ain't ruinin' shit. I'm good. I gotta make sure you straight."

Fallon smiled, surprised at Outlaw's gallant behavior. She had never seen this side of him, but she was impressed. This certainly wasn't the dude that she remembered. It was certainly a big contrast in comparison to the way he'd acted the last time they went to the club.

"I think I just drank too much," Shantreis said, trying to downplay the situation. Honestly she was wondering if Fallon was right. She never missed a pill and always took them as scheduled but she had been feeling nauseous lately. Since Shantreis' period wasn't regular anyway due to the birth control, pregnancy was something she had never given any merit. She passed it off as a stomach bug.

"Either way, come on, girl. We going," Outlaw insisted.

"Can I talk to Fallon real quick, baby?" she asked. "Then I'll go."

He nodded before leaving her side reluctantly. "I'll be right outside the door."

"Look, if I'm pregnant…" Shantreis started when she felt the coast was clear. Tears spilled from her eyes and cascaded down her pretty face. "I'm in some big ass trouble. I don't know who the hell the father is…"

Chapter 20

"What happened with your girl?" Cash asked Fallon as she returned to her spot next to him.

"She was sick. I guess she drank too much," she said casually not wanting to divulge too many details. She was still reeling over Shantreis' confession. Fallon couldn't believe that she had been so stupid as to have unprotected sex with the both of them. Shantreis insisted that she and Blaze always used condoms but Fallon wasn't convinced. She thought that may have just been something that she told her so that she wouldn't look down on her.

"Damn. Hope she feels better." He shook his head. "Ay, I'll be right back. I gotta handle somethin' real quick."

Fallon nodded before walking back over to VIP and taking a seat. Without her girl there and Cash absent from her side, she felt awkward standing alone. She'd searched the crowd for Strap, but she didn't see him. Ghost had apparently disappeared too.

The music suddenly cut off amidst a few protests until Cash's voice resonated through the speakers. "Ay, I just wanna say 'preciate it to ev'rybody that came out tonight." He smiled, exposing his perfect teeth. He knew that none of the clubgoers knew the real reason for the celebration, thinking that it was just a going away party for Cash and that Outlaw was hosting it. They had no idea that it was much deeper than that.

"Ya'll coulda been anywhere else but y'all here fuckin' with me. Celebratin' with me and shit."

A few women shouted, "No problem, boo" and "Anytime". Fallon had to roll her eyes. Could they be any more obvious?

"My nigga Outlaw had to go home but I'm sure he appreciates y'all coming out and showin' love too." More women screamed as though they were at a Trey Songz concert. "And to my lady, Fallon, thank you, baby, for holdin' me down even though you ran out on me one time before." He chuckled and so did a few others in the audience.

Fallon blushed, mortified as a spotlight put her on display for everyone to see. She became self-conscious when she noticed her image in the many TV screens decorating the club.

"I'm gonna make sure you don't leave me this time though." Reaching in his pocket, he pulled out a ring box and opened it. The screen did a close up of the huge ten carat ring. It was adorned with smaller diamonds in a platinum setting. It sparkled under the light and paired with Fallon's sequin dress, it would really be a sight for sore eyes. "You gonna marry me, girl?"

The crowd erupted into screams and Fallon squealed, "Oh my God, Damontrez! Yes."

A few people laughed at her reaction while others clapped or 'awed' .

"Got damn, homie."

"He must really love that girl."

Fallon glided down the stairs, almost unable to see due to the tears in her eyes. She made it to the stage, feeling nervous at all eyes being on her but focused her attention on Cash. He placed the ring on her finger and once again, everybody applauded.

"Free drinks on me all night," Cash yelled before he jumped off the stage, helping escort Fallon down. "Aiight, Vic, cut that shit back on." Young Jeezy's 'I Do' blared from the speakers and he had to laugh at the selection.

Fallon pulled him close, giving him a kiss. "I can't believe this!"

"Believe it, baby girl. And don't go changing your mind either. You stuck with a nigga."

She laughed. "You're the only one I wanna be stuck with."

"Ay, man, lemme holla at ya," Strap said, pulling Cash to the side. "Look, I'll be back. I think I need to take Ghost back to the crib… He fucked up."

That was an understatement. Ghost's eyes were red and his arm was draped around a petite female who looked like she was struggling to hold him up. Without her, he probably wouldn't have been able to stand. His button down shirt had been completely discarded and now only his wifebeater hugged his chiseled muscles.

Cash had never known Ghost to get sloppy drunk, much less drink. Weed had always been his drug of choice so to see him showing out like this had him infuriated. He knew that Ghost had done it just to get under his skin.

"I can't believe this nigga," Cash seethed, clenching his jaw in anger. "I'm a' handle his lil' ass." He turned to Fallon. "Let me check on my brother and I'll be back. Stay here with Strap."

She nodded obediently, already knowing that something was about to go down. Cash could only take three steps before Ghost had headed in his direction. The Nia Long beauty he was with was still acting as a crutch.

"Congrata-fuckin'-lations!" Ghost boomed, clapping his hands at every syllable. His voice was so loud that a few other patrons turned in their direction to see what was going on. "New-New, you gonna be one bad ass bride…" He looked her up and down with an overtone of lust in his eyes, completely disrespecting the female he was with, as well as Cash. "I tell you what though. You picked the wrong muthafuckin' brother to fall in love with."

"Watch it," Strap hissed at Ghost, worried that he was going to say something he would regret later.

Cash only smirked. "Ghost, didn't we have this talk before, nigga? But you still talkin' shit?!" In one split second he had rushed his little brother, yanking him by the straps on his wifebeater.

Ghost looked him directly in the eyes and then laughed loudly. "Fuck you, Cash," he spat—literally.

"Aww shit," the small crowd surrounding them gasped, looking at the gob of spit on Cash's cheek. The loud rap music had subsided and all eyes were focused on Cash and Ghost. Everyone was in shock at what had gone down and was, without a doubt, curious to see what would happen next.

The spit barely had a chance to dry before Cash's fists were pummeling into Ghost. His younger brother could hardly fight back due to the liquor in his system. His reflexes were off, allowing Cash to get the best of him.

Strap stood watching in shock before Fallon's cries knocked him out of his trance. He attempted to break up the scuffle but Cash was determined to give Ghost the ass whupping that he should've been given a long time ago.

"Muthafucka, you wanna die?! I'll lay ya ass out right here, nigga!" Cash yelled, as he finally stopped raining blows on his brother's body. "Matter fact." His chest heaved in and out as he pushed his Desert Eagle up against Ghost's temple.

Cash looked around at the crowd, realizing the scene he'd created. "Ev'rybody get the fuck out!" He raised his gun to the ceiling and let off a shot.

Instantly screams filled the club as people frantically rushed out, nearly running each other over in an attempt to exit the packed building.

"Calm down, baby!" Fallon yelled, "Please don't do this!" She turned to Strap in despair, praying that he would do something.

"Ay, chill," Strap intervened. "C'mon, Cash. Stop it. He's fucked up, man. He don't know what the fuck he sayin'!"

Ghost's breath was ragged but his gaze didn't falter from his older brother. He stared Cash in the eyes, barely blinking. If it was one thing he possessed, it was heart. He'd gotten his ass beat but he still wore a smirk on his face. "Fuck yo' bitch ass."

"Delonte…" he called Ghost by his real name. "Tell me why the fuck I shouldn't body ya ass right here!" Cash rarely lost his composure but spitting had pushed him over the edge. To him that was the highest level of disrespect.

Ghost shrugged, looking at him maliciously. Despite having a gun pressed to his head, he showed no fear. "No reason why you shouldn't," he replied nonchalantly before grinning impishly, "but the fact is that you ain't."

"That's what you think, huh?"

Again Ghost only shrugged. "Am I right… or wrong?"

"Chill, Cash, chill," Strap reminded, noticing the

incensed look in his brother's eyes. "We blood! Y'all need to quit this shit!"

"Fuck that shit. Get this sorry ass nigga out of my fuckin' face. You dead to me!" Cash bellowed. "Keep the fuck from 'round me, Ghost, or I swear I'll merk ya ass on sight!"

Finally removing the gun from his head, Cash shoved his .357 back into his slacks. "Funny I was gonna say that same shit," Ghost smiled devilishly, knowing that Cash had fucked up by letting him live. His time was coming and now he would *really* enjoy it.

"C'mon, bae," Fallon said reaching for Cash's hand as his brothers' exited the club. "Let's go home. Please."

"I got some other shit to handle right quick, baby. You go on to the house, aiight?"

"What? What do you have to handle that I have to leave for? You're not gonna do anything to Ghost right?"

Cash was quiet, lost in his own thoughts.

"Hello? *Damontrez*, you don't hear me?" Fallon placed her tiny hands on her waist.

"Yeah. Don't worry about Ghost." He kissed her forehead. "If I was gonna kill him, I would've done it."

Fallon exhaled a sigh of relief. "Good because I almost thought you were for a second."

"Nah." Cash just hoped that his decision wouldn't come back to bite him in the ass. He had too much shit going for himself to be taken out by a knucklehead like Ghost.

"The car is waiting for you, baby. Go on," he urged.

There was something unsettling about his behavior and after what had happened tonight, Fallon didn't know what to expect. All she could pray was that Cash would keep his promise to her and stay out of trouble. They had come this far and she would never forgive him if he did something to destroy that.

She hugged him and they kissed one last time. "I know you're plotting something, Damontrez Hardy. But let me give *you* warning, don't mess up what we're trying to build."

"I won't, baby. I love you."

"Love you too."

Chapter 21

"Man, fuck that nigga," Ghost slurred, ignoring the 'voice of reason' Strap was trying to be. He held his head with one hand as he leaned against the passenger side door of the Charger. "He *always* thought he was the shit. Nigga ain't never done me no fuckin' favors."

"Where is this shit coming from? For real," Strap asked. He couldn't say that he hadn't expected Ghost's outburst but he didn't think that things would turn out like this. Ghost and Cash had always had their small rifts but nothing on this level.

"Fuck you mean? You actin' like you ain't seen the shit!" Ghost waved him off. "Fuck it. I don't know why the hell I'm havin' this conversation wit' you fo'. You all on that nigga dick and shit."

Strap sucked his teeth. "Ghost, you trippin'. Y'all need to dead this beef shit. It ain't even worth it."

"Fuck that. Cash think he the fuckin' boss—"

"He is!" Strap stressed. "That nigga pays us to do what the fuck he says! You just always want to do your own thing so that's why y'all always fallin' out! He tryna look out for us."

"And you cool with doin' what the fuck some other nigga tell you to do?" Ghost asked, raising an eyebrow. He completely ignored Strap's logic. No matter how Strap presented the facts to him, he never would understand. "My nigga, I wanna be my own fuckin' boss. Bein' up under another nigga ain't some shit that I was built for."

"Too many chiefs and not enough Indians," Strap muttered under his breath. "Look, I want to—*and I'm gonna*—be my own boss but until then, it is what it is."

"What the fuck you gonna do, Strap?" Ghost laughed condescendingly. "The fuck you know about anything except killin' niggas?"

"I don't, but I'm gonna learn. I'm looking into startin' my own franchise. Ownin' a McDonalds or somethin'." He shrugged. "I was thinkin' about goin' back to school too."

Ghost snickered. "Fuckin' pipe dreams."

"It ain't a pipe dream," Strap defended, "Not everybody has dreams of bein' hoodrich and shit. Hell, we ain't gonna be twenty forever, Ghost. You still gonna be doin' this shit when you in ya thirties?" He didn't wait for his brother to respond before continuing, "You need to get on the shit that I'm on. You can't tell me that with the way we livin', that you don't think we won't be locked up or dead before we turn twenty-one."

"Only if we get caught slippin'!" Ghost asserted. "Fuck outta here, Strap." Then he nodded his head knowingly. "I know what it is. New-New got ya head all fucked up, right?"

"I wouldn't call it that. Fallon just really got me thinkin' about a lot of shit. I ain't think I could do shit else but the street life… She got a nigga believin' in himself." Upon hearing Ghost's silence, Strap waved the conversation off. He knew that his brother wouldn't be able to relate, so he wasn't sure why he'd even bothered to go there. "I just don't wanna look over my shoulder all the time... This street shit is overrated."

"You love her?" Ghost asked finally.

"Drop it, Ghost," Strap warned. He wasn't in the mood for Ghost's tasteless jokes.

Ghost shook his head. "Nah… I'm serious. You love this bitch—" Seeing the look on Strap's face, he quickly changed his wording, "I mean, *girl,* but you gonna let Cash have her? There ain't too many bitches out here made like shawty. Believe that."

"You think I don't know that shit?" Strap pounded on the steering wheel to emphasize his point. "It is what it is though."

"Nah, nigga! Let her choose! Fuck Cash!"

"*'Fuck Cash'* is the only reason why you sayin' this shit."

"That ain't the reason why. Real nigga shit," Ghost denied.

"Anyway, she *did* choose. She with Cash ain't she?"

"That's cuz ya punk ass don't say shit to her." He shrugged. "Hell. It's yo' life. But if Cash marry that bitch you gonna resent his ass too."

"You right… But it is what it is," Strap reiterated in a tone that signaled that the conversation was over.

"She gonna be a widow if she stays by that nigga side though," Ghost mumbled with a smile.

"Wow… What did I do to deserve this?" Shantreis joked as she eyed the spread in front of her. Outlaw had brought her breakfast in bed and went all out. Pancakes, bacon, scrambled eggs, and freshly squeezed orange juice on the side.

"How you feelin'?" Outlaw asked, ignoring her question. He perched on the side of the bed, gazing at her intently.

"I'm good," she lied, ignoring the queasy feeling in her stomach. "I told you I think I just drunk too much."

"I ain't never seen you like that though… I was worried as hell."

Shantreis smiled as his thoughtfulness. "I'm good, baby. Thanks for getting me some IHOP."

"IHOP?" he grinned, "Who says I ain't cook that?"

"Cuz you can't cook, nigga." They both laughed, knowing that she was telling the truth. Outlaw could cook dope but food was a completely different story. Shantreis cut her pancake into tiny squares hoping to buy time. Her stomach still hadn't settled and truth be told, the smell of the eggs was making it worse.

"Fallon texted you too. She been blowin' up ya phone all damn morning," Outlaw informed her as he passed her vibrating cell phone from off the nightstand. "She probably tryna see if you straight."

"I wonder what's going on." Shantreis took the phone and tried to hide the surprise on her face when she saw '*Fallon Home*' as the incoming caller.

Why the hell is Blaze calling me so early? she thought. "I'll just uh… Call her back after I finish eatin'." She quickly pressed ignore and tossed the phone next to her.

Outlaw eyed her suspiciously, not missing her nervousness but brushed it off. "Look, I got some business to handle with Cash but I wanted to make sure you was straight first. If you ain't, I can stay home witchu."

"No, baby," she replied quickly after taking a small sip

of her orange juice. "I told you quit worryin'. Trust me. I'm good."

He nodded his head before leaning in to steal a kiss, "Aiight then. I love you."

"Love you too." Shantreis waited until he left the room before she shot up from the bed and rushed over to their adjoining bathroom. She barely had time to close the door behind her before vomit was spewing out of her mouth. She gripped the sides of the toilet as she continued to release the contents of her stomach.

Shit… This morning sickness is no joke, she thought. No sooner than it entered her mind did Shantreis dismiss it. It just had to be the liquor from last night… She took her birth control daily and on top of that, Blaze always wore a condom. Outlaw pulled out every time. She'd always been told that wasn't effective but it had worked faithfully since the start of their relationship. Shit just wasn't adding up to her.

When Shantreis' stomach was finally emptied, she grabbed a towel and wiped her mouth. She would clean up her mess later. Right now she just wanted to get dressed and run to Rite Aid for a pregnancy test. She needed to know for certain and then she would figure out the best way to deal with it.

Shantreis didn't bother rummaging through her crowded closet, instead slipping on a pair of flipflops. She knew that she looked like shit: her hair could use a comb and other than brushing her teeth, she hadn't taken care of her personal hygiene. In fact, Shantreis was still wearing her wrinkled dress from the night before. At the moment she didn't give a damn, she just wanted to be in and out of the pharmacy and back to the house as soon as possible.

Just as she'd slung her bag over her shoulder and headed out the bedroom door, her phone started ringing. *Almost left it,* she thought, picking it up from its place on the bed. "Hello?"

"Ay, baby," came Outlaw's voice, "You'll look for my chain right quick? I thought I had it on."

Shantreis rolled her eyes. "I don't know how you managed to lose it when you wear it every damn day." She didn't mean to come off with as much attitude as she did, but she was in a rush. She definitely wasn't trying to play seek and find with Outlaw's chain this morning.

"Baby, just look for me, please," Outlaw begged uncharacteristically. "I hope I ain't leave it at the damn IHOP. I'm a' be madder than a bitch."

"Where you think you left it at then? On the bed?" Shantreis smoothed back the covers but came up empty besides a few food crumbs. "It's not there."

"Check my drawer then."

Shantreis sighed as she made her way to their dresser. Pulling out the drawer, her eyes searched quickly for his Ace of Spades chain. "Nothing here either… I don't know where you left it, Outlaw, but I'm tryna eat," she lied.

"Ay, my bad, baby, but this is real important. You know how many stacks that chain set me back? Shit. I don't know how the fuck this happened. Ay, check the living room real quick—by the IHOP bags."

"What the hell?" Shantreis mumbled in awe as she entered the living room. "Are you serious?"

Outlaw chuckled. "I guess that means you see it, huh?"

She nodded as she cupped a hand over her mouth and shook her head. Sitting on the middle of the coffee table was a small black box with a red bow on top of it. *It can't be…* Cash's words echoed in her head and Shantreis knew what was inside without even having to look in the box.

"So…?" he asked eagerly, his smile could be felt through the phone.

Shantreis was silent as she opened the box slowly. Her mouth dropped when she saw the beautiful ring inside. It was a stunning white gold ring with a huge rock shaped like a heart. Shantreis estimated that it had to be at least ten carats.

"Oh my God, Outlaw," she gasped.

"I'm saying, what's up?" His voice began to echo, indicating that he was nearby. Stepping into the living room, Outlaw approached her slowly as he placed his phone in his pocket. "You gonna leave a nigga hangin' or you gonna say yes?" he joked before his voice took on a solemn tone. "I always knew that I was gonna make you my wife, I just ain't know when. And I know it took me a long ass time to get it together, but I swear, baby, you won't be makin' a mistake if you say 'yes'."

Shantreis nodded her head, barely unable to get the words out. "Yes. I will."

Outlaw slipped the ring on her finger slowly then smiled wider than Jay-Z did when Beyonce announced that she was carrying his baby. Pulling her close for a kiss, he felt like the luckiest man in the world. "Damn, baby, you 'bout to be Mrs. Travaris Robinson."

"I know," Shantreis whispered softly. "I can't believe it." She couldn't but not for the same reasons as Outlaw thought.

Chapter 22

"He's your *brother*, Cash. I know y'all are mad right now but you've got to think about what's more important. Y'all are acting real childish," Fallon said as she stood in front of Cash with her hands on her hips.

"Fuck that nigga, Fallon. I told you to drop it already but you won't stop talking about it. I'm not discussin' this shit about my brother with you."

"Why not?" she asked, slightly offended.

"Because you don't understand Ghost. I probably would a' been better off merkin' his ass at the club. He lucky that I let him live to see another day."

Cash laid back on the bed with his hands behind his head. They'd been having this conversation all night and all morning but she still wasn't letting up. With each word she spoke, it only served to remind Cash of their incident last night and make him even madder. He didn't want to have his brother's blood on his hands but if push came to shove, *this time* he wouldn't have a problem pulling the trigger.

"Are you serious?" Fallon was shocked. The way he could speak so nonchalantly about killing his brother was bothering her. "How can you be so cold?"

Cash sighed. "I told you that you wouldn't understand."

"You're right. I don't understand the type of person you are anymore."

"What?" he asked, jumping up from his place on the bed. "Why the hell are you trippin' so hard? I spare his lil' ass and you're actin' like I laid him out on the concrete!"

"Because you don't see anything wrong with what you're saying. We're talking about somebody's *life*, Cash. And your *brother's* at that!"

"Fallon, do you really think that nigga got any regard for human life? He's the trigger-happy mothafucka that's always—"

"Doing whatever the hell you tell him to! I honestly don't know what's worse: Him pulling the trigger or pulling it at *your* command?!" Fallon shook her head. "I don't know how the hell I thought that this would work." She sat down at the edge of the bed and buried her face in her hands.

Cash sighed as he took a seat next to her and wrapped an arm around her shoulder. "Baby, you're really thinkin' too much into this shit. I'm still the same nigga."

"Exactly, Cash! The same nigga that I broke up with a year ago! You haven't changed!"

"How the fuck I ain't change?" he asked, now

incensed.

Cash arose from next to her and took a place directly in front of her instead. "I'm gettin' out the damn game for you but I ain't change?! Fallon, I handled that shit in less time than you even fuckin' gave me. I'm missin' out on *millions* of dollars by giving that shit up! But I'm doin' that shit for you! You think I give a fuck bout gettin' out the game? Hell no! I changed for *you*!" Cash shook his head. "You on that bullshit."

"*I'm* on that bullshit, Damontrez?"

The fact that Fallon was calling Cash by his first name let him know that she was just as pissed off as he was, but he didn't care. Some shit she would never comprehend because she wasn't about that life. Fallon had lived with a silver spoon in her mouth until her parents died. Even then she didn't have to live a hard life due to him stepping in and helping her out.

"Yeah, you are. *I'm* ya nigga, not Ghost and you up here pityin' his ass. Fuck him. I told you I ain't gonna do nothin' to his ass but you—"

"Promise me then," she interrupted.

"Say what?"

"Promise me that you won't do *anything* to him."

When Cash was quiet, Fallon decided to explain where she was coming from, "I've changed a lot since we broke up, Damontrez. Even when things had started getting rocky when we *were* together… It's a lot of things that you did that I always turned my head and pretended not to know about but I can't do that anymore. I can't be with somebody that can kill a *human* just as easily as they could kill a roach scurrying across the floor." Fallon looked him directly in the eyes. "Promise me, Damontrez."

Cash returned her gaze before he began, "Look, Fallon, you know I've never broken a promise to you. That's somethin' I'd *never* do…" He paused briefly before letting out a sigh, "That's why I just can't promise you that."

"Then I can't promise you that I'll still want to marry a monster," Fallon responded heatedly. She may have been acting irrationally but her emotions were running high when she slipped her ring off her finger and placed it in the palm of Cash's hand. Without another word, she spun on her heels and charged out the door.

Cash didn't even bother to stop her.

Shantreis' heart sank as she stared at the two lines that had formed on the First Response pregnancy test she'd picked up from the store. Her worst fears had been confirmed.

What the hell am I gonna do? she thought before the bamming on the bathroom stall door interrupted her thoughts.

"Sweetheart," a raspy voice called, "You've been in there for ages! There are people waiting!"

Shantreis rolled her eyes before she chucked the test into her oversized Hermes Birkin bag and flushed the toilet for good measure. She had been in such a rush that after she'd purchased the pregnancy test, she had driven to the first place with a restroom—that just happened to be

McDonalds. She didn't want to take it at Blaze's house, where she was headed. Shantreis for damn sure couldn't wait until she got back home in case Outlaw saw it either. Right now she just wanted to keep the discovery of her pregnancy a secret—from *them* anyway.

"Finally," a few of the women muttered as Shantreis exited the stall and headed over to the sink.

Shantreis didn't bother to respond. She had bigger things on her plate to worry about than cussing out a bunch of old ladies that were salty about having to wait for the handicapped stall.

"That's a really nice ring," a lady commented as she took a place beside Shantreis at the sink.

"Thank you," Shantreis managed.

"He's got to really love you if you bought you a ring that big! Did y'all set a date yet?"

"Not yet," she answered, quickly drying her hands so she could leave. Shantreis knew the woman meant well but she wasn't really in the mood to talk about it.

As soon as Shantreis got into her Jaguar, she whipped her cell phone out and dialed Fallon's number. She needed to speak to her voice of reason. Most times Fallon could make sense of any situation. Or at least give her something to think about.

"Hello?" Fallon asked, picking up on the first ring.

"Ho, we gotta talk," Shantreis greeted as she backed her car out of the parking spot and drove in the direction of Blaze's apartment. "Outlaw proposed to me today."

"Oh my God! Are you serious?" Fallon squealed, "Wow. I can't believe it."

"I can't believe I said *'yes'*." She sighed. "I mean… I'm all fucked up. I took a pregnancy test today and I *am* pregnant."

"Damn… So what are you gonna do?"

"I gotta get rid of it. Fuck you mean? I'm 'bout to call *Planned Parenthood* and get an appointment."

"Don't do that!" Fallon shouted quickly—more so than she'd intended to.

"Damn, bitch. You talkin' like the shit's personal. Outlaw ain't bout to whup my ass if the baby ain't his!"

"You really think he would do a test though?" Fallon asked rhetorically, "I doubt it. He would never know."

Shantreis couldn't believe Fallon. She had always been such a goody goody but here she was, encouraging her to pin—what possibly could be—another man's baby on Outlaw. "Let me find out my best friend be on that scandalous shit," she joked. "But seriously though, he did one on Kaleesha's baby so—"

"Because she was a jumpoff. Not wifey! Besides that, despite the fact that you've been sleeping with Blaze, Outlaw doesn't know that. You haven't given him a reason not to trust you!" Fallon sighed. "Look, I know it sounds crazy, but you don't wanna do something that you regret later…"

"You really gettin' worked up about this shit," Shantreis commented, wondering where this was coming from.

"I've been there, done that and I wish I hadn't."

Shantreis' eyes grew as wide as balloons. "Bitch, you ain't tell me! Where the fuck was I?"

Fallon was quiet before speaking up, "Just think it over before you go making an appointment. Talk it over with Blaze or do whatever you have to do. But just be sure and be ready for the consequences—of either decision."

Fallon's words echoed in Shantreis' mind as she pulled up to Blaze's apartment complex. He lived in Cameron Courts in downtown Raleigh. The buildings were vintage and entirely constructed out of brick. His apartment itself was decent but the outside was a different story.

Shantreis turned her nose up at the strong smell of dog feces in the air and stepped over the litter on the grounds. *Of all the places in Raleigh,* she thought. *Blaze chose here.* She climbed the stairwell, which reeked of marijuana and was littered with junk mail flyers. Just as she'd reached Blaze's apartment, the door swung open.

"What's good?" he asked with an impish smirk.

"Damn, nigga, you anxious, huh?" Shantreis matched his look as she tried to ignore how good he looked in that instant. A wifebeater clung tightly to his lean, but muscular build and a pair of basketball shorts sagged off his waistline.

"Nah. A nigga ain't *never* pressed but I was 'bout to head out to the courtyard."

"For what?" she wondered as she slid past him into the tiny, six hundred square feet apartment.

"To wait on yo' ass," Blaze joked. "You said you was comin' through over an hour ago."

Shantreis nodded. "I know. I got sidetracked… But I got some important shit to talk to you about."

"Yeah?" he asked, raising an eyebrow and plopping down on the futon in his living room. His apartment was a typical bachelor's pad. Blaze only had the necessities for living, nothing too fancy: an oversized plasma TV, game consoles, and liquor.

She sighed. "Yeah." Taking a seat near him, but at a distance she began, "We gotta talk about us."

"Aww hell. What is it this time, 'Treis?" Blaze shook his head. It seemed like no matter what they would decide on, Shantreis was always going back and changing things. Like now, they were playing the role of fuck buddies. It wasn't an arrangement that he was completely happy with—after all, he could get pussy from anywhere—but Blaze took what he could get when it came to Shantreis.

"I-I just…" Shantreis stammered before rising from her chair. She covered her mouth with her hands and ran out of the room abruptly.

No sooner than she had reached the bathroom and bent over the toilet did the feeling subside. *False fuckin' alarm,* she thought bitterly. Sure, Shantreis was overjoyed that she didn't have to spend her time worshipping the porcelain god, but she knew that Blaze would undoubtedly have questions that she didn't want to answer.

Shantreis rose slowly and checked her appearance in the mirror. Her eyes were still a little watery but other than that, she still looked well put together. After Outlaw had come back to the house, she went ahead and made herself presentable to the public. Since she'd also decided to see Blaze, she didn't want to look a hot mess either. That would raise even more questions. Quickly, she slipped off her engagement ring and slid it into her pocket, then exited the bathroom.

"You straight?" Blaze asked when she entered the room.

"Yeah. I'm good." She retook her seat on the sofa and sighed.

"So you got some shit to tell me?" His expression was somber and his gaze on her was unfaltering. When she didn't speak, he continued, "What happened to that nice ass ring that nigga got you?"

"I don't know what you're talking about," she lied.

"Cut the bullshit, Shantreis!" Blaze thundered, "What the fuck else did you come over to talk about?"

Suddenly she couldn't find the words. Shantreis was speechless for one of the first times in her life.

"If you ain't gonna say shit then *I* will! I can't believe that you told that nigga 'yes'! Are you that fuckin' shallow that you would marry a nigga that you don't love just for some fuckin' money?"

"You're wrong!" she shouted, finally finding her voice.

"Oh yeah?" Blaze asked, standing up. Making his way towards Shantreis, he crouched down in front of her, forcing her to look at him. "Tell me that you love that nigga then! Look me in my muthafuckin' eyes and say that shit!"

"I do, Blaze, okay?" Shantreis looked at his face but couldn't bring herself to make eye contact with him. She pulled Outlaw's ring out of her pocket and slid it on her finger for emphasis.

Blaze chuckled and shook his head dismally. "Man, you changed."

"I ain't change!" she insisted. "I'm the same ol' Shantreis Teasley from Gilpin Courts!"

"Hell nah." Blaze took a spot near the window and stared outside. "I don't know who the fuck this is. Some brand new Raleigh chick but you ain't my 'Treis from Richmond."

"Fuck you, Blaze! I don't give a damn what you think! I know exactly who I am!" Shantreis grabbed her bag off the floor and started for the door.

"That's it, huh?" he asked sullenly, walking towards her.

Her voice came out shaky. "Yes. That's it."

Blaze grabbed her hand, pulling her back towards him. Feeling his body so close to hers momentarily made her forget why she was leaving. Shantreis wondered if he was going to make love to her, right there. She couldn't say that she would have put up much of a struggle if he had. But what he whispered in her ear, made her realize that his thoughts were far away from that.

"Answer me, Shantreis," Blaze demanded. "You weren't gonna tell me about the baby huh?"

"You've been snoopin' through my stuff?" Shantreis asked, jerking away from him.

Blaze ignored her. "Is it mine?"

Shantreis was quiet.

"It is, ain't it?" he prodded, stepping closer to her.

"Whether it is or not, me and Outlaw will be raisin' this baby." Shantreis turned the doorknob. She was unable to face him after what she'd just said. She knew that it was despicable but what other choice did she have? She wasn't sure about aborting it because Fallon was right—she *wasn't* sure that she would be able to live with herself if she did.

Blaze shut the door just as quickly as Shantreis had gotten it open. "I'll be damned if you gonna have my seed call another nigga daddy!"

"Listen! I don't even know if it's yours or not!" Shantreis screeched.

"I do!" he shouted firmly. "And if even you don't, the fact that you just—just *decided* that no matter what, it's Outlaw's…!!!! That's some scandalous ass shit!"

"Look at how you livin', Blaze! You got this cramped ass apartment that I bet you can barely even afford! Shit, you wouldn't even have that damn Denali if ya momma hadn't kept it for you when you got locked up! There's no way you could—"

"Could what?" he interjected, daring Shantreis to say it.

"There's no way you could take care of a baby. They're expensive… Outlaw could give our child—if it *is* yours—a better life than you ever could," she said quietly. It was her attempt at softening the blow.

"Shantreis, you don't know what the fuck I'm doin'!" Blaze roared. He couldn't believe the hurtful words that were coming out of her mouth.

"Tell me what you're doin' then, Blaze?! Because I

think I know. You're workin' at UPS in the damn warehouse making minimum wage or some shit! And *I* don't have a job! *Please* tell me how you could take care of us!" Shantreis demanded.

Now it was Blaze's turn to be quiet. He nodded his head and walked back to the sofa. "You right."

"Blaze…" Shantreis said softly, knowing that she had went too far. She had just wanted him to see things from her point of view, but she had gone too hard. Shantreis had made it about bashing him instead of enlightening him.

Blaze raised his hand to silence her, not even bothering to look back at her. "You can let yourself out, shawty." He didn't exhale until he heard the door close behind her.

He couldn't believe all that she'd said. He called himself 'doing the right thing' by staying on the straight and narrow, but here Shantreis was belittling it. Blaze had served about five years at DMCC for his role in the robbery committed back when he was eighteen and vowed that he would *never* go back. Blaze had since done his best to do right. It was so tempting to go back to the streets, but he would never risk his freedom for a second time.

Then again, if he could just hit one more lick and be set for a while, why not do it? He would be lying if he said he wasn't sick of UPS and rubbing pennies together to make ends meet.

Blaze pulled out his cell phone and scrolled through his call log. Finding the number he was looking for, he pressed 'send' to dial the number. "Ay, what's up?" Blaze paused. "Yeah… About that… Listen, I want in. I'll do it."

Chapter 23

"Ay, ain't that New-New?" Ghost asked Strap. He looked out the window of BP on the corner of Capital Boulevard and Spring Forest Road.

"Where?" Strap asked, moving back slightly so that he could see.

"Out on pump 3 with them itty bitty ass shorts on." Ghost stared for a second before turning his attention back to the cashier and paying for his cigarillos. "You gon' holla at her?"

"There you go again." Strap waved him off as he headed towards the door on the opposite side. They hadn't parked on the same side as Fallon so she didn't even have to know that they were there.

Ghost snickered and collected his change. "You better say something before I do. Quit bein' a pussy. Fallon ain't got on Cash ring either."

"Say what?" Strap could barely get the question out before Ghost bopped out the door. *Damn,* he thought, hating the position his brother was putting him in. Their earlier conversation had Strap really reconsidering a lot of things that he'd initially decided against. He was actually *afraid* to get too close to Fallon because he feared he would do something he would regret.

"Whassup, New-New?!" Ghost yelled boisterously, making his way towards Fallon's pitch black 760i.

"Hey, Ghost," she greeted, glancing at him briefly before turning her attention back to the credit card reader. After putting in her zip code and selecting 'premium', Fallon focused back on Ghost. "What are you doing all the way on this side of town?"

"Shit. Just cuz we live in Zebulon don't mean we gotta chill there all the time, right?" Ghost asked leaning against her car. He looked back at the gas station and saw Strap was still in there bullshitting.

This nigga here, Ghost thought. He didn't know what Strap's problem was but he was about to push him in the right direction.

"What's up with you and my brother?" Ghost prompted. His eyes were focused on her ring-less finger. Fallon quickly hid her hand in the pocket of her Citizens of Humanity cutoff shorts.

"We just had an argument…," Fallon answered quickly. She didn't really want to get into the specifics with Ghost, not knowing how he would take the information. Telling him what transpired would probably only make things worse. "I'm just going to go back to my house. I'm a little nervous though because I had a little incident there a week or so ago. I really don't know what to expect."

Bingo. "Shit. Strap with me. He can go with you and

make sure shit checks out. I'd go too, but I got this shawty I'm hooking up with later," Ghost lied.

"Really? Where is he?" Fallon asked hopefully. Since her altercation with Kevin, she constantly checked her rearview mirrors whenever she had to go out alone. Cash wanted her to start carrying a gun but she refused. If she ever feared for her life that badly, she would move away. Besides that, with Fallon's luck, her captor would end up with the gun instead and she'd be a sitting duck. Not having a gun made life less complicated for her.

"In the store."

As soon as the words left Ghost's mouth, Strap came waltzing out of the gas station. "Hey, Fallon."

"Hi, Strap." She smiled brightly and her grass-green colored eyes lit up. "You look cute today."

"'Preciate it," he thanked her nonchalantly. "You do too."

Ghost had to stop himself from laughing aloud. He thought that Strap looked soft in a beige V-neck and fitted Levi jeans that were crisp and starched as hell. Lanvin hi-top sneakers were on his feet and Strap wore an opened button-down shirt for decoration. That was Ghost's guess anyway. It resembled some shit Trey Songz would wear for a preppy magazine shoot, not a nigga that did the shit they did on a daily basis. Ghost was dressed more appropriately, in his opinion. Jeans two-sizes too big, a black wifebeater and a pair of Jordan's was his style.

"Ay, Strap, I told shawty that you would make sure her crib was safe. She worried about that pussy ass nigga from Waffle House I was tellin' you about."

Strap exchanged glances with his brother. Ghost knew just as well as he did that they had long ago squashed the issue with Kevin. Cash put in the orders to have him killed the same night of the incident with Fallon. Kevin hadn't been hard to find either. Right after they'd gotten rid of the girls' bodies, they put two bullets in Kevin's dome.

"If it's not too much of an inconvenience anyway," Fallon added, noticing the reluctance on Strap's face.

"Nah. Not at all," Strap replied quickly.

"Look, you ride with her cuz I gotta go see shawty I was tellin' you about." Ghost didn't give either a chance to object before he strolled off. "Get at me when ya'll done!"

"So what's up?" Strap asked, staring at Fallon intently from the love seat. She sat adjacent from him on the accent chair. The moment they'd arrived at her apartment and ensured that it was "safe", Fallon confessed that she had something that she wanted to speak to him about.

"It's about Cash… I know you noticed that I wasn't wearing my ring but I'm glad you didn't ask."

Strap nodded. He would have been lying if he said he wasn't interested in knowing why. In fact, it was a question he'd wanted the answer to since Ghost first mentioned it at the gas station.

Fallon drew in a deep breath as she prepared to get it off her chest. She'd wanted to tell Shantreis about it, but Fallon knew that she was caught up with her baby daddy drama. She would have felt selfish to throw her own problems on top of that. Still, she needed someone to talk to and Strap had always lent a listening ear.

"Let me know if I'm wrong but I told Cash that I didn't want to marry him because of what he said about Ghost..." Fallon paused. "He was talking about how he wouldn't hesitate to kill Ghost and I just can't believe it! It's like Cash is so nonchalant about it." She threw her hands up in disbelief. "What the hell is wrong with him?"

Strap sighed. "I mean, Cash had a different momma so we didn't see him much. We didn't even know we had an older brother until we were ten. Cash used to sneak and see us at school or pick us up from the bus stop. We looked up to him but Ghost *really* did. That nigga was like his fuckin' hero.

"That changed when Ghost got sentenced to juvie. Cash threw money his way but never came up to see him much. He was busy. It wasn't personal but Ghost didn't understand that. It felt like a big 'fuck you' to him so he started working on being *better* than Cash instead of being *like* him. When Ghost got out last year, I thought shit would get better. We were all gettin' along but Ghost hardheaded as fuck. He wanna do his own thing. Ghost wants to be the fuckin' boss and he ain't scared of shit."

Strap shook his head. "They just keep butting heads because they're too damn alike. It's like a love-hate relationship, really. I don't think they would seriously hurt each other but with the way Ghost been actin', I don't know. So Cash ain't that far off base with his logic. It's just the way it is, unfortunately."

"That is so petty." Fallon couldn't believe her ears. Despite Strap's rationale, she still had mixed feelings about everything. *Nothing* was that serious. Not getting spit on or an overinflated ego. "So what are you saying? That I shouldn't give Cash such a hard time? Was I wrong for giving the ring back?"

"Why do you feel like you have to be with Cash?" Strap asked suddenly.

"I mean… I don't think that. I just—"

"Keep looking for any excuse not to be with me," Strap finished.

Fallon looked at him in surprise. "Damien…"

"Nah, Fallon. I been trying real hard not to go there but I can't forget the shit as easily as you can. I know we're supposed to pretend that it never happened but it's not workin'!" Strap stood up for emphasis and looked Fallon directly in the eyes. "You wouldn't have slept with me if you didn't feel the same way, Fallon, even a *little* bit. I know enough about you to know that!"

"It was an accident, Damien," she reminded, shaking her head. Fallon couldn't believe that he'd brought it back up. It had happened over a year ago, back when things had gotten really rocky between her and Cash. Strap had given her a shoulder to cry on but things had gone wayward quickly. After the fact, they'd both promised to never speak on it again—not to each other or anyone else. "I was drunk and depressed…"

"That's not how I remember it! It wasn't a damn accident, Fallon!" Strap raised his voice unintentionally. He hated that she refused to acknowledge it for what it was. It had been *Fallon* that pushed up on him. She'd been unsure of herself, doubting her beauty and her ability to satisfy Cash. Fallon felt that he wouldn't spend so much time in the streets if he was happy with her.

Strap had reassured her that she was everything that a man would want and more. Fallon told him that she wished Cash was more like him and the next thing Strap knew, he was kissing her and Fallon didn't put up the slightest bit of resistance. He'd made love to her in a way that he was sure no other man had and he couldn't forget. Strap knew that Fallon couldn't either, whether or not she'd admit it.

"You know I've loved you since I was fifteen and you know that I'm closer to being the nigga that you want than Cash is! Cash will *never* be the man that you want him to be, Fallon! That's my brother. I know!" Strap's chest heaved in and out and his voice wavered with emotion. "I would *never* put anything before you! Not the money, not the game, not *anything!* You would've *never* had to make an ultimatum with me!"

Fallon was quiet, not really knowing what to say. Her heart went out to Strap but what could she do? While she cared for Strap, her feelings for Cash overrode that. She knew that Strap was right though. He had proved himself on more than one occasion and had been there for her in many instances that Cash hadn't.

"What's stopping you?" Strap asked, not believing that the words were coming out of his mouth. He'd crossed the line already and he was too far gone to turn around.

"Damien, maybe you should go," she said finally.

He knew that the conversation would go something like this, but somehow he'd expected something different. "Just don't settle for less because you think you have to."

Fallon nodded her head meekly. "I won't but I—"

Strap placed a finger to her lips to silence her. "I really wish you'd let me be the nigga to put a smile on your face and a ring on your finger." He leaned down and pressed a kiss to the corner of her mouth. He was so close that he may as well have kissed her lips.

Fallon's heart was racing out of her chest and she couldn't stop herself when she turned her head slightly, allowing his lips to land on hers.

Their eyes met and Strap looked confused until she drew back, "What was that for?"

"I'm sorry," Fallon apologized, unable to make eye contact with him anymore. She couldn't believe that she'd just done that. "Now you *really* need to go."

Strap nodded understandingly as he made his way towards the door, "Just don't forget what you told me: You can't live your life based on other people's actions. You have to do what you want to do because it's what *you* want. That goes for *anything*."

Chapter 24

"The fuck you mean?" Cash's voice boomed from the opposite end of the phone.

"Chill and just listen to me," Strap started in an attempt to calm his brother down. "I'm just saying that you know Fallon ain't built for this lifestyle."

"I know! That's why I said I'd put it away for her! As soon as Outlaw picks up the clothes then that's it!" he shouted, speaking in codes. "And in no fuckin' time I did that for *her*. So what the fuck do you mean?" Cash was still unable to get his temper under check.

Strap sighed. "Cash, remember that you called *me* asking for advice."

"I know. I know." Cash had needed to speak with someone and he didn't want to talk to Outlaw about it. Although he was now a "reformed player", Cash couldn't say for sure that Outlaw knew how to handle this situation. Strap, on the other hand, had known Fallon before he did and Strap always had a knack for understanding women and their wants and needs.

"Do you really think that you could leave the street shit alone though?" Strap started again, "Seriously. I know you, brah, and—"

"Nigga, I would do *whatever* to put a smile on that girl's face!"

Strap's next words were struggling to come out of his mouth but he knew it was the right thing to do. No matter how bad he wanted her, Fallon was already taken. "Well, if you feel that way, man, then don't let her get away. Don't 'not' say shit to her or you'll lose her again!"

Fuck it, Strap thought. *If me and Fallon are supposed to be together, then we will be. I'd rather her choose than to pick for her.* Besides his own coveted feelings about her, he knew that taking his brother's girlfriend was grimy as hell. He was starting to regret what he'd done at Fallon's apartment earlier that day. Oddly enough, he couldn't regret their sexual encounter.

"I know, man…" Cash sighed. He wasn't feeling at all like himself because Fallon had never avoided him like this. His calls went unanswered, and truthfully, he hadn't known what to say anyway. Cash just knew that he needed Fallon with him like a cancer patient needed treatment.

"If you know then tell her and stop tellin' me."

Cash was silent before finally speaking up, "Shit. I don't know if I can face her though. She took off my fuckin' ring! Do you know how that shit feels?"

"I got a damn good idea but so the fuck what? You gotta make that shit right. Just don't make no promises that you can't keep. Don't break Fallon's heart again, man. She's a good girl."

Cash chuckled, finding slight humor in his warnings, "You sound more like her brother than mine."

Yeah, but I'd rather be her man, Strap thought. "I'm just on some real shit. If I had a female like Fallon, I would *never* give her *any* reason to leave me. All I'd ever be focused on is making her happy, feel me?"

"You right," Cash said finally, not knowing just how right his brother was. If Strap had the opportunity, Cash wouldn't stand a chance.

"What the hell?" Shantreis cursed as her phone rang. The ringtone was shrill and loud, interrupting her beauty rest. She'd ignored it several times, without even bothering to check the caller ID. The ringtone wasn't familiar so she knew it wasn't anyone in her address book, therefore they had no business calling her. Yet, they were persistent and Shantreis didn't want to cut off her phone so she went ahead and answered, "What?"

"You're a stupid ass bitch, you know that?"

"Excuse me?" Shantreis asked, glaring at the number on her caller ID. She rolled her eyes as she realized that it was Kaleesha on the other end of the line. Shantreis didn't have her number saved, but it was one that she knew by heart. It was to no surprise since she was always blowing up Outlaw's phone.

"It's midnight. Do you know where the fuck your nigga is?" Kaleesha continued before Shantreis could get a word in, "You don't but I do. He's laid up with me right now instead of at home with you. And you're the stupid ass bitch that's gonna marry him."

Shantreis was pissed off because Outlaw told her that he was out *handling* business. He hadn't showed his ass in a while. If anything, he'd been the picture perfect fiancé. She hadn't heard any bullshit about Outlaw up until now. The fact that he *wasn't* there and had been gone for a couple of hours made her suspicious.

"I just thought I'd give you the heads up because I'd want somebody to look out for me," Kaleesha said in a syrupy sweet voice.

Dirty ass dog, Shantreis thought angrily. Still, she refused to show her hand to Kaleesha. Shantreis was sure that her only objective was to make her mad and she wouldn't give her the satisfaction.

"Bitch, please. I know *exactly* where Outlaw is and his ass isn't over there."

"Oh yeah?" Kaleesha taunted before laying it on thick, "Guess you haven't peeped my driveway then cuz I got a badass Blu Oceano Maserati sittin' in mine. I know for a *fact* that there's not one in your garage. If he's your man, come get him." Kaleesha laughed. "You know where to find him."

Click.

"That lyin' ass, nigga!" Shantreis wasted no time dialing up Outlaw. After the phone rang about five times, she was sent to voicemail. This continued for about three times in a row before she finally decided to give up. If there was ever a time that Outlaw looked guilty, it was now. Fuck packing his shit and leaving it by the door; she was going to leave it outside of Kaleesha's house. He could stay there for all she cared.

"Fuck that nigga," she cursed aloud. Shantreis felt stupid for believing that he had changed. She had dissed a good nigga like Blaze for him and here Outlaw was, showing his true colors, yet again.

She hopped out of bed and threw on a pair of flip flops. Grabbing a suitcase out of the closet and sloppily throwing a couple of his clothes into it, she couldn't stop all the thoughts that were racing through her mind. Why did he always have to run back to Kaleesha of all people? Shantreis would've preferred a new bitch over her. His baby momma was like a slap in the face.

In less than ten minutes, Shantreis was out the door and into her car. She sped towards I-540 blasting K97.5. Keyshia Cole's song 'Enough of No Love' was on and it was the story of Shantreis' life at the moment.

"Here we are again, cuz you're wrong again. You're tryin' to tell me that you love me, but your actions say another thing," Keyshia's soulful vocals thundered through her speakers. *"What we had is now hers, let her know she can have it. Cuz I can't stay here if there's no love..."*

Real shit, Shantreis thought. Singing along to the chorus calmed her momentarily, but tears were falling down her face. She tried hard not to give a damn but she loved Outlaw more than she cared to admit. *That* was the main reason why she just couldn't bring herself to ride into the sunset with Blaze.

BOOM!

"What the fuck?" Shantreis' body jerked suddenly as she felt her car being slammed from behind. The impact wasn't hard enough to deploy her airbag, but if there had been another car in front of her, she would've surely rammed into it as well.

Frowning, Shantreis looked in her rearview mirror, squinting from the car's bright headlights. She had just merged onto I-540 and didn't know what she was more pissed about: the fact that this accident would slow her down from confronting Outlaw or the damage that her precious Jaguar had no doubt sustained.

Her first thoughts were to call Outlaw but if he wasn't picking up for her earlier, Shantreis doubted that he would pick up now.

Probably still laid up with that bitch... she thought bitterly as she pulled over on the shoulder. Shantreis didn't need him anyway because what the hell could he do? As long as she called the insurance company, everything would be taken care of. She had full coverage so she wasn't that worried about it, but that wouldn't excuse the other driver from the curse out she was going to dish out.

An old, rusty Ford truck had pulled up behind her but the driver had yet to get out. It was hard to see the driver but she was sure they were panicking. She would too if she'd hit a car that indisputably cost more than their yearly salary.

I bet they don't even have insurance ridin' in that piece of shit. Shantreis' grimace got wider. She got out instead of waiting to be approached, slamming her car door as she did. The highway was nearly empty, save for a few tractor trailers rumbling down the road.

"Ay, sorry about that," Shantreis heard a man's voice as she surveyed the back of her car. The left taillight had broken and there was a noticeable dent there. On top of that, her trunk was partially caved in.

"I can't believe this shit! I hope you have insurance," she huffed, with her hands on her hips. As Shantreis spoke, she was still looking over the damage.

"No, I hope *you* do…" the man retorted.

Shantreis looked up furiously, finally acknowledging his presence. What she saw made her do a double take. Her eyes grew wider than the sky when she noticed that the man was wearing a ski mask. He was tall and wore gloves on his hands. The spot for his mouth had been cut out and displayed his sinister smirk.

"*Life* insurance, that is," he told her. That was the last thing Shantreis heard before she felt something solid make contact with her head and everything went black.

Chapter 25

"What the fuck type of bullshit do you be on?" Outlaw asked with a frown.

"No, that's exactly what I wanted to ask you!" Kaleesha shouted. "I can't ever get in touch with you anymore so dammit, if I have to say Monet's sick to get you to come over here then I will!"

"What is so important? I told you that if it wasn't about our daughter then we don't have shit else to talk about." Outlaw started for the front door but Kaleesha tugged at his red jacket.

"It *is* about our daughter," she said quietly as he turned back around. She took a deep breath before motioning towards the living room. "Can you just sit down for a second?"

"Hell nah, 'leesha. I gotta get home to my ol' lady. I ain't 'bout to get in trouble cuz I been fuckin' with you."

Outlaw had only gotten in the door about five minutes ago, but he'd been gone for hours. The only reason he'd dropped by in the first place was because Kaleesha said Monet was sick and wanted him. Outlaw could never deny his baby girl. He wasted no time rushing over there. Now that he knew it was a false alarm, he just wanted to get back home and lay up with Shantreis.

He knew that Shantreis was probably pissed and while he wanted to call her, he wasn't in the mood to get cursed out. His battery was low and he wasn't trying to waste it on an argument when there could possibly be more pressing matters to tend to.

"Why are you marrying her?!" Kaleesha blurted out, unable to hold it in any further. News traveled fast and the rumor mill was going crazy gossiping about the new engagement. It made her sick to her stomach to think that Outlaw was really going to make things official with Shantreis. Desperate times called for desperate measures and she just needed to talk to him in person to find out why….

Outlaw sighed. "Kaleesha, let's not start with the bullshit tonight, aiight? You *know* why."

"No the hell I don't!" Her voice started to quiver and so did her body. "She doesn't deserve you."

"And I suppose you think you do?"

Kaleesha bit her lip. Her feelings for Outlaw were still mixed. She loved him and hated him all at the same time. "I have your daughter, Outlaw! I know that's got to count for something! We should be a family!"

"You gotta quit fallin' back on that shit, ma. Any bitch can give me a baby. We been through this. You wasn't thinkin' about us bein' a family or no shit like that before you fucked Eric," Outlaw reminded her.

"So if that shit with Eric hadn't happened, then what?" Kaleesha demanded to know. She wanted answers and was praying that this time he would give them to her.

Outlaw shrugged. "I don't know. If you would've acted right then maybe you would've been the one with the ring. I just can't wife no bitch that fucked my homeboy… Much less a nigga I know. Damn that," he reconsidered, "If she fuck another nigga, *period*, while she with me." He shook his head. "Hell nah. I'd never do that."

You already are, her insides screamed, but she wouldn't dare say a word. Right now wasn't the right time. If Kaleesha so much as breathed a word of it then things could go awry. His refusal to move past what she'd done was enough proof that she was making the right decision. "You're full of shit, Travaris. You're gonna live to regret this though. Watch and see."

"Yeah I doubt it. Don't blame me, blame yourself. If you was more like Shantreis then we wouldn't be having this conversation."

"Oh yeah? Well let me tell you—"

Hearing Outlaw's cell phone going off interrupted Kaleesha's rant, and truthfully she was grateful for the distraction. Just that quickly she was ready to renege and spill the beans. She couldn't help it. Any and all comparisons to Shantreis got under her skin.

"Who the fuck is this?" Outlaw muttered, glancing at the private number on his phone. Usually Kaleesha was the main one playing those types of games but the fact that she was standing next to him cancelled her out of that equation. It was probably one of his former females. Ever since he'd hung up his player's card, they were calling constantly trying to find out what happened.

"Wifey calling you?" Kaleesha snorted. She crossed her arms and shifted her weight to one side.

"Shut the fuck up." He placed his finger to his mouth. Shantreis sometimes tried little shit like that and seeing that he had several missed calls from her, it was feasible that she was on the other end of the line. If she heard Kaleesha then she would flip. "Hello?"

Kaleesha inched closer to him in an attempt to eavesdrop. Outlaw was so engrossed with whatever he was hearing on the opposite end that he didn't bother to push her away like he would've normally done.

"Who the fuck is this?" he shouted. "Nigga, I will fuckin' kill yo' ass!" Outlaw suspended his threats momentarily as he continued to listen, "Say what?"

Kaleesha was ear hustling hard and managed to catch the last of the exchange. The caller's voice was raspy and warned Outlaw, "I want two hundred and fifty thousand in one hour. I'll give you more instructions later, but let me warn you not to try any funny shit. If I don't make it back safe, then neither does your bitch."

"You okay?" Kaleesha asked when Outlaw hung up, pretending that she hadn't overheard the bulk of the conversation.

"I gotta go," Outlaw replied finally before leaving. She could hear the sound of his engine roaring before he peeled out of the driveway. Presumably to go save his damsel in distress.

Bitch, Kaleesha thought as she locked the door behind him.

Shantreis opened her eyes, but all she could see was darkness. She tried to speak, but something—probably a towel—was stuffed in her mouth, preventing her from doing so. Her arms and legs were bound with duct tape, so tightly that she couldn't even rub her wrists together. Underneath her she felt a cold, concrete floor and figured that she was probably in some warehouse or basement. The old, musty smell further agreed with her assumption.

Her first instinct was to move around or to make some sort of a noise but after hearing a man speaking on the phone, Shantreis decided to be quiet and listen.

"Yeah I got her. Things goin' according to plan so quit trippin'. You said that nigga left quick as hell, right?"

Shantreis couldn't identify his voice, but she for damn sure recognized the next name that came out of his mouth.

"Kaleesha, stop bein' so paranoid. That nigga gonna pay up, without a doubt." The man was quiet. "I'm with her right now and he's on his way to get the money. This shit is foolproof." He listened to her for a few more minutes before finally disconnecting the call.

Kaleesha? Wow. So that bitch got somethin' to do with this, Shantreis realized in amazement. She knew the girl was scandalous, but not to these lengths. It made her wonder if they had enough heart to kill her. It would be in their best interest to because after it was all said and done, *somebody* was going to die behind this shit. Better them than her. They thought they were making a come up now, but that would be short-lived. Outlaw didn't play about his money or his woman... in that order.

Even if Outlaw was cheating on her that night, his feelings for her were undeniable. She couldn't say that she could say the same about him if it was true, however. She felt that if it wasn't for him, she wouldn't be in this predicament in the first place.

The gag in Shantreis' mouth being removed put her thoughts on pause. She could feel someone hovering over her and felt his hot breath on her face. He slapped her face roughly, assuming that she was still knocked out. After she let out a squeal, he spoke up, "Listen, I'm 'bout to call Outlaw and let you talk to that nigga, aiight? Make sure he knows this shit ain't a game."

She nodded her head in agreement and felt him place the phone near her ear on speaker.

The phone rung only once before Outlaw answered impatiently, "I got the money but I ain't givin' up shit until I know Shantreis good. If you put one muthafuckin' hand on her--!!!"

"Nigga, I'm the one that's calling the shots right now. The sooner you realize that, the better off you'll be. Tell him how you doin'."

"I'm okay, Outlaw," Shantreis assured him.

Outlaw heaved a sigh of relief. "They ain't put they hands on you, did they?"

She started to tell him about the slap, but let it go for that moment. "No… Just give this muthafucka whatever he wants so I can go home."

Her voice came out a little more emotional than she'd intended. Shantreis couldn't say that she was scared, in fact, not a thing about this clown truly frightened her. She could tell that he wasn't about this life or he would've done far worse to her. Being with Outlaw, she was already prepared and understood that things like this would and could happen. It was all a part of being a drug dealer's wifey. She had long ago accepted it and embraced whatever her destiny would be.

Only when she thought about the child growing in her belly did she feel a little sorrow. Her child didn't deserve this. Shantreis' bladder was threatening to explode and she knew that asking to use the bathroom was out of the question.

"You heard your bitch," the man barked at Outlaw, taking the phone back. "As long as I get my quarter mill, everything is everything."

Are you kiddin' me? Shantreis thought. They were risking their lives for that measly amount? She would've gone hard or stayed home. Outlaw kept that kind of money lying around the house as chump change.

"Bring the money to Gattis Street in Durham," he continued to describe which house before giving Outlaw fair warning, "Drop it off and take your ass back home. I'll deliver the bitch to you after I'm sure the money is all there. Remember what I told you, if you try any funny shit, it's lights out for your bitch!"

Filthy snickered as he hung the phone up, finding the whole thing hilarious. He wished that he had gotten the bright idea to do this before Kaleesha had. That way he wouldn't have to cut her into the profits. Then again, he didn't *have* to.

"Look, I need to use the bathroom," Shantreis cut in on his thoughts. Hearing only silence as a response, she swallowed her pride, "Please."

"How about this? You do something for me, I do something for you. Deal?"

Against her will, her mouth opened and she said, "Yes."

"I'm glad we've reached an understanding…" Filthy's fingers traced the side of her face. "You a bad ass bitch, you know that?"

"Are you gonna let me go or what?" Shantreis asked, pissed. She rocked back and forth impatiently. Not being able to see was bothering her, but the fact that he was dawdling about freeing her from her makeshift shackles had her pissed.

"Did you forget? It's 'you do something for *me'* first," Filthy reminded her.

Shantreis could hear the sound of a belt unbuckling and a zipper being jerked down. "Fuck that shit, nigga!" she bellowed. "You got life fucked up if you think I'm gonna suck ya dick just to use the bathroom."

"Nah. I ain't think that," he snarled, "But you gonna gimme some pussy though."

Filthy grabbed her by the waist and pulled her close to him. Yanking her cotton shorts down crudely and eyeing her bare juice box, he smiled. "I see why these niggas can't leave you alone." He pulled his dick out through the fly of his boxers and began stroking the length. Seeing Shantreis squirm and try—unsuccessfully—to get away, turned him on more.

He gave no second thought to going in raw. He was sure she was clean. She was too pretty not to be, in his opinion.

Just as Filthy had prepared to enter her, he could feel her wetness dripping on his dick. "Got damn, ma, you…" His voice trailed off and his lips curled with repulse when he realized that it was urine that he'd felt.

"You nasty ass bitch!"

"Fuck you, nigga." A smug look was on Shantreis' face. She was disgusted by her act of defiance, especially feeling the puddle underneath her knees, but she would be damned if she didn't try to do something.

Her victory was short lived when Filthy swiftly smacked her fiercely, causing her head to slam into the cold, hard floor.

She was down for the count.

Chapter 26

Blaze shook his head as he reclined in the front seat of a nondescript, 1970 Chevelle. The car fit in with the street he was parked on, surrounded by dilapidated and abandoned houses. The tint, coupled with the darkness of the night, made it hard to see inside. His setup was perfect for what he'd come to do.

When his cousin Filthy first suggested that they kidnap some bitch for a come up, he was against it. Blaze had been trying to do the right thing but realized that sometimes you have to take risks for a bigger payoff. Since they were dealing with the streets, jail time was the least of his worries. The only thing at stake was his life. At this moment, Blaze could care less whether he lived or died, but he knew that if he lived then things could only go up from there.

Besides, they weren't going to hurt anybody so what was the big deal? The only thing that would be hurting was some nigga's pockets after he came off this money they were hitting him in the head for. With Blaze knowing that, he was down.

Blaze had been waiting there for nearly two hours. He stopped by earlier in order to familiarize himself with the area. Plus he'd wanted to be there before their target arrived so that there would be no funny business. He couldn't afford to fuck this up. Every time he thought about what Shantreis had said to him, he grew infuriated. She wouldn't have shit to say after they pulled this off.

"Showtime," he murmured to himself. Outlaw's Maserati turned down the street and idled in front of the house he was watching.

Outlaw exited the car with a duffle bag hoisted over his shoulder and his other hand was fixed on his beltline. No doubt he'd had his hand near his gun. He surveyed the area warily before dropping the bag on the front porch and sprinting back to his car.

Just as quickly as Outlaw had come, he had left. Still Blaze remained glued to his seat. He wouldn't take the money immediately. He had to make sure there were no surprises waiting for him. Blaze pulled out his cell phone and called Filthy.

"You got the money?" Filthy asked eagerly, picking up on the first ring. He couldn't wait to stare those dead presidents in the face.

"I'm 'bout to get it in a second… I just wanted to holla at you about somethin' real quick."

"What's up, cuz?"

"My girl aiight?"

"You mean Outlaw's bitch?" Filthy responded nonchalantly. "Yeah. She straight."

His tone wasn't convincing enough for Blaze. "Whatever, man. I know one thing though. You better not have done shit to her. She's pregnant!"

"So what? That bitch bein' pregnant ain't got shit to do with us." Filthy was still pissed from the stunt Shantreis had pulled earlier. To his knowledge, she was still out cold and he'd knocked her out nearly twenty minutes ago.

"The baby is mine! If she's fucked up then *we* gonna have problems!" Blaze threatened.

No matter how hard he tried to suppress his feelings for Shantreis, he couldn't. Not even after hearing her scandalous plans with their child. He wanted to believe that she'd only said that in the heat of the moment, but he would get the *real* answer soon enough.

Blaze knew that Shantreis was unsure about him being the father, but there was no doubt in his mind. As bad as it sounded, he'd actually poked holes in the condoms they used. He wouldn't call it "trapping" her, but she needed a push to see where she needed to be. Outlaw wasn't right for her. *He* was and always had been.

"Ain't nobody did shit to that bitch," Filthy stated disrespectfully. "Just hurry the fuck up with the money."

Blaze could tell that his cousin was really feeling himself. He would let him have his moment for now but they were going to be rocking to a different tune when he showed up.

After Blaze collected the money, he was driving down Martin Luther King Jr. Parkway on his way to Filthy's mother's house off Dunn Avenue. He had stopped briefly at Westgate Plaza to thumb through the bills to ensure that everything was on the up and up. Blaze had never seen that much money in his life and was more than ecstatic about spending it.

On the down side, he felt like he'd done Shantreis dirty, all for the love of the almighty dollar.

"Are you fuckin' kiddin' me?" Shantreis asked upon hearing footsteps enter the room and a man's voice—Blaze's voice, say, "It's all here."

"Damn, cuz. You really had to do her up like this?" Blaze commented in disapproval. "And what the fuck is that smell?"

"I did what the fuck I had to do," Filthy replied as he took the duffle bag from Blaze. "Got damn. If I had known this nigga would really come through then I would've asked his ass for more."

"I hope your life was worth it for them pennies," Shantreis scoffed, feeling angered to see that Blaze was cohorts with her kidnapper.

"Chill," Blaze told her as he cut through the duct tape on her legs and hands.

"Fuck you, muthafucka," Shantreis spat at him. "I can't believe you had somethin' to do with this!"

Blaze sighed, knowing that they would have this conversation. "It's a long story but I'll tell you in the car." He removed the bandanna that was covering her eyes, much to Filthy's dismay.

"Nigga, what you thinkin'? You gon' let that bitch see my fuckin' face and shit! Pussy whipped ass."

"I ain't gonna be too many more bitches," Shantreis warned.

"Chill, man. She cool." He looked at Shantreis, who was still mugging the hell out of him. She nodded reluctantly but she didn't mean it and Filthy could tell.

"Hell nah. We gotta merk her! This bitch could put our fuckin' lives in danger! I ain't do all this not to be able to spend the money I just came up on."

"Fallback. For real." Blaze turned to Shantreis again. "I'll take you back home… Or wherever you wanna go. You ain't gotta go back if you don't want to." His voice was hopeful but Shantreis shut him down.

"I don't wanna go *anywhere* with you, Blaze. I'll walk my ass back or call Amigo Taxi." She started for the rickety wooden staircase in the corner of the room.

"Cut that shit out!"

"You must got your money already?" Filthy grumbled, noticing that there wasn't nearly as much as he'd expected in the bag.

"Yeah. Fifty percent, nigga."

"Fifty?! I said thirty-five!"

Blaze shrugged, not paying his cousin any mind. "I'd say we both did equal work."

Filthy wanted to argue but decided to stay calm. He and Kaleesha were in agreement for fifty-fifty and he couldn't appreciate going from 125,000 to 62,000. There was no way in hell. He would find another way to make up for what he'd lost.

"Y'all niggas a piece a work," Shantreis piped up, with her arms crossed against her chest.

"We'll talk in the car, Treis," Blaze said. He attempted to take her hand and escort her out but she pulled away from his grasp.

"Cover ol' girl's eyes so she won't know where my momma lives. Can you at least do that?" Filthy asked sarcastically, accepting the fact that Shantreis would be leaving with her life.

Blaze nodded. "Yeah. I can do that." He looked at Shantreis. "You mind?"

She sucked her teeth. "Would it really matter if I did or not?"

Ignoring her response, Blaze tied the bandanna back around her eyes. This time when he reached for her, she accepted his help. After they'd gotten into Blaze's car and made it on TW Alexander Drive, he allowed her to remove the bandanna.

"Treis?" Blaze asked impatiently.

Shantreis' gaze remained focused out the window and she refused to make eye contact with him. She'd been playing the quiet game ever since she got into his car. While she didn't want to accept his ride, she didn't have her purse so a taxi was out of the question. With the night chill, her being clad only in a pair of shorts and fuzzy bedroom slippers, and the fact that Raleigh was twenty or more miles away, Blaze was her only option.

"Damn, so you just ain't gonna talk to me?" Blaze prodded again. Taking her silence as a response, he sighed with agitation. "Why the fuck you actin' like I ain't tell you about this shit?"

"Because!" Shantreis snapped, unable to be quiet any

longer. "*You* said that we were going to do it tomorrow, not tonight!!! And you for damn sure didn't mention your cousin or *Kaleesha's* shiesty ass! I thought this was your come up, not everybody and they damn momma! I would've never agreed to help you out if I knew all this!"

Shantreis knew that she must have been smoking on something when she decided to help Blaze set up Outlaw. Things were supposed to go much different. She was supposed to go check in the Hilton and chill until Blaze got the money. Then she would go home without incident. She definitely wasn't supposed to get knocked out not once, but *twice* and end up peeing on herself. She was beyond pissed!

The whole time she kept thinking that Blaze had something to do with it and while it alleviated her fears, it served to elevate her anger. She kept telling herself that this *had* to be a separate incident. Especially when she heard Kaleesha's name. It had her wondering what was fact and fiction. Had Outlaw really been cheating with his baby momma that night, or was it just a ploy to get her out of the house? Knowing Outlaw's old tricks, it was probably a combination of both.

Blaze started to speak but Shantreis was running her mouth like bathwater, "But hell, it don't matter now cuz you did it without my muthafuckin' help *anyway!* Fuck you, nigga, for puttin' my life in danger for some money… A hundred and twenty-five sorry lil' stacks at that!"

"Things just changed last minute. You actin' like such a—" He stopped before he could complete his thought. Shantreis chose that exact same moment to speak.

"You put our *child's* life in danger, Blaze."

"Oh so it's *our* child now, huh? You're bein' dramatic."

"Nah, nigga. You're not bein' dramatic enough! That nigga steady hittin' me upside the head. He 'bout to gimme a damn bladder infection cuz he won't let me use the bathroom." Shantreis threw her hands up in the air for emphasis. "This nigga almost raped me, Blaze. Where the fuck was you? Out doin' some shit that you had no business doin'!"

Blaze flexed his jaw. "Why the fuck didn't you tell me that shit back there?"

"Cuz it wouldn't have made any difference," she replied indifferently. "What's done is done and I'm gonna have Outlaw handle that ass. Trust and believe me, nigga."

"*I* could've handled that shit for you! Fuck Outlaw!" He banged his hands on the steering wheel angrily. His annoyance heightened when he looked at the ring that still adorned her finger. It was a constant reminder that she'd given herself to Outlaw. "Matter fact, I got a question for you too."

Shantreis shrugged, becoming mute again. Her gaze had returned to the window and she turned her body slightly to the right.

Blaze nodded his head knowingly before pulling over on the side of the road.

"What the hell are you doin'?" Shantreis shouted.

He forced her body towards him. His hands gripped her shoulders firmly. "You can't say that I can't take care of mine anymore. That goes for the baby—and you! Now what the fuck you got to say?!" Blaze stared her into doe-shaped eyes, awaiting her answer anxiously. "You still don't wanna be with a nigga?"

Chapter 27

"I don't know if that's a good idea, Cash," Fallon said softly, shooting his suggestion out of the sky.

"Why not?" Cash prompted. He stood on the opposite side of the door feeling defeated. He hadn't meant to come over that late at night but he hadn't been able to get in touch with her earlier that day. He'd tried to wait but he knew he wouldn't be able to sleep until they spoke. Cash was prepared to make things right. "Just gimme a few minutes, Fallon."

Fallon sighed. She still had the security latch on and spoke to him out of the tiny crack the door allowed. She wasn't afraid to let him in because she thought he would hurt her, quite the contrary. If it was one thing that she knew about Cash, he would never even dream of putting his hands on her.

She just felt guilty for what had transpired with Strap earlier that day. Fallon may have given Cash his ring back, but she knew just as Cash did, that they were still together. She had just acted in the spur of the moment. Furthermore, Strap's mention of what they'd done over a year ago made it harder for her to face Cash.

Fallon had pushed it to the back of her mind for the longest. She had been so successful in doing so that she'd even managed to forget that it'd happened. But now she felt like Cash could see right through her and her betrayal.

"Okay," she relented. She closed the door to remove the latch and then allowed him access.

"How you been?" Cash asked cautiously.

Fallon laughed lightly. "I'm good, Cash. It hasn't been that long. It's barely even been a day. I am tired—"

Before she could complete her sentence, Cash had pulled her into a tight embrace, "Baby, I'm sorry. I don't like him right now but I love my brother. More importantly, I love you more so if the shit is that serious to you then I can *promise* you that I won't hurt Ghost. Just please don't leave a nigga like this. I lost you once but I'll be damned if I do it again."

Cash's eyes pled with Fallon to believe him. He felt a wave of relief when she returned his embrace. He inhaled her perfume greedily before reluctantly pulling back from her. Reaching into his pocket, he revealed her ring and reached for her finger. Cash looked at her, seemingly waiting for permission.

"Cash, I'm sorry too… For everything, okay?" Fallon asked, knowing that he wouldn't understand the true meaning behind her words.

"You ain't got no reason to apologize. *I* fucked up… I

talked to Strap earlier," he admitted, "And he helped me see that I was wrong. I'd do anything for you, Fallon, you know this! But sometimes you just gotta back off and let me be the man. There's some shit I'm always gonna handle and you may not like the way I go about it, but it has to be done."

"But not the Ghost thing, right?" Fallon asked with a smile as he slid the ring back on her finger.

"Yeah. That lil' nigga straight with me," he said half-heartedly. He hoped his promise to Fallon wouldn't come back to bite him in the ass. As long as he wasn't caught slipping, he'd be alright. "But ay—"

The sound of Fallon's phone ringing interrupted their reunion and she excused herself to answer it, "Hello?"

"Fallon, can I stay over there tonight?" Shantreis' voice huffed through the receiver.

"What's going on?" Fallon asked, surprised by her odd request.

"Just some bullshit… I don't wanna be here right now."

Fallon could hear Outlaw shouting in the background and figured that they were fighting again. "Sure. You can come over." She ignored Cash shaking his head and mouthing 'no'.

"Let them work out they issues," Cash whispered loudly.

"Tell Cash I can hear his ass!" Shantreis joked, "But I need my friend so tell him y'all better get a quickie in before I get there. I got a lot of shit I need to get off my chest."

"Okay, girl," Fallon giggled, "I'll see you when you get here."

"Well damn," Cash cursed when she hung up. "Guess we better get started before she gets here then huh?"

"What the fuck are you leavin' for?" Outlaw asked, grabbing Shantreis by the arm roughly. Ever since she'd walked in the door she'd had a stank ass attitude. She didn't want to give him a hug and she didn't seem happy or thankful to see him.

"Where the hell were you tonight?" Shantreis asked, looking him square in the eyes.

Outlaw's frown disappeared. "The fuck you mean? Out paying some niggas a quarter mill so they don't kill ya ass, that's where the fuck I was!" He looked her up and down angrily. "You should be grateful instead of trippin' on me. Damn!"

"Nah. You was—" She raised her hand and shook her head as thoughts of Kaleesha filled her mind. "Never mind. Don't worry about it cuz I'm not in the mood to talk about this shit."

Shantreis brushed past him to their bedroom, looking for her suitcase.

"Are you okay?" Outlaw asked finally, figuring that she was probably mad that he hadn't asked her that initially.

"Just peachy," she responded sarcastically.

"Look, did one of them muthafuckas put they hands on you?" He thought that he'd done a pretty thorough onceover of her body and she appeared fine, but Outlaw needed to know for sure. Somebody would definitely be getting their head bashed in then. "And how did you get home?"

"My car…" Shantreis sighed. "I really don't feel like reliving this shit right now. I just wanna go to bed."

"Then sleep here! Fuck you goin' to Fallon's for? You actin' like you mad at me!"

"Well maybe if it wasn't for ya bitchass baby momma!" Shantreis shrieked, spinning around to look him directly in the face. "Then *none* of this shit would've happened! Nigga, you ain't changed a bit."

Outlaw sucked his teeth, silently wondering how she'd known about that. "What do Kaleesha got to do with this? Did she call you on some bullshit?"

Shantreis remained silent, wanting for him to give an explanation.

"Ay, man, she said Monet was sick and I'm *always* gonna be there for my daughter. If you can't understand that then you need to kick rocks, seriously. But Kaleesha was lyin'. She just wanted to talk about our engagement and the usual shit. She mad cuz she wants your spot but she can't have it."

Outlaw shook his head. "I can't believe you still think that I'd do that to you. When I asked you to be my wife—matter fact, after that shit with Blahzay or whatever the fuck that nigga name is—I gave up all that wild shit. You don't trust me at all!"

"No it's not about that," Shantreis corrected. "If that's why you was there, then cool. But I overheard that nigga that kidnapped me talkin' on the phone to Kaleesha about it. *She* had somethin' to do with this. She called me up to get me out the house and then set it up from there…"

"Nah… You sure about that? Kaleesha ain't that grimy… Is she?" Outlaw was in denial.

"I'm positive. Ain't that many Kaleesha's in the damn world and this too much of a coincidence, don't you think?"

Outlaw grabbed his keys off the dresser and started for the door. "I don't know but I'm damn sure about to find out. That bitch better pray to God that she ain't had nothin' to do with it."

"Nigga, where is my money?!" Kaleesha shouted impatiently. "I know Outlaw done paid up by now."

"Damn. Calm the fuck down. I got your cut," Filthy assured her, but he was lying through his teeth.

"Good," she snapped. Kaleesha had been blowing up his phone all night but he had been ignoring her calls. She just wanted to touch base with him and ensure that they were on the same page. "Are you on the way now?"

Kaleesha had been plotting on how she wanted to spend her money the whole day. Since Outlaw was paying her rent and other household bills, she was free to do whatever. She was no dummy though; if she was constantly buying things it may raise red flags. For now she would only splurge on a new wardrobe and put the rest into her savings. She had to ensure that no matter what, she would be straight. With or without Outlaw.

"Yeah," Filthy lied.

"Call me when you outside. And don't try no funny shit, nigga, or I will blow up your whole spot," Kaleesha said anxiously before hanging up in his face. As soon as she got her money, she was through with Filthy. His services were no longer needed.

Goofy muthafucka, she thought before lying down on her bed. When she closed her eyes, she could still see Outlaw and hear his voice, *"If you would've acted right then maybe you would've been the one with the ring."*

Fuck him and that bitch. Kaleesha was bitter. Her love for Outlaw couldn't be controlled like a light switch where she could just cut it on or cut it off. She didn't know if it was due to him being her baby daddy or just being in her life as long as he had.

She heard her bedroom door open and opened her eyes drowsily, "You okay, baby?" she asked, assuming it was Monet. Her door wasn't visible from the bed due to the small entryway. Seeing Outlaw she shook her head. "Shouldn't you be at home with your fiancée?"

Outlaw's chest was heaving in and out. He'd heard every word of her conversation with Filthy, he'd just been waiting for the perfect moment to come in. "Bitch, you robbed me?!" The question came out more like a statement.

Kaleesha didn't respond. She was like a deer in headlights. She grabbed for her cell phone, prepared to call 911 but Outlaw slapped it out of her hand. He grasped her auburn colored weave and pulled her towards him until he could get a good hold on her neck.

"You scandalous bitch. All the shit I do for ya ass! You would rob me, bitch!"

Kaleesha opened her mouth to speak but she couldn't. Her eyes silently implored him to release her but Outlaw didn't show any signs of letting go. He looked crazed and like he was in another world.

Just when she felt herself about to pass out, he loosened his hold, "Answer me, bitch!"

"What are you talkin' about?" Kaleesha asked, hoping that she sounded convincing.

"Playin' dumb huh?" He nodded his head. "So you ain't had shit to do with Shantreis bein' kidnapped?"

She shook her head 'no' and his grip tightened around her neck. "Please," Kaleesha managed, realizing that he wasn't playing games. "Let me tell you."

"I'm listening," Outlaw informed her.

"It was Filthy. He told me that if I didn't help him out then he would kill me."

"Do you really think I believe that shit?"

"I swear on Monet," Kaleesha said.

"You ain't worth a damn, you know that?" Outlaw asked rhetorically. "I overheard your stupid ass when you first called that nigga but you would *still* lie to me. And then put it on our daughter? Bitch, you must forgot who the fuck I am."

Outlaw was talking but Kaleesha couldn't understand a word that he was saying. His mouth was moving but nothing was connecting in her brain. She knew that it was due to him nearly crushing her throat. All she could do was wheeze and reach for him weakly, none of which helped to return her flow of oxygen. Before she knew it she had passed out.

Kaleesha woke up several hours later. She was in her bedroom surprisingly enough and everything looked intact. The house was quiet, save for her TV that was still playing *BET* softly. For a brief moment she wondered if Filthy had dropped by, but decided that was the least of her worries. She needed to ensure that Outlaw had gone for good and wasn't waiting in the shadows to finish what he'd started.

Vigilantly she exited her bedroom. Her front door was wide open, letting in a breeze of cold air. Quickly shutting the door and locking it behind her, Kaleesha rested her back against the door and buried her face in her hands.

What the fuck did I get myself into? she thought. *Do I need to call Filthy and warn him?* She dismissed that notion quickly. *Fuck it.*

Little did she know that she didn't have to. Filthy had gotten out of town just as quickly as Blaze and Shantreis had left the house. He wasn't going to be a sitting duck whenever Outlaw pieced together the puzzle.

Thank you, Jesus, for not letting that crazy nigga kill me. Now Kaleesha just wanted to go sleep with her baby girl. First, she peered out of the window in her den overlooking the parking. She was comforted by the fact that his car was gone. However, when she reached Monet's room to find the bed empty, she went into panic mode.

Letting out a scream, she picked up her cell phone and dialed Outlaw's number. The phone rang several times before he answered nonchalantly, "What, bitch?"

"Outlaw, where is Monet? Do you have her? I woke up and—"

"Yeah. I got *my* daughter with me where she belongs."

"Please bring her back, Outlaw!" Kaleesha begged. Although her reasons for bringing Monet into the world were less than admirable, it couldn't be denied that she loved her daughter—more than she even loved herself.

"Hell no. I don't want a shiesty bitch like you raisin' her."

"You can't do that!" she sobbed.

"I just did, didn't I? Consider that the reason that you were able to keep your life," Outlaw advised her. He felt that if Kaleesha could lie about that, she could lie about anything. She would definitely be a liability to him as long as she had his daughter with her. He would be damned if she would pull the wool over his eyes again.

"You come near me *or* my daughter and I'm killin' you, bitch."

Chapter 28

"You aren't afraid that Outlaw might try to kill her?" Fallon asked Shantreis after she'd spilled the beans on the night's prior events.

The duo was in Fallon's bedroom sitting on top of her bed. Although Fallon had been exhausted, hearing Shantreis share what she'd been through perked her up.

Shantreis shrugged. "I got more important shit to worry about… Like Blaze."

"What about him?" Fallon wondered curiously.

"Well, you know he got that money now… And that had been my excuse for not bein' with him," she said slowly, "So he wanted to know if I would be with him now that he's paid."

"What did you say?"

Shantreis' face fell. "I didn't know what to say… I just got quiet as hell. If I would've said 'yea' then I would've looked like a greedy golddigger. He was mad that I wouldn't say shit but I couldn't." She shrugged. "He stopped askin' and just took me back to the car."

"Are you still keeping the baby?"

"I don't really know about that," Shantreis admitted. "Don't give me another lecture just cuz you aborted Cash's baby." She rolled her eyes. "Did he know about it?"

"No. He doesn't know because it wasn't his," Fallon said quietly.

"You cheated on Cash?! Bitch, why am I just now findin' out? With who though?" Shantreis had never seen Fallon with anyone else so her confession had her shocked. She never deemed her best friend as the underhanded, devious type but it seemed that there was a lot more to her than met the eye.

"It was Strap."

"Damn…" Shantreis was silent as she shook her head. "That's fucked up, Fallon."

"How can you judge me?" Fallon asked quickly, hating the way her friend was looking at her. She felt ashamed and embarrassed. It was probably something that she should've taken to the grave.

"I ain't. I'm just… Damn, Fallon," she repeated.

"You're cheating on Outlaw with Blaze!"

"Oh well. At least he ain't Outlaw's *kid* brother," Shantreis reminded.

"I should've never told you," Fallon frowned.

"Chill out, girl. I mean, it's really fucked up, Fallon. I always thought Cash was a good nigga," Shantreis said. "Outlaw is the damn dog but not Cash. I'm sure you had a good reason. I just would've never guessed it… Damn. What other secrets you got?"

"I kissed Strap the other day," she blurted without thinking. "I don't know what I was thinking but it won't happen again."

The two were silent for a moment, both reflecting on their predicaments. Being torn between two lovers was one of the hardest things to deal with.

"You feelin' him like that or you was caught up in the moment?" Shantreis asked her finally.

"Honestly, a mixture of both," Fallon divulged. Her feelings for Strap were something that she couldn't comprehend. For years she had only looked to him as a little brother, but he was determined to show her that he was a grown man. Fallon had long noticed the way that he looked at her—there was always love and admiration in his eyes. It was the little things that he would do that let her know just how deeply he felt about her.

"You know I've loved you since I was fifteen! Cash will never be the man that you want him to be, Fallon! I know! I would never put anything before you! Not the money, not the game, not anything! You would've never had to make an ultimatum with me!"

Strap's words echoed in Fallon's mind. She knew that he was telling the truth but the taboo of their relationship would never allow them to be together. *What am I saying?* she thought. Strap was sweet and his love for her was sincere, but Cash was her first. He had done nothing but provide, protect, and take care of her. He'd put a ring on it and he'd *never* stepped out on her. And this was the way she thanked him? Fallon didn't feel that she deserved Cash. He would have *never* betrayed her the way that she had him.

"Let me ask you this..." Shantreis asked, breaking the silence. "Could you see yourself with Strap if he wasn't Cash's brother?"

"I don't wanna answer that," Fallon answered almost as quickly as Shantreis had asked the question.

Shantreis nodded in understanding. She knew why. Undoubtedly the answer would be 'yes', but to admit it would be another form of betrayal.

Fallon gazed down at her engagement ring, twisting it around in a circle. "Why are we getting married when we have so many secrets?" She sighed. "What about Blaze?" It was her attempt to change the subject and get out of the hot seat. Fallon's contrasting views on the Cash/Strap situation had her feeling lower than dirt. "What's the real reason you won't be with him? I know y'all got history."

"I don't know," she lied. Truthfully, she was afraid of starting all over. Even though Outlaw's fucked up countless times, they'd moved past that and he's been the man she wanted him to be. There was a soft spot in her heart for Blaze, but it wasn't enough to make her leave her stability. He would just have to chalk it up as a loss. $125,000 would be more than enough for him to get over losing her and the baby.

"Damn, so you ain't heard from that bitch yet?" Ghost inquired. "No offense on that 'bitch' shit."

"Nah," Strap answered. It had been a week since he'd

revealed his feelings for Fallon and he hadn't heard from her since. Truthfully, he hadn't expected her to but kept wishing she would surprise him and do the opposite. "It's straight though."

"Maybe if you wasn't so busy tryna school Cash on how to get her back." Ghost shook his head. "Why you did that backwards ass shit, I'll never know."

"Cuz the shit was wrong, Ghost. You was the main one warnin' me that I was playin' wit' fire."

"That was when I thought you just wanted some pussy, but you in love."

Strap sucked his teeth in response.

Ghost chuckled. "What? A nigga like me can't believe in romance and shit?" he asked unconvincingly.

"Nigga, your heart is colder than Antarctica."

"You right but it's on you. If you don't give a damn, I don't give a fuck."

"Where you at anyway?" Strap asked, ready to shift things away from him and Fallon. He was trying to respect her space—and most of all, his brother. It had been hard especially when he'd spoken to Cash and discovered that they'd reconciled. Fallon was avoiding him, making herself scarce anytime he had to get up with Cash. That was okay with Strap. He wouldn't have been able to face her himself. Not without remembering all that had transpired.

"I'm out," Ghost replied simply. "I'm a' holla at you later." Without awaiting a response, he disconnected the call with his twin brother.

Currently he was sitting in the parking lot of Wal-Mart in Wake Forest. For the past few days Ghost had been following his older brother around. A week ago Cash had called and told him that he wanted to squash their beef. Ghost pretended to accept his truce, but he didn't give a damn about that. The simple fact of the matter was that he'd been disrespected and Cash would have to answer for that. Ghost had been letting shit slide for too long and he was ready to check Cash.

As soon as he watched Cash get out of his Bentley and head inside, Ghost whipped out of the parking lot unseen. His brother wasn't hard to find or to get up with, but Fallon had been stuck to him like flypaper. On the strength of Strap's love for her, and the fact that Fallon was a pretty cool female, he waited for her to bounce. Now that she was out of the picture, he was good to go.

In less than three minutes, Ghost was pulling up towards Cash's residence. He parked on the side of Dunard Street off New Falls of Neuse Road. Instead of his flashy rimmed up Caprice, he was riding in an older model Mercedes-Benz. It was his current jumpoff's car and she'd had no problem letting him borrow it, especially when he'd promised to see her that night.

Bitches too easy to please, Ghost thought as he walked towards Beauvoir Street. Normally Cash was on his shit so he would notice if something was amiss. Taking every precaution, Ghost decided to go the rest of the way on foot. He wouldn't be surprised if Cash knew which cars his neighbors drove and kept in their driveways. Ghost didn't want him to see it coming.

He had even adjusted his usual attire. He was dressed more preppy in an attempt not to draw any more attention to himself. A black man with dreads was always stereotyped—especially in these types of neighborhoods.

Ghost walked up to Cash's front door and rung the bell. There was only one person that he knew was still home and would be his ticket inside.

"Hello, Delonte," Roger greeted him by his real name.

"Wassup, Roger?" Noticing his apprehension, Ghost smiled, "You gonna let me in?"

"Damontrez isn't home… Do you want me to tell him you dropped by?"

"Nah, nigga. What the fuck? You actin' like I ain't welcome in my own brother's house," Ghost brushed past him forcefully. "I'll wait for him in here." He walked into the living room and took a seat.

Roger sighed and closed the front door. He would be sure to let Cash know that Ghost was there. He had never cared for his younger brother, viewing him as too troubled and reckless. Roger's assumption wasn't that far from the truth. To say that Ghost made him uncomfortable was an understatement.

"Ay, man, you'll get me somethin' to drink?" Ghost asked with a sneer. When Roger looked at him indignantly, Ghost's smile got wider and he clapped his hands together. "Chop chop. Last time I checked you *are* the butler."

Roger walked past him, headed in the direction of the kitchen. Before he could take a step onto the hardwood floor of the dining room, Ghost sent a bullet whizzing into his chest.

"I never did like you," he commented. Ghost dragged his body into the dining room and underneath the table so that he wouldn't be visible whenever Cash arrived. The long tablecloth ensured that. The light carpet was still soaked with blood but that wasn't Ghost's problem.

Hearing the garage door opening, he realized that show time was coming sooner than he'd thought. Ghost crouched near the dining table. It gave him the perfect view of the door that Cash would be entering from.

When Cash walked in carrying a couple of grocery bags, it took everything in Ghost not to pull the trigger right then. *I don't wanna sneak up on this nigga,* he thought, *I want that muthafucka to look me in the eyes when I merk his ass.*

Standing up, Ghost swaggered into the kitchen with his gun raised as though he belonged there. "Whassup… *brother*? Don't drop shit or I'll drop you," he warned in reference to the bags he was holding.

"What the fuck, Ghost?" Cash exclaimed, but he followed his instructions. He stood about six feet from the door and about ten away from his brother. "I told you I'm not beefin' with your ass so what is this really about?"

"Nigga, you said *you* weren't beefin', *I* didn't."

"Just chill out, Ghost, before you do some shit you'll regret." Cash looked towards the door nervously.

"Oh don't run, muthafucka. You supposed to be such a 'G' but when you starin' down the barrel of a gun you ready to take off like a bitch."

"Never that," he replied coolly but the look in his eyes said differently. They darted back and forth from Ghost to the doorway. "I could never fear a lil' nigga like you."

"I can't tell. Nigga, how do it feel to know that I'm

more in control of your life than you—"

Suddenly Cash turned his head towards the door and dropped his bags. Anticipating his next move out the door, Ghost didn't hesitate to fire. It was only when he realized he missed his target that he regretted what he did.

Ghost had just hit Fallon.

A high pitched scream reverberated across the room. He could hear the familiar thud of a body dropping along with the sound of plastic bags hitting the floor. The blood leaking from underneath the bags seemed to be moving in slow motion. Cash was yelling in anguish as though *he'd* been hit too. The sound brought him back to reality.

Fuck, Ghost cursed before bolting in the opposite direction and out the front door. He was running faster than Wilma Rudolph. It was the first and hopefully only time that he'd felt sorry for shooting someone. He didn't know if she was dead or alive, or where he'd hit her at for that matter, but he would be damned if he would stick around and find out.

Reaching the Benz in a record of one minute by crossing through the neighbors' backyards, he skirted out quickly. His cell phone was vibrating constantly. Ghost had five missed calls. He didn't check them until he'd merged onto I-540, headed to his jumpoff's house in Knightdale.

Three of his calls were from her. The other two were from Strap. He wasted no time calling his brother back, "Ay, Strap, shit didn't go right at all!"

"What?" Strap asked confused, he couldn't ever recall hearing his brother like this. He was definitely shaken up and uncharacteristically so. "What didn't go right?"

"Fallon got shot by accident." Ghost wouldn't dare say that he did it because he never knew if the Feds or someone was listening. He knew that Strap would be able to fill in the blanks though.

"How the fuck did that happen, Ghost?" he practically yelled. "I can't believe this shit... Is she okay? What the fuck?"

"I don't know. I left soon as the shit happened! You said she was at work! Fallon wasn't supposed to be there!"

"So what?" Strap shook his head. "Why couldn't you just leave that shit with you and Cash alone?"

"Hold up now, nigga." Ghost's voice took on his usual hard edge. "You got me fucked up. I had decided I wasn't gonna fuck with that nigga Cash after he called me on that truce shit. It wasn't until *you* kept talkin' about how if that nigga died you could bag Fallon, that I said 'fuck it'. I don't give a damn whether or not that nigga lives or dies, but *you* did. Or did you forget?"

Chapter 29

"Please, can I ride another one?" Monet begged, looking up at Shantreis with big puppy dog eyes.

She sighed, unable to resist her cute expression. "Okay," Shantreis relented as she placed three more quarters into the Bob the Builder ride that Monet had jumped on.

They were upstairs at Crabtree Valley Mall, near the food court. Outlaw was at Andy's getting them some strawberry shakes. Monet couldn't get enough of the rides so Shantreis stayed behind with her. It was a nice family outing.

They'd had several outings that week since Outlaw had taken his daughter from Kaleesha. She was constantly calling but she wouldn't dare come over to the house. Outlaw's words to her that night had her shook. Monet was oblivious to it all, believing that she was just living with her daddy for a little bit… the way she used to with Kaleesha. At least that was how he'd explained it to her.

Shantreis had tried talking to Outlaw about it but he wouldn't hear her. Sometimes he would even try to flip it around and act as though Shantreis just didn't want Monet around. That couldn't be further from the truth. Shantreis and Monet had always had a good relationship despite the way Kaleesha had tried—unsuccessfully—to get her daughter to dislike her.

Looking at Monet laughing and having fun made her smile. Shantreis couldn't help but think about how her own child would look and act when it got to be that age. After much consideration, she'd decided that she wanted to keep her baby. Now Shantreis was just waiting for the perfect time to tell Outlaw about it. Her morning sickness had subsided marginally but she was constantly hungry. In that week alone she had gained about seven pounds but the weight agreed with her.

Surprisingly, Blaze hadn't been in touch with her since their conversation in the car. It was Shantreis' assumption that he was finally giving up. She felt bad about it but her mind was made up. There was nothing that he could do or say to change it… At least she didn't think so.

Right now, things between her and Outlaw were going fine and would continue to as long as Blaze stayed in his lane. Outlaw didn't even know that Blaze had helped with the kidnapping. His cousin was MIA so Outlaw decided to kill Filthy's mother instead. He didn't tell Shantreis but after seeing the news report on TV, it wasn't hard to piece together. It was too much of a coincidence.

Shantreis was so caught up in her thoughts that she didn't realize they had company until Monet's little voice piped up, "Stranger danger!"

"Huh?" Shantreis turned to face Blaze. Her heart was

beating out of her chest. "What the hell are you doin' here?"

He gave her an impish grin. "Last time I checked anybody can go to the mall, shawty."

Blaze looked and smelled like new money in an Alexander McQueen Raven Skull T-Shirt, True Religion jeans, and some sneakers that Shantreis had never seen in Footlocker. In short, he looked good.

"Are you one of my daddy's friends?" Monet probed, looking at him quizzically.

"Hey, Monet, why don't you get on this ride next?" Shantreis suggested, pointing to something resembling a school bus. She didn't have to ask the toddler twice before she jumped on. Shantreis inserted another three quarters and looked over in the direction of Andy's nervously.

"Blaze, we're here with Outlaw… I don't want no problems from you."

He shrugged nonchalantly. "Quite frankly, sweetheart, I don't give a damn what you want." Blaze placed his hands in the pockets of his jeans and stared in her eyes piercingly. "I thought about it and I just can't let this shit ride… I don't know how you could even think I would be down for lettin' another nigga think my kid is his."

Blaze shook his head and adjusted his snapback cap. "You got me fucked up. You know, shawty, most women *want* they baby daddy to take care of they kid. They *want* them in their life."

"I already have him in my life. Blaze, this baby ain't yours!" Shantreis looked around again before hissing, "Me and you always used protection!"

"I'm a' put it to you like this… You better tell that nigga or I will."

Shantreis didn't believe that she'd heard him correctly. *This nigga must lost his mind!* "Are you crazy, Blaze?! Why the hell would I tell him somethin' now when we don't even know!"

"Eventually you're gonna have to tell that nigga when you start showin'. Which version sounds worse…? You tellin' Outlaw before you have the baby so *he* can know what he's dealin' with or afterwards, when he's already thinkin' this kid is his? After he's spent all this money on you and got his emotions involved?"

"Is this another attempt to get me to be with you because if—" Shantreis asked, dodging the question.

"Hell no," Blaze chuckled condescendingly. "I really thought about that shit… for a long time. I really loved you, Treis, but you too damn dumb or too damn greedy, one, to acknowledge that. I *always* looked out for you back in Richmond and now this nigga got you brainwashed. You lightweight scandalous too. That was some shit I didn't know. So riddle me this, why would I want to be with that kind of female?"

Shantreis had never felt so insulted. She felt her hands balling up into fists. "Well, if you feel that way about me then why the fuck do you care so much about havin' a baby with a "scandalous" bitch?"

"I never called you a 'bitch', Shantreis, but like I told you. This ain't about you." Blaze shook his head. "That's ya problem now. You think it's all about *you.* I just wanna be there for my child. That's it. Any more questions?"

Shantreis rolled her eyes at the sarcasm in his voice.

"You need to go."

Blaze walked close to her, his arm side by side with her shoulder. "Just remember what I said. You can tell him on your terms, or I'll tell him on mine." With those last words, he headed off in the direction of LIDS.

"Shan-Shan, who was that?" Monet asked. The ride she was on had stopped, and she'd been watching the whole exchange quietly. She didn't know what they were talking about but she knew enough about facial expressions to tell that Shantreis was mad… maybe even sad.

"Nobody," Shantreis answered quickly, wiping the water from her eyes. Then she stooped down to the little girl's level. "But, you can't tell daddy about that, okay?"

"Why not? Daddy will beat him up for bein' mean to you!"

Shantreis giggled slightly. "Let it be our little secret—just between us girls, okay?"

"Okay."

"Pinky promise?" She held up her pinky finger.

Monet nodded eagerly. "Pinky promise."

"Shantreis," she heard Outlaw's voice, startling her. She looked up at his stern expression, nervously. Had he seen what transpired between her and Blaze? She felt like he'd gotten there pretty quickly and wondered how much of their conversation he'd overheard.

"What's up? Why you lookin' like that?" she asked timidly.

Outlaw leaned towards her, whispering in her ear, "Fallon got shot. She's at Wake Med… Cash just called me to let me know."

"What the hell happened?" Shantreis shrieked as she entered Wake Med. Cash had agreed to meet her out in the lobby. Outlaw stayed with Monet at the mall, not wanting her to get caught up in the drama they were dealing with.

"S-she got shot," Cash choked out. His eyes were red and his body was slightly shaking. She could tell that he was really torn up about it.

"So what are they sayin'?"

"Nothin' yet. They won't tell me shit until the doctor comes out."

"Where was she shot at?" Shantreis demanded, upset with the lack of information he was giving her.

"Excuse me, sir," the new voice entering their conversation greeted, "You were the one that brought Ms. Hall here right?"

Cash eyed the police officer suspiciously, already having an idea of where this was going. His guard was up, prepared for whatever. He nodded his head slowly.

"My name is Officer Dunwoody and this is Officer Thurmond. We need to ask you a few questions." They escorted Cash over to an unoccupied area of the waiting room. Officer Thurmond pulled a small notebook out of the breast pocket on his uniform. "What exactly happened?"

"Look, I'm not answerin' any questions until I find out about my fiancé so you can leave ya card or whatever and I'll be in contact," Cash told them gruffly, regaining his composure.

"It's procedure, Mr. uhm… What did you say your name was?" Officer Thurmond asked nervously, attempting to regain control of the situation.

"I didn't."

"So… asking you any more questions would just be wasting our time huh?" Officer Dunwoody remarked sarcastically.

"You got it." Cash took the card grudgingly.

"We'll be back to interview your fiancé when she's feeling better," Officer Thurmond notified Cash before they left.

Cash watched their retreating figures and shook his head. He had no plans of getting in contact with them and he was sure that they understood that as well. He pitched their business card in the nearest trash can. Whenever Fallon woke up then Cash would coach her on what to say. He didn't want to give them any leads towards his brother. Ghost was a problem that he wanted to handle on his own.

I knew I should've just merked him when I had the chance and then this shit wouldn't have happened, Cash thought, feeling a pang of guilt. It was his job to protect Fallon and he'd failed. Why didn't he just deal with Ghost in his own way? She would've been mad, but she would've gotten over it. Why didn't he tell her not to come in? Why didn't he do something?

The more Cash thought about it, the angrier he

became. Each time that he closed his eyes he could see Fallon writhing on the floor in pain. The big puddle of red blood resembling paint covering a canvas… Her eyes pleading with him to do something and her scream of pain when the bullet entered her side.

Sparing Ghost's life would be a promise that he'd have to break. He was sure that this time Fallon would be able to understand.

"What happened, Cash?" Strap asked, entering the hospital. He looked just as miserable as Cash felt.

"Yo' dumb ass brother," Cash seethed, "I'm gonna merk that nigga with my bare hands when I find him…" The veins on his neck looked ready to burst at any second.

"Where was she shot at?" Strap decided to change the subject. He felt especially responsible since he'd played a quintessential role in the shooting, even though he hadn't pulled the trigger himself. He felt horrible. While he hadn't *told* Ghost to kill Cash, he knew that was how his hot-headed twin would take it. Strap was ashamed for even wishing that on his brother.

"Her side… But there was so much fuckin' blood…"

"Mr. Hardy?" they heard.

"Yes?" Cash and Strap asked at the same time.

The nurse smiled. "The doctor would like to speak with you."

Cash looked over at his brother and Shantreis before following the nurse. The doctor stood with a stoic expression and a clipboard in hand. He was an older man with graying hair and a stern look.

He made Cash think the worst.

"Well, Mr. Hardy, your fiancé has lost a lot of blood so she may need a blood transfusion. But I am glad to say that her injuries aren't life-threatening so she'll be fine after surgery."

Cash let out a sigh of relief. "Thank you, Doctor."

It took about five hours of waiting in the ER before they were notified that Fallon was being transported to ICU. They were told that she was weak from surgery but luckily, she hadn't needed to have the transfusion.

"Can we see her now?" Strap asked eagerly, before Cash could even form the sentence.

"Only family members," the nurse told him nicely.

"We *are*," Shantreis spoke up quickly, almost daring the woman to question her. "Where is her room?"

After getting the room number, they were rushing down the corridor. When they opened the door, Shantreis wanted to faint. Fallon was laying on the cold, hard hospital bed with an IV attached to one arm and other devices connected to her body. Strap's heart was in a million pieces and Cash had to choke back his tears again.

"She's… She's asleep, right?" Strap whispered, almost like he was afraid to speak any louder. Her eyes were closed and hospitals always had a way of making him feel like the Grim Reaper was nearby.

"The thing is beepin'," Shantreis replied in an equally low tone as she pointed towards the heart monitor.

Cash took a spot near Fallon's bedside and held her

hand in his. Shantreis could tell that he wanted a moment alone, but probably didn't know how to ask them to leave after they'd all waited those agonizing hours. She nudged Strap's shoulder, "C'mon. Let's go outside for a second."

Strap was reluctant but nodded his head and followed Shantreis out of the door. "Look, Strap, I know how you feel about her but you gotta chill. She *is* with Cash, after all."

"That doesn't even matter." Strap pulled away from her. "She was there for me when I got shot so I should be there with her… Know what—just let me know when he leaves then."

He took off down the hallway but before he reached the elevator, he turned around. Strap walked back towards her like a wild man. "Fuck that. I got just as much of a right to be in there as he do."

"Strap…" Shantreis started, but he'd already let himself into the room.

Chapter 30

"Ay, Strap," Cash started, trying to find the words. "You mind, man?"

Strap shrugged as he pulled up a chair next to Fallon's bedside anyway. He honestly felt that it would be in Cash's best interest not to say shit to him about it. The way he was feeling right now, he had no more fucks to give. He was liable to say anything.

Cash sighed. "I meant can you fall back, bruh?"

"No disrespect, *bruh*," Strap matched his brother's annoyed tone. "But you're not the only one that gives a damn about Fallon."

"I know you do, too, but this is different."

"Really? Cuz I think this is the same."

"Fuck is yo' problem?" Cash asked as his tone became confrontational. "Why the hell is you takin' this shit personal?"

"Cuz I care about her too, Cash!" Strap was like a ticking time bomb and the countdown had just ended. He exploded. "You ain't the only nigga in her fuckin' life! *I'm* the one that's been there from the very beginning! Nigga, you *just* showed up!"

"How you figure that?" Cash's face was twisted in confusion. He didn't know what the hell his younger brother was talking about but he was getting out of pocket. At first Cash figured that Strap's anger was just due to the circumstances but now it seemed personal.

Strap shook his head. "It's nothin', man. I'm just..." He paused. "Nothin'."

"Nah, nigga. Speak what's on ya mind!" Cash was riled up now and stood toe to toe with his younger brother. "Tell me how I *just* showed up!"

"I loved her since I was fifteen, nigga, that's how you *just* showed up! What's worse is you knew how I felt about her! But you *still* went after her. I even tricked myself into believin' that you didn't do it on purpose, but I think you did."

Cash was baffled. "Are you kiddin' me, Strap? You mad cuz you was crushin' on her but she chose me?" If Strap had come to him in a different manner then Cash probably wouldn't have responded to him like that. But Strap had stepped to him with disrespect so he would return it. He could care less about his feelings at this point.

Strap's blood was boiling but Cash wouldn't stop running his mouth. "Fallon wanted a grown ass man and she got the right one! I didn't force her to be with me!"

"And I didn't force her to be with me either!" Strap yelled.

"That's obvious, ain't it? She ain't with you," he retorted.

Strap shook his head with a small smirk on his face. To Cash, it clearly read 'I-know-something-that-you don't' and he was ready to wipe that smug expression off with his fist.

"Yeah. You right," Strap nodded knowingly. "You got it."

His nonchalant behavior had Cash feeling that something wasn't right but he didn't question it. He was probably just trying to get under his skin. Strap was succeeding in that.

"Hey… Why are y'all yelling?" Fallon asked weakly, finally coming to. She was a tad disoriented and her vision was a little blurry. The morphine the doctors had given to her had done its job of knocking her out but now that the drug had subsided, she was awake and feeling a dull pain.

Cash cracked a smile as he came closer to Fallon's bed, temporarily forgetting his spat with Strap. "Damn. What's up, baby?" his voice indicated how happy he was to see her awake. "How you feelin'?"

"I'm a little thirsty," she admitted, "I do feel some pain but I'll live." Fallon smiled wanly.

"Do you remember… what umm… happened earlier?" Strap asked cautiously as Cash handed her the glass of water near her bedside.

She shook her head vigorously. "All I remember is hearing somebody say I got shot?" Fallon asked, thinking that she was mistaken. How could it have happened? Fallon could recall pulling into the driveway behind Cash. She had gotten off of work early and decided to surprise him. She'd walked into the doorway and then everything after that was a blur. She could hear someone screaming but didn't realize it was her until the moment she felt something hot piercing her skin.

Oh my God… I really did *get shot,* Fallon thought in a panic. It showed on her face and Cash tried to calm her down. Tears were streaming down her face like it had occurred all over again. "Who shot me?"

Both men were silent as they exchanged glances. Strap swallowed the lump in his throat. There was no way he was going to throw Ghost under the bus, but he wasn't sure if Cash cared to protect him. He opened his mouth to speak, but Fallon beat him to it.

"Why are y'all looking like that? And don't tell me you don't know because I know you do! Who would've been in your house that wanted to shoot me, Cash?" she yelled hysterically. Fallon looked like she was about to hyperventilate. "Oh my God, is somebody after you? You didn't really get out of the game did you?"

"No," Cash answered, "I mean, nobody's after me. Calm down."

"I'm not gonna calm down, Damontrez! *You're* not the one who was shot minding your own business. *I* was!" She looked back at Strap who was standing there speechless. Fallon hadn't expected him to know anything since he wasn't there, but they were brothers and that was reason enough to suspect that he was hiding something too.

"I'm gonna find out and handle that shit though," Cash assured her.

Fallon shook her head vigorously. "You just don't get it! When will this all stop? They attack, you retaliate, and the circle continues! I don't want that kind of life, Cash. I want to be able to walk around without fearing for my life. I'm no gangster and I refuse to have to look over my shoulder like I am one!"

"Baby, it's not that serious. It won't be like that at all," Cash tried to convince her fruitlessly.

"No, Cash. You *promised* me but now we're back to the bullshit. Get out!" She pointed towards the door for emphasis.

"Fallon, you don't know what you're saying…"

She pressed the buzzer to alert the nurse. "I think I do. I need a minute to myself to sort all this out."

Cash sighed, knowing that her mind was made up for the moment. "I love you, baby." He kissed her on the forehead. "The police might try to question you later, just tell them you don't know shit."

"That won't be too hard for me now will it?" Fallon asked sarcastically.

Cash headed to the door without another word until he realized that Strap wasn't behind him. "C'mon, Strap."

"Do you need me to stay here with you?" Strap asked, ignoring Cash. "You know that's not a problem, Fallon. I'm here for you when you need me."

Fallon shook her head 'no'. "But can you please call Shantreis and tell her to come up here?"

"You got it. She should still be here." Strap tried to linger for a bit but Cash kept calling his name louder and louder. Strap wanted to tell Fallon that he loved her but despite the lack of respect he'd shown Cash earlier, he couldn't bring himself to just come right out and say *that* in front of his brother.

Telling Cash that he loved her and saying it directly to Fallon were two different things. That would probably be enough to get him hemmed up. He didn't want to make Fallon uncomfortable either. She'd been adamant about keeping things between them a secret and he would never go against that. Not until she was ready to let the cat out of the bag.

Reluctantly, Strap followed Cash out of the door. Seeing Shantreis in the waiting room he called out to her, "Fallon wants to see you."

"Okay." She nodded. Noticing them walking towards the exit she asked, "Where y'all goin'? Y'all ain't gonna stay with her?"

"She just wanted you," Strap answered simply, noticing that Cash wasn't going to speak up.

The two brothers walked in silence until they reached the parking deck. Strap was headed towards his car and Cash called out to him, "Since I know how you feel now don't let me catch you around Fallon! Just like Ghost, I'll kill you if you step out on some disrespect shit again."

Strap nodded. "You got it." Cash had just made things easier for him. The guilt of having betrayed his brother weighed heavily on him, but Cash's decision to sever their ties took away the bulk of that load. Strap realized that everything Ghost had been telling him was true.

He hated that he hadn't spoke up for himself sooner. Strap would put gaining true love over him and Cash's relationship any day. His woman could be his best friend, his lover, his family, and his homie all rolled up into one. And that woman would be Fallon, he'd put that on everything.

Shantreis had stayed with Fallon for the three days that she was in the hospital. Now that Fallon had finally been discharged, Shantreis couldn't wait to sleep in her own bed. The cot they'd provided for her to sleep on didn't have anything on her TempurPedic mattress at home.

"We missed you, Shan-Shan!" Monet squealed the moment she walked into the door.

Shantreis smiled as she swept the toddler up into her arms. "I missed y'all too!" She surveyed the room. It was littered with toys and *Bubble Guppies* was on the television, but there was something missing. "Where's your daddy?"

Monet pointed in the direction of Outlaw's study. It was a room where he discussed the majority of his business and the place that he went when he wanted to be alone. Normally Shantreis wasn't allowed in there but she missed him and didn't give a damn about any of his silly rules.

Rapping on the door softly, she entered without waiting for permission. When Outlaw saw her, his eyes lit up but he motioned for her to be quiet. "Yeah. I'll be ready for it. Aiight. Yeah." He ended his call and his lips curled up into a smile.

"I missed you, daddy," Shantreis purred as she made her way over to his chair. Straddling his waist, she tilted her head forward and sucked on his bottom lip before taking his tongue into her mouth. She could feel herself becoming moist as she grinded on top of him. When she felt his dick harden in his pants, she grinned and pulled away.

"Damn, girl," Outlaw muttered, "What you stop for?"

"To do this," she said seductively, pushing his chair backwards and positioning herself between his legs. Shantreis unbuckled his pants before pulling his erection out. She twirled her mouth around his tool like she was licking a Tootsie Pop. She knew that she was doing a good job when he moaned and placed his hand on the back of her head.

Since being pregnant her sexual appetite had definitely heightened. Going three days without Outlaw had been agonizing. Coming home to him and getting her freak on had been all that she could think about.

"Damn, baby," Outlaw praised her skills. "Sit on it for me."

He didn't have to tell Shantreis twice. Lifting up her maxi dress and pulling his A.P.C. jeans lower, she situated herself over his magic wand.

"Shit. You ain't got no panties on?" he commented, appreciating the sight and easy access. It turned him on more.

"Nope," Shantreis giggled before he pulled her down on his length. "Damn, bae." She bit down on her lip to keep from howling with pleasure. She didn't want Monet to hear them and fuck up everything.

Outlaw thrust in and out of her slowly… alternating between going up and down, and from deep to shallow. The two moved in unison to a beat playing in their own heads. Not even ten minutes later, it was over but it was undoubtedly the best ten minutes they'd spent that day.

Shantreis had managed to get two orgasms before Outlaw bust one.

Their sticky bodies remained stuck to one another until Monet started banging on the door, "Daddy, did you hear me? I wanna watch Dora!"

"Aiight! Daddy be right there!"

Sluggishly, they fixed their clothes. Outlaw smacked Shantreis on the ass playfully. "See, you keep actin' like that and I'm a' jump on ya ass again," she flirted.

"Shit… I want you to," he eyed her up and down with a wide grin. Outlaw had been feening for her just as much as she had him.

"Well, what about…" Shantreis placed a finger near her chin thoughtfully. "You get Monet taken care of and then meet me in the bathtub for round two."

"Bet." They both exited the room, headed in their own respective directions.

"Now what did you wanna see?" Outlaw asked Monet.

"Dora, daddy," she said matter-of-factly. "Don't you remember?"

He laughed as she pretended to be exasperated with him. "I think Diego's cooler than her."

"Diego's for boys!" Monet reminded.

Outlaw nodded. "I know, I know."

He adjusted the channel for her before rising to leave the room. The constant ringing of a cell phone stopped him. His was still in the study so he knew it was Shantreis' phone that was blowing up. Outlaw reached his hand inside of her Gucci bag, searching for the iPhone. Whatever it was seemed to be urgent and he figured that it was Fallon. Hell, Shantreis didn't have any other friends.

Seeing her name on the Caller ID confirmed his theory. "Shantreis!" he shouted. The phone vibrated again, but this time it was a text message labeled as urgent. *It must be.* He noticed that Fallon had called about ten times in a row. Outlaw thought nothing of opening the message but what he saw blew his mind:

Look, Treis, I'm tryin 2 be a man bout this n handle mine. I don't wanna show my ass but I will if you keep playin wit me. Fuck outlaw. I got money now so don't use that excuse. If he kicks you out after you tell him then I'll take care of you. You won't have to worry about shit while you carrying my baby. Let's talk about this... like adults... before it gets out of hand. Plz don't stop me from bein a part of our childs life... Sry for the way I acted at the mall too.

Sent: 4:00pm

Chapter 31

"What?" Shantreis repeated, as though she hadn't understood him perfectly the first time.

"I said 'Are you pregnant'," Outlaw spoke slowly as if he were speaking to a small child.

"Why you askin' me that?" she asked, attempting to dodge the question.

"C'mon, Shantreis, are we really gonna play that game? Just answer me."

Shantreis sighed. *I should probably go ahead and get this over with.* "Yeah… I am."

"How long you knew this? Why you didn't tell me about it?" he prodded.

Shantreis sat on the edge of the bathtub half-naked. She'd been undressing for their underwater rendezvous when he entered, asking about her pregnancy. Outlaw stood in front of her with a humorless expression. He didn't seem to be too thrilled about the news. Honestly, she didn't even know how he felt about having more kids. It was a topic that they'd never touched base on because at the time, Shantreis hadn't wanted kids. Now that it was happening, she felt differently.

"Because I didn't know what you would say… You seem like you're mad, honestly," Shantreis told him while fiddling with her thumbs nervously.

"I mean I would a' been excited…" Outlaw looked her square in the face, "if it was mine."

"Fuck you mean?" she asked, pretending to be insulted but inwardly she was terrified. *Oh hell naw!* Shantreis thought. Her heartbeat was racing and she could feel her blood pressure rising.

Outlaw smacked her upside her head. "Bitch, don't play dumb with me. Some nigga texted ya phone about the shit." He smacked her again.

"Stop, Outlaw!" she stood up from the ledge of the bathtub. Her hands shielded her head in an attempt to block the blows. "Nigga, you better quit puttin' ya hands on me! I know that!"

"Who the fuck gonna stop me?" Outlaw snarled before knocking his hand against her head again. "You triflin' ass ho! How the fuck you gonna be pregnant with another nigga baby? I should beat that shit out of you!"

"It *is* yours," she insisted. Shantreis covered her stomach instinctively as she backed away from him.

"Tell me another fuckin' lie." Outlaw grabbed her hands forcefully and pressed her backwards until she landed on the bed. His body weight pinned her down and his hands tightened around her wrists. "You was fuckin' that nigga today? Huh? That's why you ain't have no fuckin' drawls on?"

"No," Shantreis denied. Tears were running rampant down her face and snot streamed from her nose. She didn't know how she was getting out of this dilemma but her guess would be in a coffin. Looking at Outlaw she felt like she was staring into the face of the Devil. His expression was deranged and wild. It was obvious that he wasn't in his right mind.

"I'm tellin' you. This is your baby!"

"Then why that nigga think it's his? You would a' told me about it if you thought it was mine. But you *didn't.*"

"That's not—"

"Who the fuck is he?" Outlaw demanded. Spit landed on Shantreis' face as he spoke. "What nigga you fucked?"

"Blaze," she said, merely above a whisper.

"That nigga from the club!" he roared. "You—"

"Daddy, somebody's at the door!" Monet's voice called loudly. "Can I answer it?"

Outlaw stared Shantreis in the eyes with contempt. "That nigga know where the fuck we stay?"

"No!" she lied. Blaze had been over their house on more than one occasion. They'd even fucked in their bed before. It sounded bad, but it was true. When Shantreis found out that Outlaw had disrespected her that way after finding a used condom in their bed, she wanted him to feel as hurt as she did, even though she planned on him never finding out.

"You been lyin' to me all night so why the fuck do you think I would start believin' you now?" He wrapped his hands around her neck, squeezing tightly. In the years that they'd been together, Outlaw had never put his hands on her but Shantreis had never done anything like this either. She was bringing out his bad side.

"Daddy, some man is at the door!" Monet screeched.

"Don't answer it," Outlaw yelled back while continuing to force the air out of Shantreis' lungs.

Shantreis tried to move her legs… to do anything to get him off of her but he easily overpowered her hundred and forty-five pounds. Each time she blinked it became harder to reopen her eyes.

"Ay, nigga, you better raise the fuck up off her!"

Outlaw released his grip on Shantreis and arose from the bed. "Nigga, you in my muthafuckin' house but you barkin' out commands?" he asked arrogantly.

"Blaze?" Shantreis choked out, surprised to see him in the doorway with his .45 raised. "What are you doin' here?"

Blaze ignored her questions and kept his eyes and gun trained on Outlaw. "Nigga, I swear I will blow ya brains out right here."

"You ain't got enough heart to do that or you would've done it already. You ain't scarin' nobody." Outlaw wasn't strapped but he was talking as if he was. No matter what type of situation he was backed into, he would never go out looking like a pussy. "If this is about this bitch," Outlaw nodded his head towards Shantreis, "You can have her. I don't give a fuck. Take her and get the hell out."

"C'mon," Blaze called out to her, holding out his free hand.

Shantreis trembled as she inched across the bed, increasing her distance from Outlaw. When she felt that she was far enough, she rushed over to Blaze's side. "Go on to the car," he instructed. "I'll be there in a minute." Noticing her resistance, he tried again, "Treis, just do what the fuck I said! I don't need you in here for what I'm about to do!"

What had transpired between her and Outlaw was fucked up but Shantreis couldn't say for certain that she wanted to take his life for it. A simple ass whupping would suffice but Blaze wasn't trying to hear it.

"Blaze, think about this…" Shantreis said in an attempt to help him regain his senses.

"You betta listen to her! Nigga, you think you gonna kill me in my own muthafuckin' house? I'd like to see you—" Before Outlaw could finish his sentence, he'd leaped at Blaze unexpectedly hoping to catch him off-guard.

BLAOW!

Shantreis' eyes widened as she watched Outlaw take a shot to the chest. His gaze never faltered from her, not even as he staggered backwards, clutching himself in a futile attempt to stop the blood. Then he fell onto the floor.

"Blaze! We-we gotta call 911!!!" she stuttered.

"The only thing we gotta do is get the fuck out of here."

"But what about Mo—"

As if on cue, Monet stood at the doorway trembling with tears in her eyes, "Was that thunder? I'm scared."

"Monet, come on," Shantreis scooped the little girl up quickly and turned out of the room. "Let's go for a car ride, okay?"

"No!" she shrieked. Monet had gotten more than an eyeful of what Shantreis had tried so hard to shield her from. "What's wrong with my daddy? Why does he look like that?" Her tiny arms and legs bombarded Shantreis with hits as she struggled to get down.

After hitting Shantreis in the face, she was freed. Monet rushed to Outlaw's side but Blaze intercepted her quickly. "Hey, sweetheart, let's go visit your mommy, okay?"

"No! I want my daddy! What's wrong with him?" Monet tried the same sequence with Blaze but his grip was firm and she could only kick her legs weakly.

Blaze felt like shit to say the least. After all, he'd just been responsible for taking away a little girl's father... a man that was probably her hero. He had fucked up but he couldn't take it back.

"Treis, get your purse," he told her, seeing it sitting on the sofa.

Shantreis did as she was told, but that wasn't going to stop the lecture she was about to give him. "Blaze, do you know how much shit we gon' be in?" Shantreis felt the need to remind him as if he didn't already realize it. "I can't believe you did that shit! And especially in front of her," she chastised loudly in an attempt to be heard over Monet's cries.

He simply ignored her as he continued out the front

door, which was still unlocked from when Monet had opened it for him. After Shantreis had been ignoring his texts and phonecalls, Blaze decided to make good on his promise at the mall. He planned on forcing her to tell Outlaw the truth.

"Your fingerprints are everywhere and so are mine! Do you think that the police won't do an investigation?" Shantreis' nerves were on edge at the position Blaze had put her in. She was happy to have her life but she knew that she would lose it in the worst way if she was charged with murder.

"Don't worry about that shit. I ain't goin' back to jail and neither are you." When they got outside, he strapped Monet's seatbelt on and enabled the childproof locks. She was no longer putting up a fight but she was still crying hysterically, drawing attention from some of the neighbors that were outside.

Blaze placed the car keys into the palm of Shantreis' hand, "Go take her to Kaleesha's house. I'm gonna call you and let you know where to come get me from, aiight? If you don't hear from me then just go to my house. I got my money stashed in the closet on the top shelf in some shoeboxes."

"What are you gonna do?" she asked, searching his eyes for answers.

"I'm gonna make sure we don't go to jail," he said vaguely, handing her her cell phone. He'd found it on the floor when he came inside. "Now hurry up."

Obeying his orders, Shantreis got into his Denali and pulled out the driveway. Her hands were shaking and Monet's howls were making her head hurt. Visions of her sitting in a courtroom fitted with handcuffs and an ugly orange jumpsuit appeared each time she blinked.

It was only when she turned onto Capital Boulevard and merged onto I-540 that she felt a tiny shard of relief. Monet had finally tuckered herself out and was dozing in the backseat. Shantreis turned on the radio, hoping that it could relax her mind. Jay Z was telling about his 99 problems.

"The year is 94 and in my trunk is raw," she rapped along with Hov, feeling a little more at ease. That was until the song spoke the truth on her situation. In her rearview mirror she could see a police car had sped up behind her with his sirens wailing. "I got two choices, y'all, pull over the car or bounce on the devil, put the pedal to the floor."

Decisions, decisions…

Chapter 32

Fallon sat on her sofa wiping the tears that fell from her eyes. She had just finished watching *The Notebook*. It was one of her favorite movies.

I want a love like that, she thought as she stood up to remove the Blu-Ray Disc. Once upon a time Fallon thought that she had that with Cash but his street life wouldn't allow for them to have a happy ending. At least she didn't see it. But if that was true then why was she still wearing his ring?

Cash had called her every day and even stopped by her apartment a few times, but she refused to speak to him. She just wanted some time to herself. Fallon needed to think and really figure out what it was that she desired before she got in touch with him. Cash had always been her weakness. He had the ability to impair her thinking. Yes, he would surely change her mind in a matter of minutes with his methods of persuasion.

Fallon was still angry about how he'd put her life in danger, however. She had yet to get any answers as to why the shooting had even occurred but she was starting not to care. Knowing wouldn't change the fact that it'd happened.

The police had questioned her like Cash warned her they would, but she honestly didn't have any answers for them. In fact, she'd completely fabricated a story of how the shooting happened rather than leading them to investigate Cash. She knew that they could possibly uncover more than a murder suspect; they could discover the truth about his lavish lifestyle. While he proclaimed to be out of the game, she couldn't be so sure. Knowing that Outlaw was still involved was another reason that she wouldn't point fingers in their direction.

Ding-dong!

Fallon looked at the clock hanging from the wall of her living room. It was almost seven o' clock and she wasn't expecting any company. *Cash,* she thought. *He just doesn't get it.*

Slowly she strolled to the door and peered into the peephole. To her surprise Strap was standing on her doorstep. His eyes were downcast and his hands were inside of his pockets. "Hey, Strap," she greeted, opening the door.

Strap smiled. "Whassup, Fallon? You mind if I come in real quick?"

"Sure." She moved aside and allowed him entry. She headed back towards her sofa. "Oh. I'm sorry that I didn't call you to thank you for the flowers." Fallon nodded her head towards the beautiful arrangement of colorful carnations sitting in the middle of her coffee table. "That was really sweet of you."

"It's nothin'," he told her bashfully. Strap had sent the flowers after Shantreis had informed him of when Fallon would be discharged. He had wanted to send her something to let her know that she was on his mind. Obviously it had worked because her anger with him had subsided. "But how you doin'? I just wanted to check up on you."

"I'm as okay as I can be given the circumstances, I guess. They prescribed me some painkillers and they're a big help." She crossed her legs and sat a pillow in her lap, wrapping her arms around it and laying her head on top of it.

They sat quietly for a minute before Fallon started speaking again, "Where's Ghost at? I haven't seen him in a while." She hadn't really expected to, but it was her attempt at conversation. She was trying to get a feel for Strap and the real reason for his visit.

Strap shrugged. "I ain't seen much of that nigga at all lately." It wasn't a complete lie. He hadn't seen him, but that was because Ghost had done exactly as his name implied—disappeared. The same day that he'd shot Fallon he'd relocated to Jacksonville, FL. Raleigh was too hot. Word on the streets was that Cash put a bounty of $500,000 on his head. Ghost wasn't scared but he wasn't a dumb ass either.

"Oh. Okay…" Her voice trailed off. "I know you didn't just drive all the way over here to check on me."

He nodded his head. "Yes I did." Strap stared at her so intensely that Fallon had to break off her gaze with him.

"Why are you looking at me like that?"

"You beautiful as fuck…" Strap said bluntly. "Not just on the outside, but the inside too,"

Fallon's cheeks turned a light rosy red before she shook

her head. "Thank you, Strap. I feel the same way about you."

"But look, I'm a' be honest, I do have some other shit that I wanted to talk to you about."

Fallon's smile faded when she heard his solemn tone. "Strap, I hope it's not about 'us' again."

"Why?" Strap persisted. "What's so wrong with bein' with me?" He took a place next to Fallon on the sofa. "If you would let your guard down and open your eyes then you would see that the perfect man for you is right here." He leaned closer to her and cupped her face gently with his hands.

"Damien… Why won't you just give up?" She turned her head away from him.

"Cuz I love you and I know that no matter how hard you try to deny it, I know you love me too."

"Damien…"

"Nah, Fallon. I'm so serious right now. I know I should a' spoken up last year. Hell, I should a' said somethin' way before then instead of sacrificin' my happiness for my brother," he said passionately. "But the point is, I'm saying it now…. If you can tell me, right now, that you don't love me or at least tell me that you don't think I could treat you better than Cash, then I promise you I will fall back."

"I d-don…" the rest of her sentence was lodged down in her throat somewhere and she couldn't force herself to say it. Her feelings for Strap had her more confused than ever. Maybe he'd just caught her at a vulnerable time?

"Just give us a try, Fallon. Stop thinkin' about what Cash or anybody else might think about you bein' with me… If you don't love me yet, I'll teach you how." Tentatively, he wrapped his arms around her waist and pulled her closer to him. Strap kissed her lips softly then jerked back suddenly, as if he'd been burned. Noticing that Fallon was just as into the kiss as he was, his lips met hers again.

Fallon closed her eyes, allowing herself to get caught up in the moment. When the kiss turned more passionate and tears dropped down her face.

"Why you cryin'?" Strap asked, genuinely concerned.

"Strap, I don't know if I can do this…" She shook her head and wiped away her tears.

"Yes, you can, Fallon." He coerced her with another kiss, savoring the feel of her soft lips. She leaned back slowly and he rained kisses over her neck and face. Fallon could feel her temperature rising as he pressed his body on top of hers.

Fallon surprised herself when she unbuttoned his shirt, never removing her lips from his. When she pulled down the fly of his jeans, it started to dawn on her what she was about to do. Could she really do it? Was she about to give herself to Strap again? The answer was a resounding 'yes'.

Strap took his time with her. No inch of her body went unexplored or undiscovered. Fallon felt self-conscious about the spot where she'd gotten shot but Strap didn't care about that. He moved from her mountains, to caressing his face in her valley and tasting her sea. He made love to her slowly, silently showing her what it would be like to be with him. It felt just as good as it had the first time, if not even more so the second time around.

"I love you, Fallon."

"I love you, too," the words had escaped Fallon's mouth before she could help it.

Those were the words that he'd been longing to hear. It was like an orgasm in itself because Strap was no longer able to hold it after she'd confessed that.

That night the two fell asleep intertwined in each other's arms. It was the best sleep that they had gotten in a long time.

The sun rays streamed through the huge bay windows early the next morning but that wasn't what caused Strap to awaken from his peaceful slumber. A gun being loaded into the chamber did.

"What the fuck?" Strap mumbled before fixing his eyes on the loveseat across from where they lay.

Cash sat there, tapping his gun against his temple. He'd let himself in with Fallon's spare key. She always kept one hidden inside of the decorative seasonal wreaths that she kept on her door. He had decided that Fallon had enough time to mull things over. Cash was going to explain himself and then bring her back home with him... where she belonged.

"Damn, Strap... I always thought it was Ghost that wanted to be like me but you did too huh?" Cash said quietly. "I understand that you love her. I really get that but the strength of the fact alone that she was—*is*," he corrected himself, "my girl—my fiancé, should've resolved that for you."

Cash shook his head and stared at Fallon thoughtfully. She was still knocked out. Seeing her lying underneath Strap in such a display of passion had him past heated and hurt. He couldn't explain how he felt at that moment but he was definitely in a dangerous place.

"I told you how I felt about her," Strap said sitting upright on the sofa, being sure to keep the sheet around him. "I couldn't cut that shit off, Cash. It may seem fucked up, but you would've done the same thing."

"Nope. That's where you're wrong. You should've voiced your feelings a long time ago!" Cash boomed. "You let the shit build up and get out of hand! All the women in this world that you could've chosen but you go after mine?!"

"They could never be Fallon."

"Nigga, I know that shit! But you could find a damned good replica!"

Fallon started to stir and rubbed her eyes slowly. "Cash?" she whispered.

A pained smile was on his face when she called his name, "It's fucked up, girl… I thought I was a good nigga. Whatever you *wanted* I did it for you… This is how you pay a nigga back?"

"Cash, I…" Fallon's voice cracked as she became overcome with emotion.

"Nah. I don't wanna hear that shit." Cash's voice sounded just as broken as hers did. His face was even more so. He raised his gun and shook his head. "Death before dishonor is the code we abide by." His eyes were fixed on Fallon as he spoke before taking aim and pulling the trigger.

BLAOW!

ABOUT THE AUTHOR

Georgia native Love N. Lee has had a passion for reading since she was in Pull Ups. It wasn't until she had to write a short story as a class assignment in elementary that she discovered that she liked to write and create her own stories. Love's parents and teachers took note of her talent, believing that one day she could become an author. Unfortunately, Love felt it would only remain a hobby since she thought it was too difficult to land a publishing deal. It would be nearly ten years before she picked up her pen again.

Love dropped out of college after having her son, and then relocated to Raleigh, North Carolina. While working at a call center, in-between calls and on her break, she would read urban fiction. Soon she began working on her own novel as her interest in writing returned. Thanks to a chance encounter, Love linked up with best-selling author Treasure E. Blue on a social networking site. He introduced her to other literary heavyweights that shared resources to help her perfect her craft and offered invaluable advice. After receiving encouragement and mentoring from Nakea Murray of The Literary Consultant Group and David Weaver of SBR Publications, she decided to bring her dreams to fruition.

Taking a leap of faith, Love quit her job and began writing full-time. Her novel 'Already Taken' hit virtual bookshelves in July and became an overnight bestseller. After much hard work, she is now the CEO and Founder of JME Publications, which specializes in romance books for the hood. Love currently lives in Atlanta with her four-year-old son. Outside of writing, she enjoys reality TV, K-dramas, and traveling.

ACKNOWLEDGEMENTS

Thank You To All Of The Readers! I Hope That You Enjoyed This Book And That You Will Stick Around For My Next Release. Thank God For Giving Me The Courage And The Talent To Write. Thanks To My Parents For Molding Me Into The Young Lady I Am Today. Thanks To All Of My Friends For Giving Me Feedback. I Know I Really Worked Your Nerves But I Wanted It Perfect. ☺

Readers, go to http://eepurl.com/rYocn To Be Added To The JME Publications Mailing List For Exclusive Sneak Peeks, Contests, And More!

You Can Reach Me At:

Twitter: @Author_LoveNLee

Email: author_LoveN.Lee@hotmail.com

Facebook: author.lovenlee

ALSO FROM JME PUBLICATIONS

Rap Star Wifeys: Miami Season 1 by Love N. Lee

Cherish by Tihanna Peach

Love Hate Thing by Love N. Lee

Street Love by Love N. Lee

Already Taken 2 by Love N. Lee

Rap Star Wifeys: Miami Season 2 by Love N. Lee

Street Love 2 by Love N. Lee

Mine Games by Love N. Lee

Beauty and the Thug by Love N. Lee

Love and the Streets by Love N. Lee

Rap Star Wifeys: Miami

Season 1

Exclusive Excerpt!

Track 1

Why I can't have a nigga like that? Lavisha wondered bitterly. *Sonya and AK ain't even been together that long. Me and Yamajesty been together for eight damn years and he still won't give me a damn ring.*

Lavisha shot Yamajesty a look of resentment, but he was too preoccupied with whoever had been blowing up his phone all night. He refused to answer it but he wouldn't turn it off either. When Lavisha demanded to know who it was, he told her to mind her business.

"Oh my God, AK!" Sonya squealed, admiring the beautiful, four-carat diamond ring that now adorned her pudgy finger. "I can't believe it!" She waved her hand across the table to show the rest of the crew.

"Ay, and when we blow up, I'ma buy you an even bigger one," AK bragged with a wide smile on his face.

They were all eating at The Cheesecake Factory at Dadeland Mall. It was Sonya's favorite restaurant, and therefore it was only befitting that AK proposed there. He'd invited the other members of his group, 5519, to attend, along with a few other close friends.

"Congratulations, y'all," Lavisha spoke up, hoping that she sounded convincing. *They probably only getting married because Miss Piggy's pregnant.* Her rationalization made her smile. *That's got to be it. Why else would AK marry Sonya now?*

Sonya had been what niggas would deem 'a bad bitch' before she got pregnant. She had the typical video vixen's body, but it was *au natural*… That's what she claimed, but Lavisha was sure that she'd gotten a Brazilian Butt Lift. In Miami, you could never be too sure. Nevertheless, Sonya was one that men drooled over with her pretty, butter pecan complexion and fashionable style.

All that changed when she got pregnant. Sonya went from one hundred and forty five pounds to at least two hundred. Pregnancy didn't agree with her in the slightest. Her nose was wide and her face had gotten round and chubby. Her svelte figure had completely disappeared. Sonya went from resembling a Coca-Cola bottle to a big bowling ball. If Lavisha hadn't known any better, she honestly would have sworn that the Sonya of the present was a completely different woman than the Sonya AK had hooked up with a few years ago. The changes were that dramatic.

Gossip sites like *Media Takeout* were always posting her before and after pictures and people commented cruelly about her weight gain. Lavisha was always sure to notify Sonya each time they posted about her, too. She rejoiced in bringing Sonya back down to earth and feeding into her newfound insecurity. Instead of being happy for her, she was envious of Sonya. It had been that way since the day they met.

Lavisha longed for her carefree life. Sonya had everything she didn't—a wonderful fiancé, a beautiful condo at Marina Blue, and was expecting twins. AK gave in to her every whim and desire whilst Lavisha practically had to beg Yamajesty for nice shit.

Maybe if I had found AK first and snatched him up, my life wouldn't suck so bad, Lavisha thought. She was far from attracted to AK, even though she could recognize that he was a good looking dude. She just wanted *her man* to be more like him. Lavisha wouldn't dare tell Yamajesty that, however. The last time she did, he'd flipped out on her. He made it clear that she either accepted him or found another man who could give her what she was looking for. Foolishly she stayed, believing that she could change him but she'd had no luck.

"Maybe you and Yamajesty will be next," Sonya beamed, knocking Lavisha from her unpleasant thoughts.

Lavisha rolled her eyes. "I wish."

"Why wouldn't he?" she continued, "He better before someone else snatches you up!"

Yamajesty snorted. "If they can hit her, they can have her!"

"If you like it then you're supposed to put a ring on it," Sonya reminded playfully.

I wish this bitch would shut up, Lavisha thought. Although Sonya didn't mean any harm, that's what it would escalate to when Lavisha and Yamajesty got home.

"You would really wanna marry a nigga?" Yamajesty asked with slight skepticism lacing his voice.

"You know I wanna get married," Lavisha said quietly.

"To me though?"

"Why not, Yamajesty?" She was starting to get irritated and her voice rose a few octaves. "We've been together since we were thirteen. We're twenty-one now. If I didn't wanna marry your ass, I would've been left you alone."

Lavisha had been with Yamajesty since before his so-called fame. Before females started screaming his name and throwing pussy at him. Before he was making a couple thousand dollars per show and wearing fly shit like Hermes belts and True Religion jeans. Even before he got his own apartment overlooking the Miami skyline.

Lavisha had *always* been down for him.

She was with him back when females referred to him as ugly. When they said he resembled the Predator, with his big unkempt dreads, chocolate chip-colored skintone, and chinky eyes. Lavisha was there when he was only hustling weed and making a couple of dollars. Back when he only wore wife beaters and Dickies with a fresh pair of Jordans. Even when he was still living at his momma's house in Deepside.

If ever there was a chick that deserved to take his last name and wear his ring, it was Lavisha Clark.

"Off rip, you know I ain't tryna get married. Shit changes when you do that," Yamajesty said, reciting his usual speech whenever the topic arose. "You said you was cool with that."

"Yeah, back when we were like seventeen!" Lavisha reminded.

"Shit. Y'all damn near married," Blood piped up. He was the third and final member of 5519. "Y'all been together for a long ass time."

AK chuckled and shook his head. "Yamajesty, you know Lavisha's a good girl. You might as well go ahead—"

"Hell nah! A bitch really gotta be something special for me to wanna put a ring on it!" Yamajesty laughed obnoxiously.

"Really, nigga?" Lavisha spoke up, not finding a damn thing funny. "I can't believe you would say some shit like that when I *been* holding your trifling ass down!"

Immediately the smile faded from Yamajesty's face, "Ay, Lavisha, you better chill the fuck out."

"Nigga, please." Lavisha arose from her chair quickly and looked him up and down as though she was sizing him up. "You better get your mind right. Flaw ass nigga." With those last words, she stalked off from the table.

"Got damn!" Blood snickered loudly. "She checked yo' ass!"

"Man, shut the fuck up!" Yamajesty snapped, visibly embarrassed by Lavisha's outburst. He couldn't believe that she had flipped out on him like that. Especially not in front of his boys. Hell, he was sure that the whole restaurant had heard her. Quite a few heads had turned in their direction. Some were concerned while others were just nosy.

"Lavisha!" Yamajesty yelled as he rushed behind her. She continued walking briskly as though she didn't even hear him. "AY!" Quickening his pace, he finally caught up and pulled her by the arm as they made it outside. "What the fuck was that back there?"

"I should be asking you! Why would you say some shit like that? And in front of every damn body?!"

"Shit. It's true. You think I'ma lie just cuz we in front of AK nem? You already knew what it was so I don't know why you'd let that bitch hype yo' head up anyway." Yamajesty shook his head. "I do shit on my time, not just because some other muh'fuckas is doing it. That's yo' damn problem, you always wanna do what the fuck e'rybody else doin'!"

"Nigga, fuck you! It ain't about what everybody else doing," she made little quotation marks with her fingers. "It's about what *you should* be doing!"

"Like I told yo' ass before, this me. Take or leave that shit."

Lavisha shook her head and tried to fight the tears that she felt coming. "Yamajesty, you ain't worth a damn."

Yamajesty only shrugged, not the least bit affected by her words. About three times a week they'd have a conversation mirroring this one, so he was immune to it at this point. "It is what it is."

"I ju—" Lavisha stopped abruptly as she felt her stomach churning. Without another word, she pulled away from Yamajesty and rushed back towards the entrance.

I gotta get to the bathroom, she thought urgently. Her eyes scanned around the room looking for the sign.

"Ma'am, can I assist you?" the hostess asked.

"Your bathroom?" Lavisha whispered as she covered her mouth slightly.

"I'm sorry, I didn't hear—"

Before she could get out the last word, Lavisha could feel the contents of her stomach escaping without her will. A couple of the patrons gasped and the hostess' face was filled with horror. Lavisha had vomited on the woman's clothes and doused her own new Giambattista Valli booties.

"Here you go, ma'am," Lavisha heard as someone passed her a napkin to wipe her mouth with.

"Are you okay?" several concerned voices rang out, along with a child that shouted loudly, "Mommy, that lady just threw up everywhere!!!"

"Ay," Yamajesty's deep voice came from behind her. "Go on to the car. I'ma tell AK we leavin'."

Lavisha nodded quickly before rushing out the door. He didn't have to tell her twice. She was mortified at what had just taken place. In between all that had happened that night, she didn't know what she was more embarrassed about.

Pulling out the key fob to their black Audi A5, she unlocked the doors and reclined the passenger seat. All she wanted to do was go home and lay down. Her stomach's queasiness had subsided slightly, but she was exhausted nevertheless.

"What's wrong with you?" Yamajesty asked as he entered the car. He eyed her suspiciously, taking note of the way she grasped her stomach.

She shrugged. "Must've been that Jambalaya pasta I ordered."

"You get that shit e'ry time we go and you never get sick like that," he objected before pulling out of their parking space.

"Oh well. First time for everything. Damn. Why are you cross examining me?" Lavisha asked with annoyance.

"I'm just makin' sure you ain't pregnant." His eyes cut over at her as they sat at the light on Southwest 88th Street.

"Funny for you to say that when you don't ever strap up anyway. You must've forgotten how babies are made," she said sarcastically.

"Lavisha, you better watch yo' mouth or I swear I'ma pop you in it!" Yamajesty threatened as the traffic cleared, enabling him to make a right. "Now answer the damn question: You pregnant?"

Lavisha was quiet for a couple seconds before managing a soft, "I don't know yet."

"What the fuck?!" he shouted. "I told yo' ass to go to

the pharmacy and get that damn Plan B pill like you always do! I don't know why you won't get one of them damn shots or take some birth control pills like everybody else!"

Maybe you should use condoms or pull out like everybody else, Lavisha thought. It was true that Yamajesty had repeatedly told her to get on birth control but she was scared. The side effects they advertised in the commercials had her shook: blood clots, stroke, or heart attack… She was good on that. Although the many trips that she had taken to get abortions wasn't any better.

"Lavisha," Yamajesty continued, "You better get rid of that shit and I'm not fuckin' playin'."

And we ain't got no worries… You see pussy right there… His ringtone went off for what had to be the fiftieth time that night, but this time he answered.

"Bitch! Stop playin' on my muh'fuckin' phone!" he yelled, then hung up before they could respond. He placed his attention back on Lavisha. "I told you to get that pill but you keep doin' whatever the fuck you want to do! I told you I don't want no damn kids! I'm tryna enjoy life, not be somebody daddy!"

Lavisha looked at him from the corner of her eye. She could see the vein on the side of his neck bulging like it always did whenever he got riled up. A tattoo of Florida was drawn around it, really making it stand out. Tattoos covered his whole body, giving him a grimy look. Even his face held a couple of tattoos. The numbers 954 were stenciled in over his eyebrow and two teardrops were under his left eye. It was sexy to Lavisha, but none more so than the big ass tattoo of her name on his chest.

They had gotten matching tattoos of each other's names right over their hearts back when they were sixteen. Those had been their first tattoos but it was also Lavisha's only one. It made Yamajesty feel as though he owned her.

"It's too late for that shit, ain't it?" Lavisha asked knowingly.

"No the fuck it ain't. I tried to give you a baby before

and you ain't want it!"

"That doesn't count, Yamajesty! Don't bring that shit up now!"

"Why not? It's true!"

"No," she protested, "We were young and we couldn't take care of him."

"We can't take care of a baby now!" he retorted.

"You make good money doing shows and shit! And you still sling drugs every now and again. Nigga, we far from broke!"

"Why do you want a baby anyway?" Yamajesty asked, changing the subject. "Look at Sonya. You wanna end up like that bitch? Fat and ugly as a muh'fucka?"

Yamajesty glanced over at Lavisha, taking in her raw cookie dough colored skin and thick thighs. An ombre-colored Mongolian weave fell past her plump behind and her gel nails were pointed at the tips. She was hood, just like he liked his women, but deeper than that, she was loyal.

He was her first and only everything and he knew that had her mind all fucked up. Yamajesty was what she was used to and comfortable with, thus the reason why she never left him no matter how bad things got between them. He'd never tell her, but he loved her for it. Because of that, there was sincerely no other female that he'd want to be with. No one could ever take Lavisha's place as far as he was concerned.

Lavisha loved him way before she knew he could rap. Yamajesty appreciated her, but he still wasn't ready to grow up. He enjoyed having the attention of the snooty bitches that called him ugly back in middle school. He knew that he was far from being 'fine' in the traditional sense, but he could dress his ass off. Money made everything look better, including him. Oddly enough, Lavisha had always thought he was the finest nigga to walk the earth and nobody else could convince her otherwise.

"Shit," Yamajesty chuckled, momentarily finding humor in the conversation. "I'ma tell you one thing, I ain't shit like AK. I ain't wifin' you up if you start lookin' like that."

Lavisha sighed. "Never mind, Yamajesty. I don't know why I would wanna have a baby by you anyway," she muttered.

"The fuck did you say?" he barked.

She was quiet, knowing better than to repeat herself but she knew that he'd heard her loud and clear.

"You don't wanna have a baby by me anyway, huh?" Yamajesty nodded his head and rubbed his chin thoughtfully.

"That's not what I said," Lavisha insisted.

"Nah. That's what you said," he spoke calmly. "I ain't mad. But since you don't want my seed anyway, make sure you set up a appointment tomorrow to get rid of it."

CPSIA information can be obtained at www.ICGtesting.com
Printed in the USA
LVOW08s1737030315

429115LV00001B/53/P